A Pride & Prejudice Reimagining

Rapture & Rebellion

Pride, Prejudice, & New Adventures
Volume I

NEY MITCH

RAPTURE & REBELLION
Copyright © 2018 by Ney Mitch

ISBN: 978-1-68046-679-9

Published by Satin Romance
An Imprint of Melange Books, LLC
White Bear Lake, MN 55110
www.satinromance.com

Published in the United States of America.

Cover Design by Caroline Andrus

Dear Reader,

Welcome to *Rapture & Rebellion.*

This story is a reimagining/variation of the actual story of Elizabeth Bennet and her immortal relationship with Mr. Darcy of Pemberly. I understand when picking up these sorts of books, that one can be surprised when things are, well, different than the original. I respect the original characters, have a great love for them, and I couldn't help but enjoy giving them an alternate journey. I hope that any new readers to this series can enjoy it as well.

Regarding Mr. Darcy's character, he initially begins in a strange place, is very flawed, and antagonistic. However, this is so that he can develop over the series as a character who, in the end, redeems himself.

Also, this story has an addition of a few characters which are not in the original book, but over time, they become integral to the series and to the characters that were Jane Austen's originals. It also includes fictitious historical events with nonfictional ones. Therefore, for clarification, there are characters in this story/events that occur, which were not initially present or didn't occur at all, historically.

The series flips between perspectives. Whenever a section

focuses on Elizabeth, it is first person narration. Whenever it is not, the section flips to third person narration.

Either way, for those of you who are willing to pick up another read, I dedicate this book to you, for it is through you that I have been able to continue. I hope you enjoy reading this alternate tale of the love of Mr. Darcy and Elizabeth Bennet, the two most romantic heroes in all of literature.

PROLOGUE

OF NEWS...AND OTHER BUSINESS OF SORTS

1810, Steventon, Hampshire, England

News was something that fueled the gossip among the neighborhood of Steventon. Whether it was news of a personal nature or a political one, any was better than none.

Yet Steventon, Hampshire, a lovely town in the country, sometimes reacted to news in the strangest of ways. Sometimes the marching of armies was enjoyable to speak of, but the excitement that could be caused by hearing news of a ball taking place caused more reaction. In many a town in England, it was normal amongst even the most well-informed of a gentleman's daughters to rejoice in news of a dance. Yet, in the town of Steventon, there was one woman in particular who had news from a letter, and she was more than happy to share.

Mrs. Phillips, an elderly woman married to an attorney in Meryton, had just received a letter in the post that had come express from London. Upon reading it, she immediately left and walked to the other side of the neighborhood, where her sister lived with her husband, Mr. Bennet, on their estate of Longbourn.

Upon reaching the house, Mrs. Phillips stepped on the pathway leading up along the comfortable estate. And the door immediately opened to reveal her sister, Mrs. Bennet. Mrs. Phillips almost never had to ring the bell, for she made her Thursday morning visit at exactly the same time of day, and Mrs. Bennet, always waiting for the news her sister always had a way of discovering, was quick to exit the house and greet her eagerly.

"My sister!" Mrs. Bennet said. "Oh, you are five minutes later than usual, and I was worried that something had happened to you. Well, get in out of this dreadful cold."

"Oh, sister, I had a hard time in coming here, you would not believe, for the road was quite blocked due to an accident a farmer had with his carts."

"Oh, what an inconsiderate thing for the farmer to do!" Mrs. Bennet cried. "For him not to care that he was holding up any passersby on the street, what a foolish thing to do."

"I know, sister, it was monstrously selfish of him."

Mrs. Phillips and her sister, Mrs. Bennet, were two elderly women who could be described both simply, as well as in a most complicated way. They were considered past their prime but had children who were described as being right in the middle of theirs. This compounded with being women who desired constant amusement in their lives, but almost never experiencing it, left them in one position. They were keen to be doing anything to make themselves busy with the trivialities that occupy their lives. They also were gossipy, silly, and women of mean understanding. Such was the binding tie that connected both sisters to each other. When Mrs. Phillips followed Mrs. Bennet inside, they both sat in the parlor. And Mrs. Phillips brandished her letter.

"Sister," Mrs. Phillips beamed, "I have the most wonderful news."

"News!" Mrs. Bennet cried, "not that I care about news, for there is always news going on here. And yet, now that you mention it, I am fine with hearing it, but still, news is not something I need at all."

"Well," Mrs. Phillips continued, used to hearing her sister say that, "I have just received a letter from our brother in London."

"Stephen has written? Of what?"

"He has somehow done a very prestigious man in London a favor, and the man has two sons."

"And how old are these sons?"

"One is thirty, and the other is six and twenty."

"And are they both unattached?"

"By some miracle, yes."

Mrs. Bennet beamed at the news, then got up and rang the bell. "Hill!"

Hill, the head maid of the house, entered and bowed. "Yes, ma'am."

"Where are my girls now? For I know that they are not in the house."

"Oh, ma'am, Miss Kitty and Miss Lydia have gone into town, joined by Miss Mary who needed to get a new book. Miss Jane, however, is simply upstairs, and Miss Elizabeth is—"

"Oh, never mind about Lizzy," Mrs. Bennet snapped, shrugging her entire frame as a sign of impatience. "I know where she would be right now, and it always vexes me greatly. Goodness me, why did I have to give birth to such a wild little thing? Jane!"

From upstairs, Miss Jane Bennet, the eldest of the five daughters, ceased her activity and stood up.

"I'll be down soon, Mama," Jane replied, "for I am just fixing the lace on one of my boots."

"Very well, come down as soon as you can, my dear."

"And yet, sister," Mrs. Phillips said, "our brother, Stephen, has actually hinted in this letter that he has plans for Lizzy as well."

"He does?" Mrs. Bennet sighed out in annoyance, "Whatever does he go favoring Elizabeth for? Oh, very well! Hill, go out into the woods and find Elizabeth. Good god, I hope she's not climbing trees again. A twenty-six year old woman and I still doubt if she's brought such a bad habit to an end."

Hill nodded and left.

❧ I ❧

IT'S A TRUTH

With caution and ease, I looked around myself and beheld the peace that came with my solitude. For here, in the dense collection of woods that bordered my father's estate, I was able to find the tranquility that comes with the state of being surrounded by none other than tree, rock, twig and leaf.

In seeing that I was alone, I smiled to myself, gathered the hem of my petticoat in my left hand and then began to climb up the trunk, making sure to step on the sturdiest of branches.

Higher and higher I climbed until I reached the very top of it and was over thirty feet above the ground. I gazed above the top of the trees and beheld the sun as it was in the middle of the sky.

"Beautiful!" I said to myself, for it was always and would always be a sight to behold. For indeed, to look upon the world above and from such a height, makes one feel far away from the woes or everyday news and comings and goings that perplex the people whom you dwell amongst.

La! If I had to sit in the parlor and hear my Aunt Phillips tell my mother news that was of little consequence, when in truth, there was tension rising between Britain and America once more—I would secretly wish to groan out impatiently. My mother, indeed, cared more for a person falling and staining their dress than about the problems that have arisen with the impressment of American soldiers, or America's continual pursuit of Canadian land, or the madness of King George, or the inability of the Prince Regent to understand how to rule our country.

And while I enjoyed the gaiety that came with the fun news of a ball occurring, of an assembly, or the pleasure of making a new acquaintance and meeting fascinating individuals, my curiosity didn't just end there and there only.

And to possess the liberty of being away from it all! And not to have to hear my mother shouting Lizzy! Or Elizabeth always!

"Miss Elizabeth!"

I closed my eyes in frustration but sighed in acceptance when I realized that it was our maid, Hill. I did my best to climb down as quickly as I could, but Hill found me as I just managed to get to the last branch.

"Ah," Hill said, "look at you."

"Yes, I know I am a sad sight to behold." I laughed as I jumped onto the ground. "And yet do you promise me what you always promise me?"

"Aye, I do miss, and I won't tell your mother anything."

"I love your sense of discretion," I replied as I smiled and walked with her, "for it is my findings, and I believe that I am not alone in thinking so, that a good maid understands that sometimes the best thing she can do is not tell the mistress of the house everything."

"And by that, you mean your mother."

"Every daughter can have her secret if the secret is innocent."

"Well, Miss Elizabeth," Hill said, touching my shoulder

affectionately, "I daresay that I am a good servant, and a good secret I can continue to keep."

Hill was always nice to me, and it was a constant comfort.

"Hill, I love every deceptive bone in your body."

"Of course, you do, Miss."

We walked back to the house where my mother was awaiting me.

❧

When I entered through the back door, Hill went directly to the kitchen, and I progressed to the parlor. The door was closed slightly for some reason—a reason that I knew.

My mother, with all desires to keep appearances as they should be, closed the door to keep privacy, but also left the door ajar ever so slightly to make sure the servants could accidentally hear anything and everything.

Her skills at appearing private while being very public about something were quite an art of hers.

I looked through the crack of the doorway and saw my sister, Jane, sitting down while my mother and Aunt Phillips were discussing plans and a letter that had clearly been sent by my Uncle Gardiner.

"Oh, Jane!" our mother cried. "It is the most wonderful news. Your Uncle Gardiner has sent word that he has received an invitation to go to Almack's, for a ball with the most prestigious and illustrious persons in all of London. You shall be able to mix with all the best of society and meet the wealthiest men, who I am sure, will be struck by your charms."

"I am indebted to my Uncle Gardiner, truly," Jane said demurely. "And I am very fortunate."

"Fortune is all that you deserve, my dear," our mother said, "for none of your sisters are even half as handsome as you, and therefore are less likely to be made such a wonderful offer as yourself."

"Mama, you flatter me." Jane blushed. "My sisters are all quite lovely in turn and have their own different definitions of goodness."

"Oh, you and your youngest sister, Lydia, are such a comfort to me," our mother sighed. "For she is good-humored, and you are kind and ever so good. Yet take heart, my dear. Remember that man in London, the Mr. Samuel Edmund Brocklehurst who was quite taken with you a year ago, and he owns a very pretty estate in Surrey, if I am not mistaken. He is said to respond to both the names Edmund and Samuel because his parents alternated with calling him by both. And what was his worth?"

"Three thousand a year!" Aunt Phillips confirmed.

"Indeed, three thousand! Well, rumor has reached Hampshire, and this Mr. Edmund Brocklehurst is still very much likely to be unattached, and if you recall, he wrote you some very pretty verses of poetry once. If we could just throw you in his company more, then there is a chance that he would make you an offer of marriage this time."

"Mama, I have no aims to be wed at all." Jane smiled bashfully. "If the opportunity does arise, then of course, I shall do my duty to you."

"Of course, you will my dear."

I closed my eyes and gritted my teeth as I stood outside the parlor. I honestly did not know how Jane could stand it! And yet Jane, born with immense beauty and blessed with the sweetest disposition, made her different than my own temper and temperaments. She was too good, so terribly angelic, and such kindness and domestic tranquility in character was never something that I or the rest of our sisters acquired. I was raised in a house where the eldest of us, Jane, had been given all the good graces that a woman could desire, while the rest of us knew ourselves to be lesser creatures.

I was Elizabeth Bennet, the second oldest in the family, and there was no perfection to me. Yet, I had one thing that I believed myself strong in—or better yet, there were two things I prided myself on—my witty intellect, and ability to laugh at anything. And as I grew older and older, I prayed that those talents of mine were enough to get me through any painful situation or harsh word spoken by my frivolous mother.

Being the oldest of five daughters, the first was my sister, Jane Bennet, twenty-eight years old and blessed with the best looks of us, a handsome face, as well as a perfectly pleasing and serene personality. Then there was myself. Then came Mary, twenty years, and then Kitty, eighteen years, and then the youngest was Lydia who was sixteen. They all meant well, but Mary was the sister who was doomed to be considered the plain one, and therefore she resolved it, within herself, to be the most accomplished of us. The constant study of books and the philosophies she could extract from them was forever her objective, whenever she was not practicing on the piano-forte. Though she meant well, it led to her being, in her own way, affected and pretentious.

And then there was Kitty and Lydia. I had loved them as much as I had cherished Mary, but as in Mary's case, I would not let my sisterly affection for them cloud my judgment, and my opinion was clear. While Mary leaned too far in the direction of being bookish and proud off her accomplishments, Kitty and Lydia had heads filled with little substance, not seeming to be aware of it themselves and, also, were of the age where their minds bent more towards dancing, excitement, parties, and men to admire than it was full of anything else. And while it could not be denied that almost every young woman's head was full of such subjects, it does not follow that one should speak of such things always, or make it their sole subject of conversation, yet Kitty and Lydia did. And while Kitty proved to be blind and foolish, Lydia just proved to be wild and sometimes vulgar.

Forgive me, for I am not being attentive to the words spoken between my aunt and mother at hand. Bending my mind toward the present, I focused on the conversation once more and gleaned more insight as to why I was needed.

"And for reasons that cannot be explained other than for strange favoritism," our mother said, "I despise favoritism of any kind, for you know I don't ever favor any of my children in particular!"

"Mama," I sighed under my breath, "what a lie."

"Your Uncle Gardiner has also requested for your sister Lizzy to join you. He is always so partial to her! Yet it is all for the best, for it would be best for you to have a sister of yours with you to serve as the perfect chaperone. Yet I confess that I daresay there is no chance of there being a man at this prestigious ball who would be taken with Elizabeth."

"Elizabeth is a most wonderful companion," Jane said, coming to my defense.

"Aye she is, when she doesn't go on in her wild ways. And yet, your Aunt Gardiner will have her eye on her."

If there was a chance that I would get to journey into town to see our Aunt and Uncle Gardiner, then I would be fully satisfied in doing so, for not only would I have temporary escape from my mother's constant reprimands on me, but also, I would be in the presence of two people who always saw the good in me as opposed to the bad.

"Yet I doubt that there will be a single man at Almack's who would be taken with her."

"If there are any unattached men at all." Jane sighed.

"There are always unattached men at balls in London at this time of year," our mother said, "for it seems like they always come out of the woodwork this season."

Before they continued to speak of news and other business of sorts, I took that as the opportunity to enter and announce that I had listened in to a great deal of the conversation.

"Of course," I smiled to all their startled faces, "for it is a truth universally acknowledged, that an unattached man in possession of a good fortune, must be in want of a wife!"

❧ 2 ❧

TO LONDON WE GO!

"Yes," our mother replied to my comment, hiding her fears that I overheard all that she had said before. "Yes, he must indeed. Now come in, Lizzy, sit down and hear all that we will have planned for you both."

Accepting my fate as the companion to my sister, I sat down and listened to my mother's latest plans of marrying off her eldest and most beautiful daughter to the highest bidder. All the while I found all the amusement that comes along with watching a master planner pull together all her machinations for something that might not be fruitful in the end.

The plans were decided very quickly that we should make our way to London as soon as was permissible and possible, which, due to my mother's wishes, was only in two days' time.

At the end of the decisions being made, I stood up and looked at my family that surrounded me.

"Forgive me," I began, "But I think it wise that I visit Charlotte and Jane before we take our leave."

"Oh, you can visit the Lucases and Austens tomorrow, Lizzy,

for you must prepare what dresses you may bring with you to town."

"I can do that as readily tomorrow as I could today," I said, putting on my bonnet and jacket.

"Mama," Jane said, "Elizabeth is correct. We have two days before our journey is to take place, and Lizzy and I have made plans with the Austens next week that now we have to tell them to postpone."

"What plans?" our mother scoffed, "you have not told us of such a plan."

"Oh, it is nothing so formal. As you know, the Austens every now and again do home theatricals that are small yet fun, and Lizzy is part of it, while I am the one who assembles the costumes."

"And we planned to do one with them for next week," I added. "Now we must tell them that we shall have to resume our activities upon our return."

"Well, go directly," Mrs. Bennet said. "Though I don't understand why Mr. Austen allows his children to indulge in such things, if you must go, then you must. Yet honestly, he is our parson at our parish, and he must learn to be more serious."

"Depend upon it, Mother," I said, "that if we humans have the ability to laugh, then I believe that God has the ability to do so as well."

"Don't mock the Maker."

"I don't mock Him, Mother. I just believe He has the ability to smile."

Jane and I put on our bonnets and outdoor apparel and left as quickly as we could.

"How bitter do you think she is with me?" I asked.

"Our Mother loves you, Lizzy," Jane said. "She just has an interesting way of showing it."

"I wonder if she had truly despised me, how would she act

then? For honestly, if she ever were to exude it, then I believe that I would not be able to survive."

After a brief walk, we arrived at Lucas Lodge, which was the home of Sir William Lucas and his wife, Lady Lucas. Sir Lucas was a very warm and open man who was cordial and loved a good conversation. Also, he was a man incapable of seeing the good of his past. Sir Lucas originally owned a shop and was in the merchant business and had quite a long and successful career, so well that he gained great wealth from it. Yet, when he was presented at St. James Court and given a knighthood, his perspective on the same life that gave him his livelihood had changed. The best parts of him were that he was a man who worked for his wealth, but the gaining of his knighthood was felt a little too keenly. He grew to look down on being a man of profession, therefore he sold it and bought some property here in Hampshire, where he brought his family. I liked him tremendously, but I do believe that if he had never gained his knighthood, not only would he be a man of means, but also one of many perspectives, other than just one.

Yet I was quite friendly with two of his children. His daughter, Charlotte Lucas, was a close friend of mine, and her younger sister, Maria, though too young for me to warm to completely, was still a nice girl. There also were three brothers, John, Peter, and Samuel.

When Jane and I arrived, Peter was home with Charlotte and Maria as well. We only spoke briefly and convinced Charlotte and Maria to join us on a visit to the Austens.

Yet, as we prepared to leave with them, Samuel, the oldest brother who was twenty-eight years old, entered.

"Miss Jane Bennet and Miss Elizabeth Bennet!" Samuel said, taking off his hat and cloak as he entered. "Well, this is a wonderful surprise, though I should always expect to find you here."

"Indeed, Samuel," I laughed. "Your sister and I have only been friends for over ten years. Yet, if the product of you forgetting that is me getting to see a wonderful look of surprise on your face, then I am happy that your mind works in such a way."

"You are happy with my blankness of mind?" Samuel laughed.

"I like that you are easily surprised."

"Well, whenever you arrive, Miss Elizabeth, it is a surprise that is most welcome," Samuel said, looking into my eyes. In all honesty, I could never tell if Samuel understood that flirting was something that a man should harmlessly do because he should always keep in practice, or if he was sincere—or if he just felt comfortable around me enough to know that he could play with my sensibilities and that there would be no harm in it.

"Are you trying to make me smile, Samuel?" I said archly, in hopes of being playful, but also in attempts to be harmless in turn.

"Aye, I am," Samuel replied. "As always."

Charlotte cleared her throat, loudly, and Samuel turned to my sister and his. "Oh, I see that you are all leaving for somewhere?"

"As always," Charlotte said. "We are on the move to see Cassandra and Jane Austen."

"Might I be your escort?"

"Are you afraid the garden hedges will attack us?" I laughed.

"I have seen them look very lethal of late."

"Well," Maria said, "you unfortunately have no choice but to remain. Father needs to speak with you about plans for buying Mr. Baker's old land next to ours so that we can take on another farm tenant."

"Duty calls my name," Samuel said, "for such is the way of gaiety." Samuel turned to the rest of us. "Enjoy your walk, ladies, and I dare say that you have no choice but to see me as soon as you always do."

"Well then," Jane said, "till tomorrow, Mr. Lucas."

When we came upon the Austen home, we were not astonished to find that they were putting on a small, fun play with their cousins who were visiting.

They were doing a scene from Shakespeare's *Merry Wives of Windsor*, and I was not surprised, for that was one of Cassandra Austen's favorite of Shakespeare's plays.

Mr. Austen was the parson of our church in Hampshire and his wife, Mrs. Austen, was both very similar and different than our mother. She was similar in the way that she had very much desired her daughters to marry well but was also a woman who understood that her daughters had the right to be forgiven if and when they didn't. Then again, she had sons as well, and since they would inherit the house when she and her husband died, she need not worry about her children's fate. She had seven children and could suffer some of them to not have fate work out in ideal ways, and her husband had accepted that fact long ago, especially since his two daughters showed that they would never get married and were past the point of doing so. For one was now almost forty and the other was thirty-six years old. Those two daughters were the friends we had, who were playing in this theatrical with their baby cousins. There, playing an old man and a damsel in distress, were Cassandra and Jane Austen.

When we entered, they both stopped the scene and turned to us.

"Lizzy!" Jane Austen cried, standing up. "Jane, Charlotte and Maria." Cassandra greeted us as well and then told her cousin that it would be a good idea to take an early tea-time and have some cakes. When they took off the costumes, we all left and began to walk through their backyard while my sister and I told them our news.

"Yet, you must believe," my sister said, "that we still wish to perform the theatrical, it just has to be postponed."

"That's unlucky." Jane Austen sighed. "And yet, I daresay that it is from our perspective, not from yours. For I can be in no doubt as to why your mother is sending you."

"You shall have fun," Maria said. "Oh, but I do so wish that I could go to London."

"And to Almack's, no less," Cassandra said. "Though I do believe that if I were still young enough, I would be too timid to go."

"Too much aristocratic attitude in one room can make anyone shake in their petticoat." Jane Austen laughed. "Yet, I daresay that I am too old to be intimidated so easily."

"Ever since we knew you, you've boasted of never being intimidated, Jane," I said. "I just believe age has made you into that more so."

"Then it's a virtue that I will never relinquish."

"I just wish that fortune may look well on me," my sister said, "so that my mother will stop sending me everywhere to continue to put me through this. I must admit, that it would be entertaining to..."

"Fall in love?" Cassandra asked.

"Yes, I suppose that it would."

"Our father once told me something," Jane Austen commented. "He said a girl likes to be tossed in love every now and again, for it gives her a sort of distinction amongst her companions. I want to believe that he was just being funny, and yet I daresay that our father does not know anything about the hearts of women."

"He should," Cassandra said with a smile, "for he is married to our mother."

"Our mother is not a woman, Cassandra," Jane said, "she's just simply our mother."

As we walked on, Jane Austen was able to come to my side and detach us from the rest a bit while we shared a quick *tete e tete*.

"So," Jane began, "you are accompanying your sister to London."

"Aye, I am," I replied, "yet I know it's because my uncle wishes to see me again, and I am happy to see him and my aunt." Jane eyed me narrowly, and it was not lost on me. "What is it? And don't reply with nothing, Jane, because I know that expression of yours."

"Yes, you have seen it often, and I only give it when I believe that there is more to something than the person I'm speaking with is giving."

"You believe me to be hiding something?"

"Lizzy, I believe you to still have hope in yourself. Or at least, I hope that you shall."

"Hope?"

"Your sister is going to London to catch a man and hope he shall fall in love with her. Why do you not have this same ambition for yourself?"

"Jane, I'm twenty-six years old. I have to accept that many might view me as a spinster at this point."

"Your sister is twenty-eight years old. As I am thirty-six. What makes her situation more profitable than yours?"

"You see how my sister appears. She is quite five times more beautiful than the rest of us and has the most delicate and amiable disposition. Men cherish such qualities. She has it in her to make men forgive her for being older than they would prefer."

Only then did I realize that I might have offended Jane.

"Oh, Jane, forgive me. I don't mean to make you believe that I scoff at your age and regard you as an old maid, for I don't believe you to be so."

"Except that the world does regard me as so. Yet I am not afraid of the world. I know what I am, even if it doesn't, and I am content with that. That would be my advice to you. Don't fear the world, and you shall not be held back. Your sister is not five times as beautiful as you. You shall come to know it before the end."

"Jane?"

"Yes."

"You would have made a man a good wife."

"There was a time when I would have wanted to be so, and yet, all that I desire now is to one day be viewed as a good writer."

"How is the book you are writing coming along?"

"I believe that I have made progress. I have taken the original way that I have written it and have found out how I wish to write the final draft. At first, the novel was written in a series of letters, yet now I have learned from my mistakes. Though tell me, in regard to characters, what do you think of the names Marianne and Elinor?"

"I hope that we shall enjoy ourselves," my sister Jane said as we were in our bedroom that night, dressed for bed. "Perhaps in town we can experience the wonderful sensations of being quiet and comfortable in our Uncle Gardiner's house."

"This, in truth, is all in compliment to you," I said. "I am quite resigned to my fate of being an old maid."

"I am older than you, Lizzy."

"And yet, fortune simply has not found you yet, and as it has been so very much pointed out, fortune was never with me."

"And why should you believe so? You still have your loveliness and bloom."

"Because I cannot tell whether falling in love is an impossibility for me, because of a defect that is within me, or because of the constant defects that I find in others. If I could but marry a man who would love me enough to accept the fact that I am so long in my years, as well as that I can only give so much to him with a dowry."

"Lizzy, we are not *very* poor."

"I am aware of the comforts we live in, but the days of living in those comforts are numbered. For with our father's estate entailed away to our cousin, the next male heir, we have little but our charms to recommend us. The only way for us to survive is if one of us marries well, to save the family. And yet—and yet, despite this necessity to marry for advantage and advantage alone, I cannot find myself able to do so. If a man were to fall in love with me and would overlook that I bring a small dowry to the marriage, if any at all, then I would also have to be in love with him. For I am determined that only feeling the deepest love for a man could make me feel prevailed upon to marry. Therefore, as I say, and as our mother hints at often... I shall end up an old maid!" I laughed. "And strangely enough, I am resolved to that."

"Do not think of yourself so meanly, Lizzy. For you have all the hope in the world."

"I have not your chances. I only have half your beauty."

I walked up to her and kissed her on the cheek.

"And yet, I am somehow content with my fate, and I can only suppose that I agree with what our dear friend, Jane Austen, said about me once. 'Good-humored, unaffected girls will not do for a man who has been used to sensible women. They are two distinct orders of beings'. And you know perfectly well that I am good-humored and sometimes have no desire to be sensible when it seems sinful to do so. Therefore, I will always be nothing more than Elizabeth Bennet."

"Then," Jane said delicately, "by your logic, I must adhere to Miss Austen's saying about me."

"You shall find love!" I said, opening the door, chuckling. "Only take care that you fall in love with a man of good fortune, for nothing less will do for our mother—or for Hampshire, or for the whole world for that matter."

"Well," Jane said, "I must not mind the world, but I believe I have a duty to the family. But Lizzy, you see everything in these matters very clearly. Therefore, can you tell me, do you think that Mr. Brocklehurst truly cares for me in any way?"

I was torn between the truth and the un-truth. For, I could not turn my mind away from what I viewed as the course of true love, and from what I recalled, Mr. Edmund Brocklehurst did not contain the symptoms of being a man in love. He enjoyed looking at her, cherished her conversation, yet whenever she left London, he did not seek to follow her, or continue the acquaintance of pursuit. If anything, it seemed to me that his inclination was very vague and of flimsy conviction. Either he didn't love my sister, but liked her tremendously, or he did love her, but didn't know if he was ready to further their course. Therefore, in my desire to be frank, but not hurt my sister's hopes, I prepared to be ambivalent about it.

"You must forgive me," I said. "Yet this is one moment where I do not fully comprehend the minds of men. I have always believed that communication is the course to true love, and he has not been very forthcoming in writing to your family to inquire about you. He has made no attempts to meet your family, and yet, it was undeniable when we first met, that he did admire you tremendously. He never stopped looking at you."

"And yet, is that enough for love?"

"No, it is not. Yet it has the ability to become something more than what it is. Therefore, let us take this invitation to Almack's to better determine his feelings for you, if you are so lucky to see him again. Maybe, by seeing you once more, it will be enough to make him wish to pursue something greater. Maybe one look will be enough to make him believe that he was wrong to not have acted sooner."

"Thank you, Lizzy. That is all the hope I needed."

I then went to bed and hoped as I went that I had done the right thing by giving her encouragement. My instincts told me that Mr. Brocklehurst was not to be trusted in regard to a more substantial tie. His manners were pleasing, but nothing of much weight, and yet when it comes to sisters or those who are close to us, telling a whole truth of your opinions when you have no facts to base it on is foolish. Hope and heart are not always the very close of comrades when it comes to mind and logic. Therefore, I resolved it within me to indulge one set and then tomorrow, I would indulge the other. I don't believe that I had the capacity within myself to be capable of handling both sets in one instance. At least, not when it had anything to do with people that I cared about.

I sat down at the desk, which had my mirror on it, and looked at myself. Sometimes, in the late of an evening or the breaking of a dawn, a woman sits down, glimpses her appearance and wonders who it is that looks back at her. There, in the mirror, the person staring back at you doesn't seem like yourself or seems not much giving of what you internally feel.

This was the woman that I was, and sometimes I saw myself in my reflection, yet in other times, I saw someone completely different. Who was the woman I saw in the mirror? Who was Elizabeth Bennet?

⚜

"It's not fair!" Lydia, our youngest sister, exclaimed when we were setting out to leave for London. "Why do Jane and Lizzy always get to go to London?"

"Aye," Kitty said, "Lydia and I have just as much right to go as they. Age difference should not allow them so much of a preference."

"If I felt it wise to do so," our father said, "then I would ship you both off to the furthest parts of the earth just to see how you would fare. And yet, since I am obliged to be wise in this case, I must declare that it is the best thing in the world for you to remain in Steventon. For society has enough on its shoulders with me releasing your sisters upon them, and they are more than enough for society to get on with without adding you to the pot of trouble as well."

"It shall not break my heart at remaining home, Papa," Mary said, "The diversions of London would have no charms for me. I should infinitely prefer a book."

"Ah!" Lydia cried. "You would say such a thing, Mary."

"I did say such a thing."

"And you would say that as well," Kitty added. While Jane and I entered the carriage, Kitty leaned into the window and kissed my cheek. "Try to remember me enough to buy me a new bonnet."

"You have so many!" I laughed.

"I could always have one more."

"And don't forget," Lydia cried bitterly, "make sure to tell her to bring me back a new pair of boots."

"You already have a sturdy pair of boots," Mary whined.

"Oh, go play on the piano-forte already! Jane, you would be kind and bring me a new pair of boots, won't you?"

"If I find a nice pair," Jane acquiesced. "Then yes, I shall buy you some."

Lydia immediately brightened, and finally, we could silence their requests, when our mother and father accosted the carriage window.

"You'll be sorely missed, Lizzy," our father said. "And you, too, Jane, for whilst you are gone, there shall be not two words of sense at the dinner table."

"Oh, Mr. Bennet!" Mrs. Bennet cried. "Don't speak of such nonsense."

"I only speak the truth," our father said, retreating away from our mother.

I never knew whether to regard our father's constant retreats away from her as a sign of fear or of cleverness. Either he was smart enough to understand that there was no point in arguing with her, or he feared to exert himself and continue to speak with her.

Though I love my father, he always spent much of his days and nights in his study and did not like to be imposed upon. Any activity that required him to check any vulgar behavior of our family was often rare, because he was in love with only one thing fully: peace! Therefore, he was at odds to administer any energy of his that might disrupt that. Such things as being stricter and checking my sisters whenever they got too vulgar or unruly or forcing our mother to curb her tongue and not always be so unguarded in her comments, were never to occur for him.

He often loved laughing at human nature and regarded the folly of others as a constant source of enjoyment. While I did inherit his tendency toward enjoying commenting on the ridiculousness in people's natures, my father's love for it was so extreme that he would rather not ever serve as a more attentive father and husband. And yet, how could he in some ways? For my mother was quite ridiculous.

He nodded goodbye one last time to Jane and me, our mother kissed us on the cheek each, and then leaned into Jane.

"Remember, my dear," she whispered, "do as much in your power to seek Mr. Brocklehurst out if you see him. And if you do, do everything within your power to entice him."

"Surely you would not wish for her to do *anything and everything*, Mama," I teased.

"Oh, yes she must!" Our mother snapped at me. "For that is the way to get a husband. But remember, my dear, to always smile at everything he says, or especially if it's not funny. It is always a great comfort to men to know that you will always be happy with them, even when they fall short in conversation. And don't go talking too much but listen to everything that they say."

"It can be quite easily supposed," Mr. Bennet said from the doorway, "that any and every art that women use to attract the opposite sex is highly revolting, my dear, but I daresay your method is quite possibly the most frightening."

"And how dare you say such a thing? For that is how I acted when I met you."

"Exactly, my dear, exactly."

"Oh, la!" Lydia cried. "Smiling is something I do well, but why should a man only be the one to speak, when sometimes they are quite terrible at it?"

"I feel the same," Kitty echoed.

"And I don't believe that," I said to Kitty. "I don't believe that you secretly feel that way for one bit. Now, may we be off? For I declare that if we continue speaking our goodbyes rather than acting on them at this rate, we shall not depart till sundown."

"Ah, well then..." Our mother then told the carriage to drive on, and we were off. She and the rest of our sisters waved to us as we rolled down the road leading out of Longbourn.

Reclining against the cushion, I smiled at Jane. "Well, it's off to London we go!"

❧ 3 ❧

LITTLE DID HE KNOW

London, Grosvenor Square

Riding his horse down the street, Mr. Fitzwilliam Darcy found himself quite content with how the day had gone. He had come to town from Pemberly and despite his father's pleas to not ride from Kent to London on horseback, he felt that it would not hurt but to break convention this once, as long as it went unknown by all that he had done so.

And yet, while being a man of much internal energy, though hesitant to ever show it in outward appearance, he could not find himself content with being driven at the present instance. On the contrary, riding was exactly the diversion that he needed to calm his excited nerves.

His father, the senior Mr. Darcy, had remained in town, yet sent him to Kent to settle a dispute between two tenants who lived on their land and worked their fields. He had done it as a test, for since his son was to inherit the estate upon his death, Mr. Darcy Senior wished to make sure that his son could handle any complications arising from being the head of such a large estate as Pemberly on his own.

The two tenants had a dispute about a bit of land in between their farms, and to whom it belonged. Mr. Darcy felt pleased with himself because he settled the matter with ease, and therefore it gave him a confidence that fueled his inner sense of self-satisfaction. Consequently, when it was time to make his way to London to attend the ball at Almack's, he felt it more beneficial to his excited spirits to ride his horse all the way and break his journey at inns along the road. Whenever it rained, he would simply remain at the inn for an extra day. Yet traveling in the rain never did him any harm and riding through whatever weather was always most invigorating.

Yet when he arrived in London, he dismounted in front of his townhouse, his horse was taken to a set of stables that were behind the long row of homes, and he began to walk up the steps. He entered his home and was greeted by the Butler, Simmons.

"Good day, Mr. Darcy," Simmons said, taking Mr. Darcy's hat from him.

"Good day, Simmons," was Mr. Darcy's curt but unaffected reply. "How is your family?"

"Very well, sir, thank you for asking. And how was your journey here?"

"The carriage ride was comfortable," Mr. Darcy lied, "yet it passed quickly enough."

"Well, your sister, Miss Georgiana, is away at the present, for she is shopping in the marketplace. Your father is in his study. Shall I announce you?"

"Oh, that will be unnecessary."

"On the contrary, sir, it will be necessary, for you have a guest waiting for you in the library."

"A guest? Already? Who could possibly be so presumptuous to call on me so quickly after I have returned to town?"

There, on the steps, was Mr. Darcy's Valet, Jefferson.

"Sir, forgive me for being comfortable to offering you a joke, but I cannot resist," Jefferson said. "There are few people who are that presumptuous, and even fewer people who knew that you would arrive here today. I shall give you three guesses as to who it is, yet something tells me that you will only need one."

Mr. Darcy thought about it and he smiled.

❦

Mr. Darcy entered the library and soon found the person that he was seeking looking among the bookshelves of the library.

"Are you looking to become a great reader, Charles?" Mr. Darcy said. The man perked up, turned to Mr. Darcy and Charles Bingley, his closest friend, showed his face.

"No." Mr. Bingley laughed, putting the book down. "I'm merely looking to appear as one. Yet I must be failing."

"You've never given much effort to appearing as something you are not. So why are you doing it now?"

"I was told that a woman likes a man who appears as smart but is not really so."

Charles Bingley and Mr. Fitzwilliam Darcy, both men in their early 30s, had been close friends since they were at university together at Cambridge.

"Then you have been listening to the wrong people. How are you, Charles?"

"I am well, thank you—except for the usual."

"And what qualifies for being usual?"

"Darcy... you've met my sisters."

"Aye," Mr. Darcy replied, rolling his eyes. "Too right I have."

"And Caroline—well, Darcy, you know my sister, and she—she keeps asking about you."

"Every relationship has its annoying additions, and my trial for being your friend is having to deal with your older sister."

"Well, I come bearing good news."

"Good news?"

"I have come here with the express desire to tell you that I am journeying to the continent."

"For what reason?"

"For fun! Naturally. I have decided to go to Spain and Vienna in Austria. There will be festivals in both countries there at this time of year, and a few of the men at our club are journeying there as well, which means that we will have loads of company. I was wondering if you would accompany me."

Mr. Darcy immediately felt elated but showed it in the customary way that he showed his emotion...which was by a curt nod and a bit of a smile.

"What time shall you leave?"

"Is that a yes then?" Mr. Bingley said, clapping his hands together in happiness.

"Well, I shall have to tell father, but of course we can go when we are done attending Almack's."

"Almack's?" Mr. Bingley asked quizzically. "Oh, Darcy, I'm not going."

"What do you mean?" Mr. Darcy replied, apprehensive. "Why would you not go?"

"I have to travel, for I have decided to begin maintaining an interest in textile trading and I have to travel to Liverpool at this time to inspect a factory. You don't think I'm foolish for continuing holding an interest in this regard, do you?"

"Not at all," Mr. Darcy replied. "You know that I see the use of maintaining such a connection that could increase your income."

"Yet you must promise to not tell anyone of my activities. My father did his very best to bring me up to be a gentleman, and he would not like that I would still like to have a profession in trade. And if it were to be spread around, it would ruin all our chances of dealing in the aristocracy, and there will be some circles in which we will not be allowed to associate."

"Your secret is safe with me, Charles," Mr. Darcy replied, "though I don't necessarily agree with your activities, I will not deny that you are the form of man who does need an occupation of some kind."

"Then you think me wrong?" Mr. Bingley looked shaken at not feeling the security that came with having his friend's support. He looked down at his hands, uncertain with himself. "Then you believe that I am wrong and that I should abandon this pursuit of mine."

"I would not recommend you having an occupation, Charles, for it does risk you being exposed by some curious socialite eventually, and that would hinder your connections with all good society. And yet, as long as we keep it between ourselves, I shall not forsake you. And if this is something that you wish to pursue, then I shall not think any the less of you. For like I said before, keep connections that could increase your income."

"Then that is comfort enough," Mr. Bingley said a little more boldly, "and if I don't have your full support, at least I have it halfway. For you know I quite rely on your advice."

"Now, back to the most important news," Mr. Darcy furthered, "you really are not joining me at the ball?"

"Darcy, I'm certain that you shall be fine. And if you please, I have no worries in allowing my sisters to join you. For though you and Caroline have an *interesting* relationship—and that's put politely—then you shall be released from the burden of having to dance often with women whom you don't know. I know how shy you can be on the dance floor."

"I am not shy!" Mr. Darcy groaned.

❦

"Indeed son, you are very shy," Mr. Darcy Sr. had said to his son when he stood in front of his father's desk. Mr. Bingley was still waiting for his friend in the parlor, hoping that they would dine together at their club and then if he could, he would tempt his friend to go to the theatre that night.

Therefore, there they were in the study, father and son, Mr. Darcy looking at Mr. Darcy and the senior was telling the junior about the one thing even he knew.

"Son," Mr. Darcy Sr. began, "you don't possess the talent of speaking easily with others who you have not been acquainted with before."

"I am making progress," his son replied.

"Indeed, Fitzwilliam, you are, and yet you have to get better at it even more so. Have you successfully resolved the conflict back at Pemberly?"

"I have, Father." Fitzwilliam then began to tell his father about how he maintained the peace between the two tenants on their estate. Mr. Darcy Sr. listened with attention and happiness.

"Very good," Mr. Darcy said. "Son, you have done well. And I'm proud of you. And yes, you have my permission to go with Bingley to Spain."

"But—you know about that? I didn't even mention that to you yet."

"Oh, your Valet, Jefferson, he was walking by at the time and I had him tell me everything that you both were speaking of."

"You had my own valet spy on me?"

"Of course, I did." Mr. Darcy Sr. laughed. "That's the wonderful thing about owning a house. Spying is impossible to do because everything in the house is under your power and gaze."

"Still, Father, that is just sad."

"I gave you life, son. It's well within my rights...and I enjoy exerting my influence. Now, I'm sorry that Bingley can't attend Almack's with you, but I trust you shall get more comfortable as the night continues. And don't forget to smile at the young ladies and overcome your shyness enough to not be afraid to dance with them."

"And how is that a wise choice? After all, I have been told since I was a child that I would have no choice but to marry my dear cousin, Anne."

"While I and your mother—and your aunt do wish that fate for you, for by marrying Anne you know perfectly well that our estate and your aunt's estate shall be merged, keeping both houses and economy in our family, I know your feelings on the subject."

"Father, I do not love Anne. And I don't think I ever could."

"I know that you don't, yet there is always the chance that you might grow to. Therefore son, attempt to try, for me. That being said, I will never deny your rights to be a young man and have fun. You still have time to grow to love your cousin, and even more time before that to be a man who has his adventures. There is nothing wrong with the idea of falling in love every now and again, having romance, and feeling tossed against the rocks of emotion."

"Father, you know I've fallen in love before, and it has never turned out well."

"Because your first thoughts were to have a future with each woman. What I am talking about is the desire to find love and don't be afraid to lose it—to enjoy something that is temporary. There is fun in what is not always permanent. Have a romance and have the fun in knowing that sometimes where it began and ended was the height of all the pleasure of it."

"Father...are you telling me to be fickle?"

"Son, are you telling me that you don't see the healthiness of such a state of mind? I am not saying to not be capable of true emotion, nor am I telling you to break a heart. I am merely telling you that you are a young man in his thirties, and maybe it might be more essential to you to have fun now, when you are unattached and free. The last thing I want my legacy to be is of a man who repressed every natural feeling of his and then when he gets married, he decides to take all his disappointed hopes out on his wife.

I don't want you to wake up when you are forty years old and leaving your wife and children home by themselves for months at a time because you waited till you were wed to partake in all the joys that every man needs. You are young, Fitzwilliam, and a father could not ask for a better son, yet I tell you from experience. While your mother lived, I loved her tremendously. I didn't at first, but I learned to. And I am one of the few men in this forsaken city that can boast of never being disloyal to her, because I allowed myself to take every opportunity of being a young man who sometimes got a little—loose in my decorum. I fell in love quite often before her, enjoyed the comfort of being tossed in love here and there, and I never hurt them, for I was always honest about my endeavors. I only say, remember decorum, your manners, discretion, and never do anything to shed a bad name on the family of Darcy. But you are a young man. Be a young man while you still can. And if your rigid father is telling you this, then you know that you have nothing to lose."

"Yes, Father."

"Now, go off and eat dinner with your friend!" Mr. Darcy said. "Tell him that I can get invitations for his sisters as well so that you won't be alone. I daresay that his one sister's constant love for you is quite taxing." Mr. Darcy smiled, and added, "Though I find amusement in watching her constantly chase you subtly, but at least you can dance one dance with both of them, and then allow yourself to be quiet and taciturn for the rest of the ball with ease."

Fitzwilliam laughed.

"That does sound like me."

"And I'm still proud of you."

"Thank you, Father." Fitzwilliam nodded to his father and left to rejoin Bingley in the parlor.

⊙⚬⊙

Mr. Darcy Jr. entered to see his friend pacing back and forth, waiting for Fitzwilliam to be done.

"Do you ever know how to sit still?" Mr. Darcy laughed.

"Do you ever know how to move with alacrity?" Bingley retorted.

"Of course not, for too much motion is a sign of bad breeding."

"And I consider too little movement as a sign of laziness. Now I can tell that you are teasing me by holding out. So, tell me, did your father give you permission to take leave and travel?"

Mr. Darcy turned and smiled. "To Spain!"

Mr. Bingley jumped up and cheered. "To Spain then!"

⊙⚬⊙

Mr. Bingley and Mr. Darcy then began to ride to their club.

"If you were a true friend," Mr. Darcy argued, "you would find a way to push back your journey into the country and then accompany me to Almack's."

"Indeed, I believe that not telling your father how you rode all the way from Kent to London is me being friend to you enough."

"But I didn't—"

"You can lie to your father, Darcy," Bingley replied, "but you can't with me. We all have that habit that we cannot break, and your desire to perpetually ride everywhere is yours."

"Well then...you are a good friend."

"Oh, correction Darcy, I am a *great* friend."

Mr. Darcy and Mr. Bingley arrived at their club, entered, greeted some friends, and then were served their meal.

Mr. Fitzwilliam Darcy, and Mr. Charles Bingley, were a friendship that came together quite out of a co-dependency of company and manners. Mr. Darcy, being born into aristocracy, was naturally of a higher rank. Yet, being born also possessing a natural habit of being too quiet, and as his father put it, not naturally possessing happy manners to recommend himself to strangers, made Darcy a fiercely loyal companion. Darcy needed someone by his side who was loyal as well but also had an open nature and happy manners that he could accompany everywhere and have them speak for him. By being friends with Bingley, he had a constant friend and all the comforts that came along with that security. And by being next to Bingley's lively and infectious charm, Mr. Darcy could be silent in company and have Bingley do all the talking for him.

With Bingley, Darcy was a saving grace. Though very different than him in attitude and temperament, Darcy was a good friend, an assertive and wise companion, while also giving out good advice to help Bingley in society. From an advantageous standpoint, Darcy was from the highest aristocracy, and Bingley came from a family that achieved its wealth through trade, making him lesser in rank. By being friends, Darcy helped Bingley be introduced properly within society and accepted amongst the highest circles. While this was not the reason that Bingley bonded with Darcy, it was a benefit to him that such a true friendship could advance him in the world.

Being two men whose destinies seemed interconnected always, they were two walking contradictions that possessed a perfection about them.

By the end of the evening, Darcy had resolved himself to the fact that Bingley could not possibly accompany him to the ball at Almack's and groaned inwardly at feeling that the night would be very painful and tedious for him.

Little did he know that London had gathered two new visitors that very day. Little did he know that Jane Bennet had just ridden along Gracechurch Street to visit her aunt and uncle, and along with her came her sister, Elizabeth.

❧ 4 ❧

A VAIN WISH

When my sister and I arrived in London, we drove along Gracechurch Street which was in the part of London called Cheapside. We passed our Uncle's factory as we journeyed on. Uncle Gardiner owned a textile factory which was quite successful, and in my opinion, made him more distinguished than those who were considered three times his rank.

"Lizzy and Jane!" Our Aunt and Uncle Gardiner exclaimed when we pulled up to their front steps. Their four children came down and greeted us as well, and it was quite a merry gathering.

"Thank you so much for inviting us," Jane said when we stepped down and were accosted by our uncle.

"And for the freedom of being from home," I added. "I dare say that your timing could not have been more perfect."

"Oh yes," Uncle Gardiner said with a laugh, "for I do know my sister."

"It is good to see you both," I added as Aunt Gardiner kissed my cheek.

"And it is always wonderful to see you as well," Aunt Gardiner said.

Their children then gathered around us, Jane and I bent down and hugged them all, and then we went inside.

⚜

Being inside our uncle's house again was a welcome relief and we were told all the details of how our aunt and uncle were able to get invitations to Almack's. While Jane was content with the news, I couldn't help but be wary.

When alone, my aunt, who always seemed to understand my inner emotions, noted my hesitation in allowing myself to be fully happy.

"I know that look," she began. "Lizzy, what is it?"

"Aunt Gardiner, you know that I am grateful for this opportunity, yet I am worried. Almack's is said to contain the very best of society, and the best of society usually requires a person to be the falsest in manners, while also being the most tasteless in regard to being open-minded. People sneer on those who gain their wealth through having an occupation, as if working is a degradation to a person's use in the world. And that is not what I find, yet they do. You don't worry that the attendees will look down on us for being a family from trade?"

"You need not fear," Aunt Gardiner reassured me, "for while aristocracy will always be aristocracy, more and more gentlemen are marrying into families of trade because they are going bankrupt. And this year, Almack's will have other merchants and their daughters present as well. The world is changing slightly."

"Still too slowly for my taste."

"Too slowly for anyone's tastes, dear. Besides, where you and Jane go, you both must be admired. For your father is, essentially, a gentleman, and you two are a gentleman's daughters."

"I have not offended you in any way, have I, Aunt?"

"You have not asked us anything that your Uncle and I have not already discussed. And if anyone at this ball is foolish enough to offend you, then your uncle and I will have no feelings of shame in leaving the ball immediately."

I kissed my Aunt on the cheek and then went off to find Jane.

That night, Jane and I were in our guest room that we shared, and Jane was combing her hair while we were preparing for bed.

"Lizzy?"

"Yes," I said.

"Is it strange that I love it here so much? And not London, I mean, but our uncle's home here. As if I would be content to be here for our entire lives. I would be content, even if I never married, to just sit here, and grow old, surrounded by family, but not be forced to change, or be considered a failure by not moving forward in what society regards as a progressive manner?"

"You wish that we were allowed to stay the same," I said and sighed. "And be accepted as we are, for what we are."

"Yes, am I foolish?"

"Not at all. Never."

"Yet it is a vain wish."

"Who knows? Who knows?"

THE FACE IN THE CROWD

The days leading up to the ball came and went. We had our gowns made and fitted for us. Our hair was done by our aunt's maids and decorated—yet not too ostentatious or flamboyant, and then the night for Almack's arrived.

Our aunt and uncle, along with Jane and I, stepped into the carriage and were off.

Through the streets of London, we eventually arrived at the ballroom that was at Almack's. We were in a long procession of coaches and barouches that had to be parked. Our coach arrived at the entrance, we stepped out in front and were led up the steps.

When we entered the ballroom, our names were announced, and all eyes turned to us. Then we stepped into the ballroom while moving gently out of the way as the next group behind us were announced.

We entered and there were already some gentlemen in the room who had been given the distinction of being knighted. They also, wonderfully, were acquaintances of my uncle's and therefore we were then introduced to them and their wives. There were also a few soldiers dressed in their uniforms and they could be rendered as nothing less than handsome as well. Jane was asked by one gentleman for the first dance, and I was fortunate enough to be asked by one of the soldiers, but during discussion, before the first dance began, my attention was directed to a most surprising sight. There, coming toward us, was Mr. Edmund Brocklehurst.

⚜

"Miss Bennet," Mr. Brocklehurst said, approaching us. "I never thought to find you here."

Jane at first didn't know how to respond for surprise was written across her face clearly, but then she smiled warmly.

"This was a fortune I was lucky enough to have been given, due to the excellent care of my Uncle and Aunt Gardiner...if I may introduce you."

"Oh wonderful," Mr. Brocklehurst said.

"Aunt and Uncle Gardiner, this is Mr. Edmund Brocklehurst, of Canterbury estate in Surrey. Mr. Brocklehurst, these are our family, Aunt and Uncle Gardiner and you remember my sister, Elizabeth."

"Of course, I do. It is nice to make your acquaintance once more, Miss Elizabeth. And it is pleasing to meet you for the first time, Mr. and Mrs. Gardiner."

"It is a pleasure to make your acquaintance as well."

Mr. Brocklehurst continued to make small conversation with my Uncle and then eventually it was time for the dance to begin. He looked saddened in seeing that Jane was engaged for the first dance, but when knowing that I was still available, for the second dance was the one I reserved for the soldier, he asked me for my hand in the first dance. Viewing it as his way of not only trying to impress my sister by showing his gallantry, but also as a way for him to get to know more about Jane through me, I willingly accepted.

The dance began, and we developed casual small talk that I

thought would grow into a discussion about Jane...and yet it never did! I was immensely disappointed when the conversation went as followed:

"You look positively beautiful this evening, Miss Elizabeth," he began.

"Thank you very much for the compliment," I had replied happily, "though in truth I think all credit must be given to the gown."

"Oh, you are too modest."

"I believe that a woman could never give too much credit to her dressmaker, for she often can make up for any mishaps that nature has done on a woman's looks. Yet I shall take your compliment, for it makes my confidence shine."

"My words help your self-assurance?"

"They inspire my self-command."

"You are witty. That is very pleasing."

"You are a good dance partner. Though my sister is the better dancer than myself."

"She is a very skilled dancer, indeed. Now how do you find the weather in London so far?"

"It has been most pleasant so far."

"And does London and all its diversions suit you?"

"I enjoy it tremendously, but I will not deny loving the ramble one can take in the country. I am, in truth, very fond of walking."

"How refreshing. It is lovely to see a woman who has enjoyed walking. Are you a horse-woman?"

"I can ride a horse well enough, but I am not skilled at it at all and have never mastered it fully. Jane, however, is a very good horse-woman."

"Is she? I had never known."

"Aye, she is."

"Very good, that is a wonderful talent to have. So, tell me, where in the country are your favorite walks?"

And the conversation continued as such, where every time that I tried to steer our topics back to my sister, he dismissed it quickly. I did not know what to make of it. Could it have been that he wanted to be discrete about his feelings, and didn't wish to give anything away? Yet another feeling that I felt was that he was a man who was very much unable to handle thinking about something unless it was right in front of him.

When he saw Jane, he enjoyed gazing at her. Yet when she was not there, he didn't seem to care to recall her. Could I have been wrong? Yet I didn't believe myself to be, for I had studied human nature for too long to be ignorant of the signs of hidden intention. And when one thought of his actions, rather than of his words, he was inconsistent at best.

He never tried to visit her whenever she left London, and only seemed to enjoy her company whenever she was in front of him only. If he cared deeply, then he couldn't just easily forget about her. Affection should not cease when distance got in the way of it. I had then decided: Mr. Brocklehurst didn't care for my sister at all.

❧

Our dance had ended, and I went toward the punch bowl and began to get myself a cup. As I did so, another person was getting some punch as well. He picked up a cup just as I poured myself some. Then I looked up at him and started.

The man was tall, his expression was fierce and piercing. He had dark brown hair and dark brown eyes that were fixed on me. I had never seen a man who was so statuesque in my life, for nothing but coldness exuded from him. In a split second's time, I felt as if I could have been knocked down with a feather, for something about him disarmed me. His features were regal, that much was certain, yet that was not the reason for his hold on me. Something in his air and manner of stance made him very difficult for me to read.

All my life, I enjoyed the entertaining prospect of taking in a person's first impression they gave me. And my first impression of him was a blank. I could not determine anything about him...except that he seemed to be a question in my mind, and I disliked not having answers.

"I..." I began.

"I..." he replied, looking deeply into my eyes. "We have not been introduced by anyone."

I waited for him to overcome his fear of decorum and introduce himself, yet he did not. And for reasons that I could not fathom, it made me a little angry. Was decorum really so essential to the present moment? For a man to make such a statement implied that he was rigid and unyielding. And yet, I immediately softened, for his expression read more like a hesitant child. He seemed uncomfortable and as if he simply did not know how to talk to me. Immediately feeling pity for him, I decided to be chivalrous. I took another spoonful of punch and poured it into his empty glass while he held it.

"I," he started, "I mean...thank you."

I did my best, but I found myself staring at him again, and he began to want to say something else yet looked confused and he walked away. Despite how irrational it would have made me look, my first instinct was to pursue him. Yet then I was able to gather my self-composure. It would have been foolish to have tried to pursue him in any way, as well as being vulgar and indelicate. I didn't know why, but I could not help but watch him as he walked to the other side of the room.

What was most frightening was knowing how I must've looked, for when I stood there, gazing at him, he turned around one last time and looked at me. Our gazes locked again, and then he turned and walked away.

I went back to my aunt's side and she needed to remind me that I had expected the soldier soon to take my hand for the next dance.

I joined him on the dance floor and did my very best to direct all my attention to him, yet there was a distraction. Further down the line, I saw the same man dancing with another woman who was clearly doing everything and anything to keep his attention on her.

As the dance continued, his eyes eventually fell on me and I was surprised that he did not look away at first. The woman he was dancing with noticed this and I could see her eyes turn into slits as his eyes fell on me. Then we turned away as quickly as we could and focused on our own partners. Yet never did I not glimpse him out of the corner of my eye, and never was he too far for me to see.

And then the most wonderful and frightening thing happened. As the dance continued and the soldier and I had to move down the aisle and switch partners, mine ended up being him. Tension felt as if it grew all over my body and I felt tingles through me. He took my hand in his and turned me around.

"I..." I began.

"I'm... I'm Mr..."

We were then separated, and the dance steps required that we go back to our own individual partners.

❧

When the dance ended, I went back to my sister who had just finished her dance with Mr. Brocklehurst. When she came back to me, her face was beaming with happiness.

"I had the most wonderful time, dancing with Mr. Brocklehurst," she began, "for he is so fascinating."

"Aye, he is," I said warily and distractedly. In truth, I just wanted to find where that man in the crowd was so that I could see him one last time.

"Indeed, he is," Jane continued, "for I have never seen a man of such liveliness and happier manners than him. He has asked to call on me one morning this week. Oh, Lizzy, isn't it wonderful?"

"It is. Yet, Jane, I must warn you, be cautious."

"You know me, Lizzy. I shall never subject myself to ridicule of manner by exposing my sentiments publicly."

"I know that you never give away your feelings, Jane, for you are modest in that way. I'm just saying, be careful. I'm not certain that I trust him."

"Trust him?" Jane said, "What do you mean?"

The third dance resumed, and Jane had to dance with another gentleman who requested her hand for the third set.

When she went off to the dance floor, and I was not engaged, I stood with my aunt who was conversing with a soldier's wife. Free from conversation, I let my eye wander, and I was happy to behold the man who I saw once more.

Only then did I notice that he truly looked uncomfortable and almost miserable. For a moment, I wondered if he looked that way because he was proud and unpleasant by nature, or because he was simply...uncertain in himself. He might've just been uncomfortable because he was bashful. I wanted to believe in the best of him, for because we had not met, I didn't want to subject him to a first impression that might have been inaccurate.

And then once more, his eyes fell on me. At first, he looked away, as did I, and then I noticed him looking at me in earnest. I am aware that I should have looked away, yet I could not. I looked upon him once more, and I found his eyes set, firm and unrelenting. Struck by an impulse, I made a funny face at him. His lips started forming into a smile, but he stopped it quickly.

Feeling as if his refusal to laugh was a challenge that I was more than happy to face, I could not deny myself the pleasure of such an attempt. It was foolish of me to do so, and yet I could not resist. I was breaking decorum in every sense of the word, and yet, when looking back on my actions, I do not believe that I would have changed my course of action.

If he did not wish to laugh, then I would do everything in my power to make him do so.

෨෫෪

Looking directly at him without shame, I pursed my lips together. He did not smile, but the sides of his lips curled up slightly, and I took that as encouragement.

I put my finger under my nose and pushed the tip of my nose up, which from what I recalled, it made me look slightly like a pig.

His lips curled up even more.

Then I quickly pulled one side of my lip to the side and distorted my face.

And then he laughed.

I had felt victorious. For I was.

The look on his face, despite his attempts to suppress it, showed that he knew I was successful. I could not tell whether he was satisfied with my actions, or if he thought me impertinent.

Yet he did not look away and that was all that mattered. However, the fourth dance began and the same woman who he danced with before had come to retrieve him.

Unfortunately, she saw me once more and her eyes focused on me narrowly again. I knew that, despite my lack of an acquaintance with this woman, that she had clearly regarded me as a rival when it was not necessary. And yet the mind of a woman in competition with another woman will always render itself blind to how it must act. I hoped that I would never meet her, whoever she was, for she would now view me as her enemy.

When the man had left to dance with her, I asked my uncle who he was. He looked to where I gestured and then glimpsed the man who danced.

"I cannot tell you," Uncle Gardiner replied, "For I have not made his acquaintance. And he clearly is in circles that are too high for me to reach."

The night at Almack's continued and eventually ended. I never got acquainted with the man who I almost met but didn't, the man who would remain nothing more than the face in the crowd.

❧ 6 ❧

FEARS & WOES

When the ball at Almack's ended, Mr. Darcy escorted Miss Bingley and her sister, Mrs. Hurst, back to their townhouse. The whole time on the way home, Miss Bingley tried to engage him in conversation, yet he did not know how to attend to her, and honestly didn't care to.

He did not mean to be rude, yet he had danced two dances with her and wasn't surprised but no less annoyed with the looks she gave that woman that he was admiring at the ball.

When dropping them both off and trying to be polite to them at the end, Mr. Darcy was left to ride in his carriage alone, and he welcomed the isolation.

All throughout the night, he could not help but look at the woman who always kept looking at him. He should have regarded her stares as a constant impertinence, for who did she think she was? And yet, he had stared back and thought nothing intrusive about her eyes on him until the ball had ended and he was free from her scrutiny.

Yet what about her did disarm him so much? She was a beauty, that much was undeniable, yet he had beheld many beauties all paraded around by their mothers during the seasons. Also, many of those gentlewomen were so lovely that this strange woman at the ball paled in comparison to them. She was lovely, but also plain when placed next to them.

And yet, her beauty seemed distinct, individual, and as if it could only belong to her.

And her eyes! They were so intelligent and full of life. They seemed to shine in the light of the candles that were along the walls. They were mesmerizing to him.

While Mr. Darcy could not separate his mind from the curiosity that this woman presented, he could not help but find her intrusion on his thoughts as very much antagonizing.

Mr. Darcy had been in love before, and each time he had suffered disappointment, for either the woman married elsewhere before he got the chance to tell her his feelings, or his regard for her was a foolish one, for she proved to be either a vain and foolish woman, or a disloyal character of weak inclination who proved to only be pretending to be in love with him because of his wealth and status in society.

Mr. Darcy reasoned with himself that this woman could be no different. And therefore, Mr. Darcy resolved it within himself to never let his curiosity trick him into seeking her out.

Attraction, true attraction in his life only led to a quick succession of fears and woes, and it should not follow that his future should mimic his past.

And this woman, whoever she was would not be his future, temporary or permanent.

7

THE TIDES HAVE TURNED

When Mr. Bingley returned, Mr. Darcy and he accompanied a group of other gentlemen to Spain and to Vienna. Eventually, when it was time for journey's end, their group felt restless and didn't want to return home to England just yet. They coaxed and brought forth their best pleas and arguments to convince Darcy and Bingley to join them.

Mr. Darcy, happy to know that his presence amongst the group was desired, as well as content in feeling that he was beginning to be comfortable around everyone enough to improve his personality, he readily agreed and sent a letter express to his father to let him know this. He sent two letters, one to Pemberly and the other to their townhouse, in hopes the letter would reach him in no less than two weeks' time.

Joining his company onward, they travelled to Italy and then went to Rome. Mr. Darcy, egged on by Mr. Bingley, allowed himself to get drunk for the very first time with the company. When he finally woke up the next morning to a painful headache, he hated the sight of sunlight temporarily, the smell of food made him sick, and Mr. Bingley along with the rest of his company met and regaled him with stories of what he did when he was inebriated. Mr. Darcy was mortified when he discovered that when he was in his cups, he liked to sing and dance. Bingley chuckled when he let him know that Mr. Darcy had a nice baritone voice and he did a strange two step when he drank his fourth bottle of wine. Mr. Darcy groaned inwardly and decided to never again allow himself to go past half a bottle in his life.

In Rome, there were many festivals at night, and they attended them. Mr. Darcy then decided to listen to his father's advice and let himself loosen his self-command temporarily—at least enough to kiss a woman. And he did! To his incredible inner sentiments, he found himself to enjoy the look of a very beautiful woman who wore a mask at first. She actually walked up to him and kissed him suddenly while his friends laughed and turned around to pursue another group of women who were standing nearby and looking at them teasingly. The woman took off her mask and she was incredible to behold.

"I..." Mr. Darcy began, "Good evening, Signora."

"Good evening?" She laughed. "Is that all that you have to say to me?" She then put her mask back on and began to walk away.

"Wait!" Mr. Darcy said, chasing her through the crowd. She took off her mask, laughed and then threw it at Mr. Darcy, who caught it in his hands. "Now you are learning some courage, whoever you are. Yet, I shall place this task on you. You may only get me if you catch me!"

She then began to run through the crowd and away from him again. At first, Mr. Darcy thought not to do so, because of his pride and self-assurance. And yet, he was not in England, but in Rome. What really were the chances of his actions getting seen and then retold back in England? As his father had said, he was a young man, and for just one moment he could be so.

Acting on an impulse that was unlike him, he began to run after her. However, when he got near to her, he felt a hand grab his arm and he turned to see his valet, Jefferson.

"Jefferson!" Mr. Darcy said, startled and a little embarrassed, "I was just—wait, what are you doing here?"

"I was sent to come and fetch you."

"Fetch me? By whom?"

"Mr. Darcy..."

"Spill it, man, time is of the essence."

"The prince of Britain, Mr. Darcy. The Prince Regent needs you."

Mr. Darcy was following Jefferson through the crowd.

⚜

"I can't believe it." Mr. Darcy groaned. "Not again!"

"Yes, sir," Jefferson said, "I know how you feel."

"I cannot comprehend the coincidence of the Prince being present here in Italy while I am." Darcy chuckled sadly. "Darn the word *chance*."

Jefferson had told Mr. Darcy why he was sent for and as soon as his narration was done, Mr. Darcy followed his valet immediately.

"Why whenever we come in the same proximity as each other," Mr. Darcy said, "The Prince feels as if he has to rely on me? Good god, I don't even like him!"

"And you have no problem in showing it."

"Precisely, he has so many sycophants around him, why must he want someone's attention who for some reason would rather risk getting my head shoved into a guillotine rather than offer him a compliment."

"I think that's why he does so, sir. Humanity is a strange thing, and very often people cling to those who we feel have robbed us all in some way. Therefore, instead of obsessing over those who cling to us, we cling to those who criticize us. In other words, he wants your approval because you very rarely ever bestow it on him."

"Jefferson, are you saying that it's our continual dislike of each other that makes him rely on me?"

"Sir, that's the best theory that I can give you."

☙❦❧

Both men passed through the crowds that were there for the festival and entered a very regal house. Mr. Darcy and Mr. Jefferson were immediately met by some royal guards, were led up a series of steps and then let into a room.

Mr. Darcy was shocked when a figure stood up from a bed and then turned to him.

"Oww!" Mr. Darcy cried when he beheld the person's face. There standing before him was the Prince Regent and he had a bloody eye and bruised cheek.

"I would ask for your sympathy, Darcy," the Prince of Britain sneered, "yet something tells me that you won't offer your condolences."

"Only after you tell me how the Prince of all Britain ended up with a scratched face, and why he is here in Rome."

"Can't I have any secrets?" He groaned, and added, "Especially since I'm royalty and you're not."

"Aye, Prince you are royalty, but I'm Mr. Darcy."

"Is that supposed to mean something?"

"I'm sure it does somehow."

"I could and should have you thrown into a dungeon and tortured."

"If you do that, then how will I be able to help you? Now, do you wish for my assistance or not?"

"I do, despite myself."

"Very well, then. So how shall we begin? Really, Prince, you must tell me what has happened."

Mr. Darcy was inwardly not only annoyed with the Prince, but also angry, for he felt as if he had been taken from being in the company of a woman who had intrigued him.

"Right, well then," the Prince said, "I am surrounded by useless sycophants, as you know, who I love to have around me because they do whatever I want. Yet when it comes to finding someone, they are useless."

"You need me to find someone? What did they do to you?"

"You do see my face, don't you?"

"Yes, but I'm sure they did something else to you as well."

"I was dining with a beautiful woman and naturally I wanted my privacy with her. So, I brought her here, and we drank somewhat. Then on the point of our intimacy getting more enjoyable—"

"Prince, these next details are things that I don't need to know."

"Don't worry, it does not get vulgar—or not in the manner of vulgarity that your mind is thinking. The woman kissed me and slid something in my mouth through hers. I ended up swallowing it and it made me paralyzed somewhat, my body went sluggish and I could barely move. She then tied me up, gagged me, and then began to steal everything of value in my chambers. All of my jewelry is gone."

"Your highness, why do you even have jewelry? You're a man."

"Because I'm royalty, you insolent fool!"

"Yet I'm sure that you have many more rings and necklaces."

"Yes, but one of these rings is custom and is known for belonging to me especially. Therefore, if this thief were to get away with it, then they would be able to show how they got the better of the Prince, and the way in which they went about it."

"So, a woman stole from you and was able to walk out of here so easily."

"Like I said, I wanted privacy. After she bound and gagged me, then stole, she then began to beat me up with her fists."

"And she gave you those lacerations?" Mr. Darcy said, pointing to the Prince's face.

"Aye, now I know you have a way of finding people, and I don't know how this is such a talent of yours."

"Yet you need my services to discover this person."

"My guards are good with protection, but not with being clever. And if you help me in this, then I shall give you two things that you enjoy most of all."

"And what is that?"

"Peace and forgiveness for all the times that you spoke to me in such a blasphemous way."

"Well, I suppose that is not really fair, but fair enough."

"Then we have a deal."

"Aye, we have a deal."

"Oh, and one more thing. You will not be looking for a woman. You will be looking for a man."

"Yet it was a woman who had robbed you."

"I... I thought she was a woman."

"Come again?"

"I thought she was a woman. Yet the woman turned out to be a man."

"Are you serious, your highness?"

"You don't understand! I had no way of knowing! He was dressed as a woman, looked like a woman, and was beautiful! It wasn't until the clothing came off a little further that I was able to make the discovery."

Mr. Darcy held his tongue and offered the Prince a farewell as he left and vowed that he would find this person. Yet when he got outside of the room, Mr. Darcy could not resist bursting out laughing.

Finding this thief was not nearly as hard for Mr. Darcy as it would have been for anyone else. There was a reason for why Mr. Darcy kept Jefferson in his employ, and it wasn't just because Jefferson was a loyal and talented valet—it was because Jefferson had a history of being a bit of a spy before, as well as having a separate life once, in America, that Mr. Darcy did not know the full extent of the secret in some way.

When he was a young man, Jefferson had a whole different life than he did as an older one. To have Jefferson under his employ was to have someone who, wherever he went, would make it a mission to learn everything about where his employer was staying. If there was a secret plan afoot anywhere near Mr. Darcy, then Jefferson knew how to figure it out.

Therefore, when given his mission, Mr. Darcy went to Jefferson who went to work immediately. Jefferson also interviewed the other people who worked under Mr. Darcy's employ as well as speak to all the servants in the house of the Prince's. They gave Jefferson information of which way the thief went, then Jefferson also sent inquiries around the owners at pawnshops, asking for a very particular ring, and to be notified immediately once it got sold to them. Very soon after a few days, the thief was discovered, and wishing to help his valet at the end, Mr. Darcy accompanied the guards of the Prince's and they arrested the thief.

After it all, Mr. Darcy still felt that he could not get his mind off the woman that he had kissed that night at the festival. At first, he could not understand why he could not get the woman out of his mind, for he did have the self-assurance and inner command to not be so moved by a woman to feel bound to her after one kiss. Yet, after a while, it then began to occur to him the source behind his obsession. The woman, who he regarded as quite lovely, had a beautiful set of fine eyes. And those dark brown eyes of hers had reminded him of the woman who smiled at him at the ball at Almack's all those weeks ago. And that woman—and those eyes of hers—had never been far from his mind.

Mr. Darcy had hoped that the distance he placed between England and himself would have rid his mind from this woman who had haunted him, yet it had not done so. Somehow, despite his best efforts, the distance he put in between himself and London didn't distance himself from his curiosity about her—and her name. Good god, he had never learned her name. At first, he had welcomed the ignorance, yet now time had worn him down, and it ate away at him.

Then, when the last time that he would see the Prince Regent arrived, he came upon the idea suddenly, and made his way to the royal house in Rome.

๛

"You're asking me for what?" The Prince said, sitting in his private chambers.

"I just wish to know the identity of a woman who was at Almack's last time I was there."

"Why don't you find this woman yourself?"

"I don't wish to appear as if I am pursuing her."

The Prince Regent leaned forward and smirked at Mr. Darcy in a way that he did not like.

"Well, my word, Mr. Darcy is taken with a woman? Could it be that the pure and annoyingly rigid Mr. Darcy has learned how to fall into the foolish traps that we other humans have fallen into?"

"You act as if love is something you know about."

"Do you think me void of every proper feeling? Of course, I

have been in love before. You are just mean for thinking otherwise."

"Then I ask you to do this for me, to even our deal."

"Our deal? Our deal is done."

"In response for my discretion," Mr. Darcy said, "and to make sure that I pay all of my servants enough to not spread any word about what has transpired this night. Do this one small thing for me, and we shall be even."

"Very well. And is there any way that I shall be able to find out how to discover this woman?"

"Aye, I know that she was with her sister at Almack's, and her sister danced with a gentleman named Mr. Edmund Brocklehurst. Yet I don't know Mr. Brocklehurst myself."

"I do. I shall write to him immediately, and then I'll have her name for you by the time that you arrive back in London. The letter of her name and whereabouts will be waiting for you back at your London townhouse."

"Thank you, Prince Regent."

"You're welcome. And by god do I love having you feel as if you owe me."

"Must you look at it like that?"

"I cherish it."

Mr. Darcy bowed and left, thinking, *well at least I didn't get beat up by a man dressed up as a woman,* to himself.

❦

Mr. Darcy and Mr. Bingley ate with their group of friends, who still did not understand why Darcy had wanted to stay in Rome for so long. Yet, when he merely gave them the excuse of courting a woman a bit, they believed it and didn't press the matter—except for Mr. Bingley.

"I know that you are not telling the whole truth, Darcy," he said.

"I know you can tell," Mr. Darcy had replied, "Yet you must trust me now. This is something that I should not tell you, and it's better that you do not know about it."

"What did you do? You didn't make love to a nun, did you?"

"God no, Bingley!"

Then they were interrupted by Jefferson who entered with a letter from Mr. Darcy's father, which had been sent by express. Mr. Darcy opened it and read it with alacrity. Mr. Bingley watched as his friend's face began to lose all color.

"Darcy, what is it?"

Mr. Darcy's eyes glazed over with rage in inner shock at feeling how the tides had turned and the moment went from one of levity to one of gravity.

"It's my father. A week ago, he fell ill, and the doctor diagnosed it as pneumonia and that if he rested, he would improve. Yet he has not, and he wants me to come home immediately."

Mr. Darcy stumbled to his feet, rushed out and Bingley followed him.

❧ 8 ❧

THE BEST OF NEWS

Over the past few weeks, I had seen Mr. Brocklehurst pay my sister much attention. He visited often and was most attentive to her, including writing her poetry. Poetry was a very ambiguous activity to me in the way of love. It could nourish a strong love, or make a weak love appear as strong. Yet I willed myself to not look on any actions of Mr. Brocklehurst and censuring them or offering my talents of ridicule. Truth be told, Jane was so happy with the attentions he bestowed on her that it increased her self-assurance.

I knew her main reasons why, which were that our mother had seen at a young age that Jane was the main beauty of our family, and therefore she would be the one who was most likely to make an advantageous marriage. Too much weight and responsibility had been placed on her shoulders that should not have been, and I was quite happy that it was a burden that I never had to bear. Even at the expense of my mother not regarding me in any special way, I was at least liberated from her constant schemes. And that freedom left me able to dwell on things that I was intrigued by, yet would never see come to pass.

The man that I had seen at Almack's was a primary subject upon which I dwelled. I could not accept or deny that inwardly, he did intrigue me, and I couldn't help but think of him often. There was a time where I resolved it within me to think of him no more...and then I was thinking of him an hour later. Accepting that my self-will was not as strong as I had hoped, I tried to distract myself by focusing only on Jane's happiness.

And yet one thing had struck me as strange one day. When Mr. Brocklehurst had visited Jane, and I greeted him in the hallway before she came down, he came toward me and greeted me warmly. He asked me about my health, I responded in kind, and then he said something that confused me greatly.

"So, Miss Elizabeth," he said, "I congratulate you. Your beauty has really gotten you further than even the luckiest of women here in the London aristocracy."

"Further, sir?"

"I will say no more on the subject, yet I must acknowledge that it takes a certain special lady to be asked about by the Prince of Britain. And while I first wondered if I might have made a mistake in leaning toward one sister, I am happy that I made the choice I did, for I would not have gotten in the way of royalty—and its tastes. Besides, Jane is ideal, and I adore her. Truly, Miss Elizabeth, your sister is perfection itself. I never comprehend my fortune, sometimes. She—she understands me unlike any other."

"I am happy that you have such views, but I still do not know to what you are referring."

"Of course, you don't." He winked at me. "Nay, I shall say no more. I shall say no more."

Jane then came downstairs and I was left in confusion over what had just transpired, and it would have been impertinent to ask anything about what I had been told. They then enjoyed their meeting in joyous tones while I sat on the other couch and sewed a design on a pillow and allowed myself to be thoroughly ignored.

After a week, I was still wondering what Mr. Brocklehurst meant by that when he came to visit. While we sat with them, he turned to our Aunt Gardiner.

"Mrs. Gardiner," he began, "would you mind if I were to request an audience with Miss Bennet...alone?"

Our Aunt Gardiner smiled and granted it while the rest of us left the room and waited in the kitchen.

"I have...doubts," I said as we sat there.

"Doubts," Aunt Gardiner replied, "of what?"

"Of Jane and Mr. Brocklehurst. I am not so sure that they both are fully in love."

"Has Jane told you she doesn't love him?"

"No, she has not, yet I am not sure that she can tell if she does. Sometimes, when a woman is flattered by the attentions of a man, she can think herself in love—but in truth..."

"She is not in love with him," Aunt Gardiner finished my words, "But in love with the idea of being in love."

"Precisely. I have seen many women make this mistake. I don't want Jane to do so as well."

"I understand your fears, but my dear, if she accepts him, then that is her choice. And you must respect that."

"Aye, tis true."

We waited and then Jane entered, smiling.

"Aunt, Mr. Brocklehurst needs to now speak to my uncle, for my father is not present."

"Aye," Aunt Gardiner jumped up, knowing the meaning of it, "I shall find him immediately." Aunt Gardiner went off to find him and then Jane turned to me.

"Well?" I smiled.

"Oh, Lizzy!" She beamed at me and we embraced. "He loves me, Lizzy, and I am now the happiest of women. He has asked for my hand in marriage."

"I take it from your reaction that you have said yes."

"Of course, I have!"

Any fears I had of Jane not being in love with Mr. Brocklehurst had ended and together we celebrated her hearing the very best of news.

❧ 9 ❧

THE WORST OF NEWS

Mr. Darcy eventually made it to his townhouse in London and Mr. Bingley accompanied him. When they arrived, the door opened, and Darcy was surprised to have been met by his cousin, Colonel Richard Fitzwilliam. Colonel Fitzwilliam was a man in his mid-thirties, who was not as handsome as his cousin, but was blessed with such happy manners that it made up for his lacking in the best of features. And yet, being amidst a painful scene, his usually pleasant expression was now dour and woeful.

"Darcy!" he said when Mr. Darcy rushed up the steps. "Thank God you have arrived."

"Richard! How is my father?"

"He is not doing any better, and he has been asking for you ever since this morning."

Mr. Darcy, Colonel Fitzwilliam, and Mr. Bingley all entered, and his friend and cousin waited in the parlor while Mr. Darcy rushed up the steps and into his father's bedroom. There at the bed was the physician and his younger sister, Georgiana.

"Fitzwilliam!" Georgiana cried, running to him. They

embraced, and Georgiana followed him up to his father's bed, where he was resting.

"How is he doing?"

Georgiana shook her head. Mr. Darcy walked up to his father and sat down.

"If you wake him up," the doctor said, "it's best that you do it now."

"Now?"

"Mr. Darcy, I want to believe that he will improve, but I will be truthful. He is not doing as I would hope. You should...prepare yourself."

Mr. Darcy halted, feeling the weight of what the doctor confessed.

"Father," Mr. Darcy whispered, "Father?"

Very soon, his father's eyes opened.

"Fitzwilliam..."

"Yes, it's me, Father. How are you feeling?"

"I am... I shall be honest. You see how I'm doing."

"You will improve. You will, for—you've survived worse."

"And yet it only takes the one time, that you cannot recover from, to best you." Mr. Darcy Sr. opened his eyes wider and looked at Georgiana. "Georgiana?"

"Aye, Father?"

"You look so much like your mother."

Georgiana held back her tears.

"And Fitzwilliam?"

"Yes, Father?"

"My will is already written, and it shall be clear."

"Please, Father, don't speak of this now."

"And yet," his father spoke over him, "There is one thing that I have left out. I thought of omitting it many times because it seemed to be something that was expressed through sentiment. Yet it's something that has been passed down from father to son for hundreds of years, even before our family came here from France—it's like an eternity. This decree is something that has never meant anything to me, and I find it foolish, but so it is. I must tell you, that if you ever meet a woman named Bennet, you owe her a debt."

"A debt? What does that mean?"

"I haven't the slightest notion. Like I said, I have ignored it myself and I have never been the worse for it. As did my father, and his father, the father before him, and so on...yet we are told to say so nonetheless."

Fitzwilliam Darcy was confused over the message that his father relayed to him. Seeing him perplexed, his father took his son's hand in his.

"Like I said, don't worry on it at all, for it has been news that meant little to me or any man that I have ever known in our family. Yet what is the most important thing of all, son—well you know my sentiments. Remember family, and the loyalties you must feel bound to, but above all, be happy, Fitzwilliam. Be happy."

Over the next couple of days, Mr. Darcy Sr. didn't get any better, and yet he didn't get any worse.

Over time Mr. Darcy sought comfort with his sister, and Mr. Bingley, but he mostly sought the counsel of Colonel Fitzwilliam. His cousin always had the best way of making Darcy feel better, and his presence there was invaluable.

"So," Mr. Darcy said as he sat with Richard, "how does military life treat you lately?"

"Same as it always does," Colonel Fitzwilliam said, "yet we should not speak of me now. This is your time."

"You think I want to speak of my father dying?"

"I think now is the time to not be afraid of speaking of what you feel."

"In truth, I feel ashamed."

"Ashamed? Of what?"

"Ashamed that I had been so disobliging in the past. He had so much advice to give and I never listened."

"Advice? What foolishness are you talking? You were a devoted son and he knows that."

"What he asked of me was something so simple. What my mother and Aunt Catherine asked of me was simple, and I have held it off for too long."

"What could you be talking about? And..." Colonel Fitzwilliam's eyes widened, and he began to comprehend his cousin's meaning. "No, Darcy, don't even think about it."

"I'm only saying..."

"I know precisely what you are saying. You are implying that to honor your father, and your mother's memory, you might give into your families' desires of marrying our cousin, Anne."

"It is a wise course of action."

"Except that you do not love Anne. And our Aunt Lady Catherine has been cruel for constantly mentioning and implying it all these years."

"Richard, you know as well as I that if we marry, we can keep our family's wealth within the family. If Anne and I marry, then we shall make sure our family remains one of the most prestigious families in Britain."

"You already are one of the most prestigious families in Britain. Wherever the name Darcy is, you will be given respect, be granted admission in the best of society, and treated in the most wonderful of ways."

"Yet if I marry Anne De Bourgh, our family will be only less than the royal family. It is a logical action."

"Yet is it the right one? We have had this discussion before. And for a man of such wealth, marrying who you prefer is something you can afford. Which makes you more fortunate than I."

"Richard, I am sorry for your situation."

"And as I said, we are not talking of me just now," Colonel Fitzwilliam said, ignoring the pain of being a man born as a second son and having to work for a living, for he would never inherit a fortune as Darcy would. "Darcy, I know your disposition, and it's not your way to marry someone that you don't feel a deep affection for. You are a man who cannot bind himself to someone so intimately and does not consider that you love her. And you don't love our cousin Anne."

"And yet, the family loyalty that I wish to maintain is not the sole reason behind my desire to marry Anne De Bourgh."

"And what is your other reason?"

"Because of my weakness."

"What weakness?"

Mr. Darcy turned to Richard and looked hopeless.

"My weakness that my history has proven is within me, and that is my weakness for falling in love with the worst form of women. Richard, you've seen it. I have formed attachments to women who just wanted me for my wealth or status, and I didn't notice until it was almost too late, and they almost had trapped me."

"Yet you figure out eventually. You always do."

"But it's risky, and I cannot be trusted. I cannot rely on my own judgment to lead me to the right form of love."

"And if you marry Anne, what then? And tell me, how is Anne's marrying you for your wealth and connections any different than what those other women did to you?"

"I see the truth, unlike the women before, where I was being deceived. Also, I felt bound to those women who society praised and then proved to be heartless creatures. How heartbreaking it would be for me to wake up and find out that the woman I love never loved me."

"So, better to marry Anne, who you know you don't love at all, and who doesn't love you, so that you won't feel any disappointment."

"I'm not a strong man, Richard. Heartache would destroy me."

"You are the strongest man I know, Darcy. Heartbreak is just something that gnaws at all of us eventually. Don't fear it so."

"I need time to think."

"Then do so and realize that you have all the time in the world."

"Yet my father doesn't."

"In this life, yes. Yet in the afterlife, he will still see you, and no matter your choice, he will still be happy for you, and proud of you."

Colonel Fitzwilliam put on his hat and left his cousin alone.

⊛

Mr. Darcy sat alone and thought about it, and he concluded that he would do his duty by his people. And who knew what the future would bring? Maybe he would learn to love Anne, and she would with him.

While sitting there, the door opened, and Jefferson entered, looking grave.

"Jefferson, what is it?"

"Sir, I..."

Mr. Darcy read his expression.

"No..."

"I am so sorry, sir."

"No!"

Mr. Darcy rushed past him, ran up the steps and into his father's room. The doctor was just placing a sheet over his father's head as Georgiana wept. Upon his entering, she cried and ran to him. He swept her up in his arms and they both held each other, each one's spirit buckling over from this weight that bore on their souls.

When Jefferson said that he would go to the coroner and make all the arrangements for Mr. Darcy, at first his employer was too stunned to reply. Jefferson took his reply as an affirmative and went off to begin to make arrangements for Mr. Darcy Sr.'s funeral.

"This isn't fair," Georgiana said, "This just isn't fair."

"No, it's not," Mr. Darcy replied.

"We just lost our mother not so long ago. I cannot bear this now."

"Nor can I. Yet the whole family must be sent for. Our Aunt and Uncle Fitzwilliam, Aunt De Bourgh... Anne. And all the rest of them."

"Aye."

Mr. Darcy then stood up suddenly and began to walk out.

"Fitzwilliam," Georgiana started, "where are you going?"

"I just need to go for a walk. Forgive me, I need to be alone. And I just—Georgiana, I don't want you to see me like this. So please don't follow me."

With the alacrity that can come from wishing to outrun a painful situation, Mr. Darcy left the house immediately and began walking to the park. He didn't know why, yet for some reason, that was the destination his feet decided to take him so that he could escape the worst of news.

CHANCE ENCOUNTER

F eeling restless one morning, I decided that I would like to walk to the park. Jane wanted to accompany me, yet she expected Mr. Brocklehurst to visit at any moment. My aunt and uncle trusted me at that point, and they allowed me to go alone. This suited me quite well, for I had two letters to read. My friends Charlotte Lucas and Jane Austen had replied to the letter that I sent them before with news about Jane's engagement.

Our parents had written to us about Jane's engagement to Mr. Brocklehurst as well, yet it was directed mostly to Jane and not really to me. In truth, I knew that Jane's marriage to Mr. Brocklehurst would make me even less visible or of any significance in my mother's eyes. Yet I was happy for Jane, and I knew that my father and aunts would not forsake me in any way. Therefore, lack of affection on my mother's side was always compensated for by the affection I received from others. And yet, I did wish, inwardly, that as she did love me, if only she could learn to like me.

Yet I walked onward and eventually reached the park. I walked through the greenery and noticed that some people who passed me were eyeing me with curiosity. It made sense, for very rarely would a woman be seen walking through the park unaccompanied. It wasn't because it broke decorum really, yet it was because women simply didn't like looking friendless or not having any popularity of any sort. Yet I never cared for such things.

As I found a bench that was a little hidden from the path, I sat down, took out my letters and began to read them. As I was reading about how Charlotte's father wanted to plan for them to travel to the continent to go on holiday, I heard a sound of footsteps coming down the walk.

Looking up to see who interrupted my privacy, I stood up and saw...

"You!" I whispered under my breath. It was the very same man who I gazed upon at the ball at Almack's. He walked down the pathway and sat down on a bench that was a little distance from mine. From his angle, he could not see me, yet I saw him clearly.

After I overcame my surprise and secret satisfaction of seeing him, only then was I able to notice his expression. He was sad—and yet sad was not the word for it. He was in despair, clearly, and his shoulders were hunched over. Then he began to weep, and my heart went out to him. Something had broken his heart, and it weighed on him terribly. Looking on him in such a state made my heart feel agony over watching him. I wished that I could ease his pain, and I wanted to walk over to him and do so very much.

Watching him as he sat there, looking so tragic, was when I had to be honest with myself finally. It had been dwelling within me for so long, yet I never let the admission get louder than a whisper in my soul, until now. Now it came to be...and I had to give my confession; I was drawn to him. I wanted him.

Yet when I immediately confessed it to myself, it frightened me. It was so, that we women, due to our position in society, had to think of such things often, yet that was not what I always indulged in. Intimacy was something I dreamed of, yet it was never something that I ever lived and truly experienced. It was a theory I often assumed but never encountered, that within a dream is where we can control a happy thought, yet when the thought became a reality it could turn into a fear. What was a blessing in your head could become a bane in the air.

And now I knew. Now I knew that love might be something too frightening for me. And for a second, when looking at him, I wanted to get away from him. And it was better that I did so, for I was intruding on his privacy during a moment that he would not want to be spied upon.

Silently, I got up and began to tiptoe away from him, slowly and surely. Unfortunately, my foot stepped on a twig and his head shot up, snapped around and his eyes fell on me.

It felt as if an eternity had occurred when our eyes connected with each other. I could tell that mine was mingled with guilt, shame, and surprise, while his was filled with shock and embarrassment at being seen crying.

Without thinking, I turned and walked a few steps, but then I stopped. Suddenly I was struck by a desire to not leave him. I wanted to remain and find some way to comfort him. Yet I did not know what to do, nor did I know if he would even take my offer of condolences.

I also did not know why my instincts had suddenly shifted from a desire to run from him, then a desire to care for him. I was momentarily being nonsensical, and I knew it.

Next, I noticed a bush of flowers that were next to me. I cannot tell you by what power I was possessed, yet I made a decision. I leaned over, tore a small branch of flowers off the bush, turned around and walked up to him. I was frightened of my own nerve and daring, yet it was too late to go back. I stopped in front of him, raised the flowers up to him to take, and looked into his eyes.

"Whatever has happened, I am sorry for your pain." I sighed, and added, "Yet I promise, you will smile again. You shall find happiness. And I promise that it will not take an eternity to find it."

The man opened his mouth, tried to say something, and then closed it again. Looking down at my hand, he took the flowers. I shuddered a bit as his fingers brushed against mine, and at first, he didn't just take the flowers, but closed his hand around mine. I looked back down at him when he did so, and all he did was look back up at me.

Then he placed them on his lap. When the silence got too heavy, I turned to walk away, but was stopped when he grabbed my hand and stopped me from leaving him. I turned to him suddenly as he placed the flowers on the bench next to him.

Suddenly he stood up and grabbed my shoulders possessively. At first, I did not know what to do, and I only looked downwards. I was eye level with his vest. He truly was very much taller than me as well as more imposing and strong. I felt his breath on the top of my head and I was filled with fear—and shock, for I never had been held like this by a man before. Then, out of curiosity, I slowly looked up at him. Being this close to him, with his tearstained eyes looking down on me, my breath caught in my throat.

Who are you? I asked myself. *Why can't I forget you? Why am I not afraid of anything that you do?*

And I wasn't. I only continued to stare up at him in wonder, at this silent man who I knew could speak, but something was holding him back, or something was within him that he would not allow himself to open up to me.

Yet I could not deny that he held a power over me. And though he was not the most ideal-looking man in the world, he was beautiful in my eyes. Indeed, I had never declared ever seeing so handsome a man in my life.

Suddenly the man began to lower his face to mine and I remained where I was, not even wishing to run away.

He was leaning down to kiss me, and I knew that I should have run or called him out for being so un-gentlemanlike, yet I could not. Was it my desire to be close to him, or was it my empathetic feeling that he needed some form of solace momentarily, some easing of grief? His lips lowered down to mine and I began to close my eyes, but then he stopped suddenly. When I opened my eyes again, I saw him looking down on me with fear and shame.

"Forgive me," he said. "I... I am being so very terrible. And you are very kind—and so very..."

Suddenly he released me. Turning away from me slowly, he took the flowers that I gave him and began to walk away from me. Then he turned and began to run away. At first, I decided to run after him, yet then people came upon me, and for a woman to run through the park would be regarded as monstrously indelicate. I had to stop immediately and when I turned to see the man who had run from me, he had disappeared from my sight.

He had run away from me once more, and that was the conclusion of the man who I got the chance to see once more with a chance encounter.

❧ II ❧

THE DECISION

Mr. Darcy ran all the way through the park, stopped when he was out of breath and turned around. Content in seeing that the woman had not followed him, he caught his breath and began walking at a quick pace.

It was a close encounter and he was happy that he had run from her, for immediately being in her presence had made him falter and lose his resolve. He had almost kissed her! And Mr. Darcy decided that his self-control was as loose as he remembered it to have been whenever he developed a strong attraction to a woman, and since he so rarely felt an attachment to anyone, his surprise at realizing that nothing within him had changed over the years was frightful.

Yet he then realized that he must've frightened her, confused her, and then had run from her. Such actions must've made her feel a great compliment to herself, then an anxiety, and then hurt—for he had hurt her feelings in running from her. And yet, Darcy acknowledged that it was necessary to hurt her and distance himself from her as much as possible. He had never met her for the first thirty-two years in his life, therefore, it would be less likely that he would ever meet her again.

For they had encountered one another by chance twice before, and what were the chances that fate would present her before him again?

❦

The day of Mr. Darcy's funeral took place at one of the largest cathedrals in London. Yet when done, his coffin would be taken to Kent so that he could be buried with the rest of the Darcys in the graveyard of the church in Kempton, which was their family parish.

Yet at the funeral, much of the aristocracy attended and the church was filled. Mr. Darcy was not even that closely acquainted with most of the people, yet Mr. Bingley was there with his sisters, as well as Colonel Fitzwilliam, his parents, and siblings, as well as many other cousins in the family. Yet what caused most attention to be drawn was the arrival of Lady Catherine De Bourgh and her daughter, Anne.

When they entered, Lady Catherine commanded as much distinction as she always did when she entered a room, looking equally ominous and stern, while her daughter entered behind her, looking as sick and feeble as ever.

When they sat down, Mr. Darcy looked from his pew over at Anne and she was as he always remembered her. She was not lively, didn't ever look anyone in the eye, and her complexion was pale. Her features were not grotesque in any way, yet nor was she marked by any special features. She was a little higher than being plain, but too low to be described as a beauty either.

Mr. Darcy acknowledged that maybe her appearance could be improved if she were allowed to get away from her formidable mother. His Aunt, Lady Catherine De Bourgh, though fond of him as well as being very devoted to family, was an opinionated, cross, and overbearing woman. Everything that occurred around her, she had to bestow her opinion on as if she were the law of everything. And that, mingled with Anne's constantly being ill, would naturally make Anne's spirits dour.

Mr. Darcy, in hopes of convincing himself that he was taking the best course of action, then began to turn his point of view into one of empathy and of helpfulness. His aunt was too controlling of Anne, and never let her live her own life. Thus, she had no choice but to not bloom into a beautiful woman. Yet, if Mr. Darcy married Anne, then he could allow her clothing to be altered to appeal to her type of beauty, he could change her diet, not have her take so much medication that he believed had been more harmful than helpful, and he would be able to free her. Surely such a reason for marrying her was a legitimate and humane one, and it was as good a reason to marry a woman as any.

❧

When the ceremony ended, and Mr. Darcy and Georgiana could return to their townhouse, he knew that he was soon to expect his aunt's entrance. And lo and behold, not more than an hour after he had entered, she made her presence known.

"Oh, my dear nephew!" she said as she entered, "You must be undergoing such a painful moment and I am sorry for your loss." She looked around the room and rolled her eyes. "Fitzwilliam, how many times must I tell you, really, this room is very unsuitable for a study? The windows are full east."

"They suit me fine," Mr. Darcy said, standing up, "How are you, aunt?"

"I am well, thanks to my employ of the best of hired help, which I still doubt that your father has been too proficient in." She sat down, filled with her own self-importance. "Yet one should not speak ill of the dead, and I was very fond of your father, truly."

"Yes, Aunt Catherine."

"So, how are you feeling? I know that the hole your father's loss has made must have you feeling vacant somewhat and being the master of Pemberly is no easy feat. As your nearest relation who has all your interests at heart, I can offer you any advice necessary to help you run your estate."

"You need not worry yourself on that score, aunt, for my father has been having me help run the estate for years now."

"Well...I am happy that he thought of that. Still, I do believe that you should visit me at my home. You should come to Rosing's Park and stay with Anne and I. Bring Georgiana with you as well, for it will not suit you to be alone at this time."

"Aunt, I know your design, and you are hoping for me to come to Rosing's so that I can increase my relationship with Anne."

"Well," Aunt Catherine said, her eyes darting quickly in response to how pointedly he approached the truth of her intentions, "if we must get to the point in the matter, then I believe, Fitzwilliam, that it is high time that you begin to fulfill the wishes that we have all hoped for you. Remember, that it is not just my desire that you and my daughter marry, but it was the express wishes of your late mother, and of your now late father. I believe that you were raised better than to not honor his memory."

"I do honor him, I assure you." Mr. Darcy did not like the way that his aunt thought she could manipulate him, yet he decided not to let his pride get in the way of making the right decision, therefore he went onward with his plan. "And I plan to make good on that score now."

Lady Catherine De Bourgh's face dropped in surprise.

"Are you saying..."

"I do, aunt. And I shall make Anne the happiest of women."

Lady Catherine De Bourgh stood up and looked proud.

"Well, you have made me proud of you." Though she was a

woman who did not know how to show ecstasy, she was very much beside herself in happiness.

"Thank you, aunt. Now I must speak with Anne about it and we should converse alone."

"Oh, you don't need to do that. I can speak for her."

"Yet, the first thing I must do is speak with her."

After more pushing, Lady Catherine allowed them to be alone while Anne entered Mr. Darcy's study and the cousins stood there, looking at each other awkwardly.

"Hello, Anne."

"Hello, Fitzwilliam. I'm sorry for your loss."

"Thank you for your condolences."

"You are welcome."

"You look well, Anne."

"Thank you." Mr. Darcy and Anne then had no idea what to say to each other. And silence threatened to reign.

"How is your health?" He asked.

"Very good, except that I still have a cough."

"Oh, I am sorry for that."

"Thank you."

Then there was another silence. Mr. Darcy realized that he had no choice but to get right to the point because conversation between them clearly was not possible at the moment.

"I have decided that we must get married," he stated bluntly and awkwardly.

"That is a wonderful decision," she whispered.

"Yes, yes, it is."

There was another silence.

"If you would like, I would like to tell you the reasons for why I wish that we should marry," he said, beginning to think of his list of requesting that they accept this union, and he hoped by listing them that it would endear him to her.

"You don't have to tell me your reasons," Anne said, still looking at the ground.

"I don't?"

"No, you don't."

"Oh."

Then there was another silence.

"Are you pleased with our union?" Mr. Darcy asked.

"Yes. Very much."

In Mr. Darcy's eye, she didn't look very happy. And this was not going as he expected.

"Well, that is very nice."

"Yes, yes, it is."

Then there was another silence.

"Well, will you and your mother like to stay for dinner?"

"I'm sure my mother would love to stay for dinner and thank you for the offer."

"Very well. Thank you for accepting my hand in marriage. We shall be very happy as husband and wife, and dinner shall be served at six o'clock."

"Thank you for telling me the time of our meal."

Anne curtsied to Darcy and then left the room.

When left alone, Mr. Darcy sat down and felt that he had done the right thing. Anne and he had no emotional compatibility whatsoever, yet the future could bring anything new.

He was interrupted however when a servant entered with a letter that was addressed to him with a royal seal. Mr. Darcy opened it immediately, but then noticed the Prince Regent's hand-writing. When he realized that it was the Prince telling him the identity of the woman he had been searching for, he closed the letter immediately. For if he was going to commit to Anne in full, then he would need to withdraw himself from any distractions. If he knew the woman's name and whereabouts, he might be tempted to find her. Therefore, he stood up, walked over to the fireplace, and threw the letter into the fire.

Watching the flames burn it completely, Mr. Darcy let out a breath. He had made a decision, and he would hold to it. He would marry Anne and forget all about the woman that he almost kissed and given his heart to so quickly.

12

PREPARING FOR A HAPPY ENDING

When I had returned to my aunt's house from the park, my heart was heavy. He had run from me—and yet he had almost kissed me. What could I make of it? Yet, at the conclusion of our scene, he had forsaken me, and I had to accept that all doors had been closed on that score.

No man had ever run from Jane before, yet one had run from me. This made me feel immensely insufficient. Why could I not be like her and understand how to charm a man that I cared for?

As I had entered, I found Mr. Brocklehurst sitting with Jane while they looked fondly at each other and clearly had just been holding hands. I made my necessary greetings and left them as soon as I could, because I was upset. How dare the strange man do that to me? I went up to my room and lay on the bed.

Feeling lost, I closed my eyes and resolved to think of the man no more.

The day soon came when it was time for us to leave London, and Mr. Brocklehurst assured Jane that he would visit her in Hampshire after he attended to some business he had to finish. This was readily agreed to, and the day of our departure came. Mr. Brocklehurst accompanied our Aunt and Uncle Gardiner and their children as our carriage set off.

After a few hours, we found ourselves looking on a familiar sight of Hampshire. As we rode through and reached Steventon, we passed the Austen's home. Cassandra and Jane Austen rushed out of their house and greeted us.

Happy to see them and feeling a comfort with being around women who were of my like mind and spirit, I asked Jane if she would be upset with me if I stepped out of the carriage and met with them while Jane carried onward to our home. She allowed me to do so, and when the carriage stopped, I ran out and embraced Jane and Cassandra. We ran around the yard of their house with glee.

I told them all about our time in London, yet I left out all news about the man who I kept re-meeting as well as almost kissed.

Jane Austen was a woman who understood that life was complicated, yet Cassandra was the sort who would gasp at the idea of me letting a man almost kiss me, and I could not blame her in full. Therefore, I kept the man as a permanent secret of mine, never to be spoken off.

Later, when I returned home, I was accompanied by both Austen sisters as well as Charlotte Lucas who we went and saw. My appearance at home made my father happy, my sisters giddy, and my mother annoyed.

"Well, Miss Lizzy!" she groaned, "I declare when Jane arrived by herself in the carriage, I was worried that something had happened to you! You do take delight in vexing me!"

"Lizzy!" Kitty cried, "It's nice that you are home."

"Yes, it is," Lydia burst out and said, "and have you brought me any presents?"

"It is nice to see you, Lizzy," Mary had said, "for as I have read in a book, 'a family without all its members feels like a family that is not complete'."

"I'm glad you are home, Lizzy," our father said, "for since you and your sister have left, I had not heard two words of sense at the dinner table."

※

Over the next few days, my mother had been planning happily for the wedding which was to take place in a months' time. The news of Jane's approaching marriage spread over all Steventon and she was the center of everyone's attention, which made her glow. Yet, if that were not enough to occupy us, soon the town was full of news that we would have a new acquaintance added to our circles.

"Lizzy, Jane and Cassandra!" Charlotte Lucas called to us as we all lay on some tree branches on a large elm tree that was off the beaten path. Jane and Cassandra Austen were two women who did not see any impropriety in climbing trees, and nor did Charlotte Lucas. Yet poor Charlotte was afraid of heights, therefore she would always lie at the base of a tree while we climbed it.

"Aye!" Cassandra Austen said, "We are here, Charlotte."

"I have the most wonderful news. It is about the estate that is on the other side of Hampshire."

"Aginfield Park?"

"Yes, that estate. Well, have you heard, it has been let at last?"

"Has it? By who?"

Charlotte then began to tell us of this new bit of news, and when her story was concluded, Cassandra and Jane Austen decided to go off to tell their family about this, while Charlotte escorted me home to Longbourn so that I could tell my family as well.

We entered, and I found my four sisters all huddled against the door that led into my father's study.

"What are you all doing standing against the door?" I whispered.

"Don't speak," Lydia hissed, "for they are speaking of news. There is talk of a new gentleman who is moving into Hampshire."

Charlotte and I looked at each other and smiled, knowing that we already knew the story. Yet that didn't stop us from tiptoeing up to my sisters and began listening in as well.

჻

"My dear Mr. Bennet," our mother began, "have you heard that Aginfield Park is let at last?"

"No, my dear," our father replied, still reading his newspaper as she spoke, "I have not."

"But it is, for Mrs. Long has just been here, and she told me all about it." Our father made no reply and our mother stomped her foot impatiently to get his attention. "Do not you want to know who has taken it?"

"You want to tell me, and I have no objection to hearing it," was his sole reply and our mother felt as if that was invitation enough.

"Why, my dear, you must know, Mrs. Long says that Aginfield is taken by a young man of large fortune from the north of England. That he came down on Monday in a chaise and four to see the place and was so much delighted with it that he agreed with Mr. Morris immediately. That he is to take possession before the end of next week, and some of his servants are to be in the house by the end of next week."

"What is his name?"

"Bingley. And he is unattached, my dear, to be sure! A man of large fortune; four or five thousand a year. What a fine thing for our girls!"

"How so? And how can it affect them?"

"My dear Mr. Bennet, how can you be so tiresome! You must know that I am thinking of his marrying one of them."

"Are you? Ah, so that is his design in settling here?"

"Design! Nonsense, how can you talk so! But it is very likely that he may fall in love with one of them, and therefore you must visit him as soon as he comes."

"Good God woman, Jane is engaged to a smart gentleman from London. Shouldn't you be content with that for the time being?"

"Why should I be, for I may have successfully married off one, yet that does not mean that that solves the problems with the other four. And if Mr. Bingley were to marry one of them while Mr. Brocklehurst was to marry Jane, then that means that two of our daughters will be wed to two men of wealth. And that would be just perfect because their marriages would throw our other girls into the path of other rich men. Therefore, you must visit him directly when he comes."

"I see no occasion for that. You and the girls may go, or you may send them by themselves."

"By themselves?"

"Which perhaps will be still better, for as you are as handsome as any of them, Mr. Bingley might like you the best of the party."

We all had to stifle our laughter at that, for we knew our father was joking.

"My dear, you flatter me," our mother said smugly, not seeing that he was speaking in jest, "I certainly have had my share of beauty, but I do not pretend to be anything extraordinary now. When a woman has five grown up daughters, she ought to give over thinking of her own beauty."

"In such cases, a woman has not often much beauty to think of."

"But, my dear, you must indeed go and see Mr. Bingley when he comes into the neighborhood."

"It is more than I engage for, I assure you."

"But consider your daughters. Only think what an establishment it would be for one of them. Sir William and Lady Lucas are determined to go, merely on that account, for in general you know they visit no new-comers. Indeed, you must go, for it will be impossible for us to visit him, if you do not."

"You are over-scrupulous surely. I dare say Mr. Bingley will be very glad to see you, and I will send a few lines by you to assure him of my hearty consent to his marrying whichever he chooses of the girls."

"You take delight in vexing me. You have no compassion on my poor nerves."

"You mistake me, my dear. I have a high respect for your nerves. They are my old friends. I have heard you mention them with consideration these thirty years at least."

"Ah! You do not know what I suffer."

"But I hope you will get over it and live to see many young men of four thousand a year come into the neighborhood."

"It will be no use to us, if twenty such should come since you will not visit them."

"Depend upon it, my dear, that when there are twenty, I will visit them all."

Our father was so odd a mixture of quick parts, sarcastic humor, and reserve that the experience of being married to him for over thirty years had been insufficient to make our mother understand his character. For her mind was less difficult to develop. She was a woman of mean understanding, little information, and uncertain temper. When she was discontented she fancied herself nervous. The business of her life was to get her daughters married; its solace was visiting and news.

⚜

However, while we wished to hear more, Kitty heard our mother huff and begin to walk.

"Move!" Kitty hissed, "She's coming out."

We all rushed to the living room and sat down on the sofas. Very soon our mother entered to find all her daughters sitting down as if we were either reading a book, writing a letter, sewing or about to play a game of backgammon.

When she beheld us, her shoulders were puffed out.

"My nerves are very vexed today!"

After her declaration, she left the room, rushed up the stairs and called out for our maid, Hill.

"Lizzy?" Mary said.

"Aye?"

"Remember when you once said that it's a truth, universally acknowledged, that a single man in possession of a large fortune, must be in want of a wife?"

"Yes."

"Well, I do believe that our mother actually believes in that philosophy."

"Ah, Mary, were you ever in doubt of it?"

☙❧

Very soon, news spread all over Steventon and Hampshire that Mr. Bingley, an unattached man of large fortune was moving into Aginfield and into our neighborhood. Therefore, while all of us here in Longbourn were preparing for a happy ending to my sister's fate, the rest of the young women in Hampshire were preparing for a happy beginning with this stranger to our town, Mr. Bingley.

❧ 13 ❧

TO HAMPSHIRE!

"Why Hampshire?" Mr. Darcy asked Bingley when he came visiting. Mr. Bingley had just told his friend about how he had chosen to finally settle down and buy a country home and he had chosen a lovely estate called Aginfield Park that was in the county of Hampshire but was also very close to Steventon.

"Well," Mr. Bingley replied, sitting down on one of the sofas in Darcy's study, "I was always wishing to buy a country home, and when I asked around at our club, this place came as highly recommended, therefore, I went down in my chaise to see the place, and I have decided to purchase it. I was hoping that you would come down and visit it with me to give me your opinion of it."

"My opinion will come too late, for you have already purchased it."

"But I would still love your approval."

"I should really go to Rosing's Park and do my best to gather a strong relationship to Anne."

"Ah, so you wish to do that thing that you secretly don't wish to do?"

"Bingley..."

"Just as you have accepted a marriage that you truly don't wish to be a part of."

"Bingley! I shall make a pact with you. Support my choice in a wife and I shall think to support this idea of a home that you have chosen."

Mr. Bingley sighed. "Forgive me, Darcy, it was not my place to judge your choice."

"Thank you."

"You're welcome. So, will you come down to Hampshire to offer your blessing on my home? Or no? And bear in mind that Anne has always been Anne before your marriage, and I think that she will excuse you joining me to go into the country."

"I daresay you are right." Darcy smiled. "And I would love to assist you. Fine then, when shall we leave?"

❧❦❧

On the road once more, Mr. Darcy accompanied Mr. Bingley in a carriage as they made their way out of London and into the countryside, eventually arriving in the town of Hampshire. Mr. Darcy immediately approved of Aginfield Park after the proprietor had accompanied them all along it.

Yet when done, Mr. Darcy asked Bingley if he could stay for a while, yet to withhold letting the people of the country know that he was now amongst their neighborhood, for he wanted to keep to himself as long as could be. Bingley allowed this, and Mr. Darcy was allowed to live in a secluded environment for a while, away from all society and he found peace in it.

"To Hampshire, I have come, and surprisingly, I am happy for the moment."

❧ 14 ❧

THE FAMILIAR FACE

Planning for a wedding was quite a lot for my mother's nerves. Yet hearing that that very wedding she was looking forward to had to be postponed was too much for her sensibilities.

My sister had received a letter from Mr. Brocklehurst that the wedding would have to be set back for a month because, due to business that he had to see to in the North, he had to leave that part of the country for a while. He told her that he hoped they could complete their nuptials in a month's time, yet not to set an exact date in case another conflict would arise.

To our mother, a postponed marriage was equal in her mind to a cancelled marriage. For the whole of the day she was pacing up and down Longbourn, railing at the inconsistency of men and especially ones with the last name of Brocklehurst.

I worried at her loose tongue, because her lack of discretion would be heard by all our servants and then the news through them would reach all Steventon, and my sister would feel shame at something that she should not have had to feel shame over.

Yet I hoped that the arrival of Mr. Bingley in the neighborhood would be enough to make anyone not care about Mr. Brocklehurst's postponement. And one day, while all five of us sisters were seated in the sitting room with our parents, my father winked at me. I knew what was going to happen, for my father had confided in me earlier that he had already called on Mr. Bingley. He just didn't want to tell us until the opportunity presented itself at its best moment. I began to sew a pillow and my father noticed.

"I hope Mr. Bingley will like it, Lizzy," he said.

"We are not in a way to know what Mr. Bingley likes," our mother said, "since you will not visit him."

"But you forget, Mama," I said, "that we shall meet him at the assemblies, and that Mrs. Long has promised to introduce him."

"I do not believe Mrs. Long will do any such thing. She has two nieces of her own. She is a selfish, hypocritical woman, and I have no good opinion of her."

"No more have I," said our father, "and I am glad to find that you do not depend on her serving you."

Kitty began to cough and as she covered her mouth, our mother decided to hurl all her aggression and rage at her.

"Don't keep coughing so, Kitty, for heaven's sake! Have a little compassion on my nerves. You tear them to pieces."

"Kitty has no discretion in her coughs," our father replied, chuckling, he added, "she times them ill."

"I do not cough for my own amusement," replied Kitty fretfully.

"Now," our father said, changing the subject, "let us return to Mr. Bingley."

"I am sick of Mr. Bingley," cried our mother.

"I am sorry to hear that but why did you not tell me so before? If I had known as much this morning, I certainly would not have called on him. It is very unlucky, but as I have paid the visit, we cannot escape the acquaintance now."

My sisters and mother all looked on him in astonishment, and it was the reaction that he had desired. There was a general uproar and our mother went from looking upset to exhilarated.

"How good it was in you, my dear Mr. Bennet! But I knew I should persuade you at last. I was sure you loved your girls too well to neglect such an acquaintance. Well, how pleased I am! And it is such a good joke, too, that you should have gone this morning, and never said a word about it till now."

"Now, Kitty, I believe that you may cough as much as you choose," said our father as he got up to leave the room. Except for Jane and Mary, the rest of my sisters jumped up in glee. Mary naturally would not want to appear as caring for Mr. Bingley's acquaintance, and Jane, I could tell, had her mind focused on the postponement of her wedding. When not thinking that she would receive any notice, she stood up and slipped from the room. Though I knew that she would wish for solitude, I thought it best to follow her.

❦

I entered Jane's bedroom to find Jane standing by the window and looking out of it.

"Jane," I began, "Are you all right?"

"I am fine, Lizzy, you need not worry about me."

"Except that I know that is not the truth."

I sat down on her bed and looked at her.

"Jane, tell me the truth, you are unhappy about your wedding being pushed back."

"Aye, I am. I know that I am being foolish, yet I cannot help it. It is so strange, for men to up and leave so easily without knowing how it makes us feel. I suppose that is the product of our circumstances. Men have the freedom to traverse up and down the earth whenever they please, and woman are expected to be fancy creatures who sit at home and have no choice but to dwell on things. Any activity that we can do to occupy ourselves forces us to be introspective and think on things and obsess over them. I know that his reasons for pushing back the wedding are probably innocent, and I have no reason to feel worry or apprehension, yet I cannot help it."

I walked up to her and held her shoulders.

"Then we must find a way to keep you from falling into your feelings of self-doubt. As we all know, the assembly dance is in a week's time, and Mr. Bingley is sure to be there. Perhaps we can use this new acquaintance in our midst as a sort of distraction and enjoy simply meeting a new person. Then we can show this Mr. Brocklehurst the stupidity of leaving you here in Hampshire while he goes off and pursues his business that he believes to be so important."

"Yes, let's believe that Mr. Bingley will be a welcome distraction—and a kind man. For all I ask is to meet with nothing else but a good neighbor. And who knows, maybe it is time that I stopped focusing on myself and paid heed to you."

"To me?"

"Yes, Lizzy, do not think me ignorant of your inner desire to be happy."

"I am happy, Jane."

"I know, yet I will not have you forget yourself. Nor will I allow you to be forgotten. I am the oldest and it's time that I dressed myself as so. This Mr. Bingley that is in our midst, if he be all that is wonderful and agreeable, then maybe he is also wise and shall like you."

"You honestly believe that I should indulge myself in thinking that my type of beauty could enrapture this Mr. Bingley?"

"I believe that he would be a fool not to."

"And yet I have no choice but to accept that while the idea of a handsome stranger sweeping into Hampshire to romance me is quite agreeable and seems like something that would fit perfectly from a novel, I must confess that the name Mr. Bingley and Elizabeth Bennet—I do not know why, yet they seem to not match up naturally in each other."

"And what's in a name, Lizzy?"

"Everything apparently." I laughed and added, "Have you never read *Romeo and Juliet*?"

"I thought that was your least favorite Shakespeare play."

"It was, and it is."

"Yet still," Jane coaxed, "this is your time now. Have a wonderful time...and get to know this Mr. Bingley."

"All I hope is that he is a wonderful dance partner."

The day continued with my sister occupying her thoughts with the idea of Mr. Bingley and myself, and she would not hear of anything else.

A couple of days before the assembly was to take place, we all received news that Mr. Bingley's two sisters had also arrived in Hampshire to keep house for him, and that Mr. Bingley was not the only male there. His eldest sister's husband was present, yet there was also another gentleman who haunted the mansion and who did not give his name to anyone. Thus, it made him the most intriguing, because he was a mystery.

The day of the assembly came, and dressed up, our family made our way to the Red Lion Assembly room where the dance immediately began. I was dancing with Samuel Lucas, while the rest of my sisters also had dance partners as well. However, the dance was interrupted by the entrance of a party of five. The one in the middle I assumed was Mr. Bingley, yet as I looked on the rest of the group, I was startled completely.

There, standing in the back of the group, was the familiar face of the man who almost kissed me in the park.

I WONDER AT THE PRIDE OF
THIS MAN

"My goodness," Kitty said next to me, "Mr. Bingley is a good-looking man if ever I saw one! He is quite comely."

"Aye," I replied, not even looking at him, for my eyes were only on the man who accompanied him.

From out of the observers, Sir William Lucas stepped forward and welcomed them to our assembly. Mr. Bingley bowed and began to acquaint him with his two sisters. Rumor quickly spread around that the oldest sister's name was Mrs. Louisa Hurst, who was married to the portly and dour-looking man who stood to her left. Then there was the other sister, Miss Caroline Bingley. I recognized her immediately as the woman who had sneered at me when the mysterious man in her group had smiled at me at the ball.

"Lizzy and Kitty," our mother whispered, "Come here."

Kitty and I went to her and stood next to Jane, Mary and Lydia who already were by her side. "Girls, do you see that gentleman who is with Mr. Bingley, the taller gentleman? Well I have just learned from Lady Lucas that he is Mr. Darcy of Pemberly, in Kent, and Bingley's wealth is nothing to his, it's ten thousand a year. Oh, my dears, isn't he just the handsomest man that you have ever seen?"

In truth, I looked around at all the other women in the assembly room and they were all looking at him with curiosity and admiration, for he did cut a handsome figure.

And Mr. Darcy was his name. Finally, a bit of the mystery was now solved.

In my revelry, I hoped that he would notice me, but our mother pulled all of us forward, and very soon we were all standing amid Mr. Bingley and his party to make their acquaintance.

"Ah," Sir William Lucas said, "Mr. Bingley, allow me the pleasure of introducing you to one of the most wonderful collection of gems that Hampshire has to offer. This is the family of the Bennets."

Mr. Darcy's head snapped around and he noticed me. At first, he looked at me boldly and I was unable to look away. It made my heart soar that he had recognized me, yet soon he remembered himself and looked away quickly. I felt pushed out of a trance and I recalled that we were being introduced to Mr. Bingley.

Mr. Bingley proved to be a nice man of ease and gentlemanly behavior, and he requested a dance with each of us, beginning with Jane. I could tell that he was taken with Jane's beauty, yet Jane seemed in hopes of getting him to notice me more.

However, the first dance began, and I went to dance with my partner while looking at Mr. Darcy beforehand. He looked at me once more and then looked away. I could not make out his expression, yet I knew that it must mean something.

When the dance had ended, I rejoined my friends Charlotte Lucas and Cassandra Austen—her sister Jane had gone and got some punch—and all the while I thought of what way that I could engage in conversation with Mr. Darcy. He was not very good at talking, it seemed, and I wondered if there was some way that I could draw him out, until I discovered that he had made the worst first impression on the people of Hampshire.

At first when he entered the assembly room, he was considered much handsomer than Mr. Bingley, and he was looked at with great admiration for about half the evening, till his manners gave a disgust which turned the tide of his popularity, for he was discovered to be proud, to be above his company, and above being pleased; and not all his large estate in Kent could then save him from having a most forbidding, disagreeable countenance, and being unworthy to be compared with his friend.

I thought of what he could have done to have warranted such a response and thought to defend him at first. In my eyes, I saw a man who just seemed bashful amongst new acquaintances and therefore did not know how to react to them. And yet, did I know him? Not at all when I thought about it. And he had run away from me before. Therefore, I thought to let the situation unfold before I chose to take sides.

Mr. Bingley was another matter. He had soon made himself acquainted with all the principal people in the room; he was lively and unreserved, danced every dance, and talked of giving a ball himself at Aginfield Park once he was settled. Such amiable qualities spoke for themselves. What a contrast between him and his friend! Mr. Darcy, on the other hand, refused to dance with any other woman besides the women he came with. I did not agree with this mentality, but nor was I disposed to write him off as a villain until what had happened next.

⁂

Because there was a scarcity of men at the assembly, and women outnumbered them, I had to sit out a few dances, and one time, I had the fortune and misfortune of sitting a few seats away from where Mr. Darcy stood. I looked at him every now and again out of the corner of my eye, and still wondered if I should go up and speak to him. I wanted to ask him so many things and above all, I wanted to ask him why he acted like we never met before. I was aware that we had never met officially and one of our meetings was not very modest of us. Yet he still could have acknowledged me when Sir William Lucas introduced us, acknowledging that he knew me at all —yet he didn't. He acted as if we never had met. In truth, while I knew that he might've done it just to save my appearance, it still hurt me. Now I knew how Jane had felt.

I was taken out of my meanderings when I heard voices coming from near me. Mr. Bingley, who had just gotten done dancing with Jane Austen, had approached his friend.

"Come, Darcy," Mr. Bingley argued, "I must have you dance. I hate to see you standing about by yourself in this stupid manner. You had much better dance."

"I certainly shall not. You know how I detest it unless I am particularly acquainted with my partner. At such an assembly as this, it would be insupportable. Your sisters are engaged, and there is not another woman in the room whom it would not be a punishment to me to stand up with."

"Good God, Darcy, I would not be so fastidious as you are for a kingdom! In truth, I never met with so many pleasant girls in my life, as I have this evening; and there are several of them you see uncommonly pretty."

"I grant you the eldest Miss Bennet that you danced with was very pretty. And her sister, Kitty, is quite lovely as well. I would say that the youngest Lydia was also pleasing in looks, yet she clearly is too wild for me to regard her as so. And I heard that the other one, Mary, is accomplished."

I could not believe it! Mr. Darcy had described every one of my sisters as beautiful, except me.

"Oh!" Mr. Bingley said, "The eldest one, Miss Bennet, she is the most beautiful creature I ever beheld! But there is one of her sisters sitting down just behind you, who is very pretty, and I dare say, very agreeable. I wonder that you had forgotten about her, for she is very lovely, witty and I find quite captivating." They didn't think that I could hear them apparently, yet I was happy to know that Mr. Bingley at least had some regard for me. "Do let me ask my partner to introduce you."

"Which do you mean?" He turned around and beheld me sitting there where I avoided his gaze, for within him, this time I felt a coldness and cruelty. Then he turned back to Mr. Bingley and sneered. "She is tolerable; but not handsome enough to tempt me, and Bingley, I am astonished in your thoughts as of now, for I am in no humor at present to give consequence to young ladies who are slighted by other men. If they don't wish to dance with her, then why should I? Go back to the dance floor and take up your dance with Miss Cassandra Austen, for I daresay that she also qualifies as your definition of agreeable, even though she seems ten years your senior."

"To be honest, Darcy," Mr. Bingley said with a smile, "age can actually recommend a woman."

"And now you have said too much."

Mr. Bingley laughed and left.

⚜

I had never been so furious in my life. He was the one who once almost kissed me! I did not ask for his attentions, nor force him to keep staring at me all throughout the ball at Almack's. It was his actions and his alone that made that choice. And now, for him to dismiss me, call me tolerable and nothing more and refuse to dance with me! He blew me away as if I were no more than a dried leaf and he were the wind, wishing to push me along with no consideration.

I stood up and walked past him intentionally, making it very obvious that I heard what he had said. Then I gathered my spirits, for it was not in my habit to become sad over such a thing; my disposition was too lively for it, and I did take delight in the ridiculous. I walked over to Charlotte Lucas, as well as Cassandra and Jane Austen, and began to tell them everything that had transpired.

By the end of my story, they all had it fixed in their minds that he was a most disagreeable man, was the most horrid and disobliging creature, and I wondered at the pride of the man.

❧ 16 ❧

TO BE TOSSED ABOUT

M y mother however was completely oblivious to what had passed between Mr. Darcy and me. She declared the night a complete success, and if Jane had not already been engaged to Mr. Brocklehurst, then she would have loved to have recommended her to Mr. Bingley or Mr. Darcy—who though she found to be the most horrible man she had met, if he did grow to favor one of her daughters, then she could forgive him anything. Yet, still, Mr. Bingley had danced with all her daughters, and though he also danced with Charlotte Lucas, which vexed her greatly, his sisters seemed to have taken to Jane and found her manners very pleasing.

"Yet, Lizzy," Mrs. Bennet said, "I heard that though he naturally thought Jane to be the most beautiful woman that he ever beheld, he also found you to be quite agreeable and lovely as well."

"He still might be in love with me though," Lydia said.

"Or me," Kitty echoed.

"And I do not have any interest in a man with too much money," Mary said.

"And that explains why Kitty and I danced every dance," Lydia said, "But you none."

"I take no pleasure in dancing. The rewards of reflection and observation are much greater."

"Indeed," I said, "And when there are none others to be had, we shall have to learn how to live by our own philosophies, Mary."

"Anyway," Mrs. Bennet said, not understanding what her daughters were talking about, "Mr. Bingley might fancy you, Lizzy."

"We cannot know his full intentions, Mama."

"Oh, don't be so prickly about it. Therefore, you must, whenever you are in his company, do everything in your power to recommend yourself to him. And don't go on showing your willfulness or being smart. Men don't like smart women."

"Well," Mr. Bennet said, putting down his newspaper, "he may very well prefer a stupid wife, as others have done before him, yet I would recommend Lizzy to not dumb herself down much, for the effects might become permanent. We must allow her to be smart sometimes."

"And when does that do anyone any good?" Mrs. Bennet snapped.

"I've been told that it's in fashion sometimes."

Our mother could not be dissuaded from her beliefs that Mr. Bingley might fancy me in some way, and she continued to speak of it and Mr. Bingley at the assembly for the next two days. When that subject was exhausted, she began to speak of his sisters, Mrs. Hurst, and Miss Caroline Bingley.

"Oh, and his sisters are charming women. I never in my life saw anything more elegant than their dresses. I dare say the lace upon Mrs. Hurst's gown—"

"No lace, Mrs. Bennet!" Mr. Bennet cried, annoyed, "I beg you. I can survive many of your speeches, but never can I undertake any interminable descriptions of finery."

When that subject proved to not be to our father's liking, our mother then moved on to berate Mr. Darcy.

"But the gentleman who accompanied him," she blurted out, "Mr. Darcy is his name, is the most disagreeable man that I have ever met."

"And is not at all pleasing," Aunt Phillips said, for she had come to visit. "So, high and conceited that there is no enduring him! He walked here, and he walked there, fancying himself so very great! Not handsome enough to dance with!"

"I wish you had been there, my dear," Mrs. Bennet said, "to have given him one of your set downs. I quite detest the man. I tried to get him to dance with our daughters, and he wouldn't do so."

"He slighted my daughters, did he?" Our father chuckled.

"We didn't care for him either, Father," I said, lying, "So we are not so much offended."

"I was offended!" Kitty said.

"And I would have been as well," Lydia said, "yet he was not to my taste. For Mother and Father, have you heard—never mind I am quite sure you have not—but a unit of militia are said to camp here soon."

"What!" Our mother said, jumping up.

"Oh, yes, my dear sister," Mrs. Phillips said, "a regiment of soldiers have come to reside in the —shire, and they already are here!"

Everyone but my father, Jane, and I jumped up in excitement. The joy could be felt all around, and I, in secret, was quite intrigued myself. A whole camp full of soldiers were here in Hampshire, which would give us new things to talk about, new acquaintances and something to occupy us, especially since Jane's wedding was postponed. I felt that this would help her to not focus on her inner disappointments.

⚜

When picking flowers in our garden while being accompanied by Charlotte Lucas and Jane Austen, my sister Jane and I were clipping roses.

"He is just what a young man ought to be," said Charlotte about Mr. Bingley, "sensible, good-humored, lively; and I never saw such happy manners! So much ease, with such perfect good breeding!"

"He is also handsome," replied Jane Austen, "which a young man ought likewise to be, if he possibly can. His character is thereby complete."

"Do you like him, Jane?" I said to Jane Austen.

"Do you like him?" she replied.

"He is very agreeable, but I give you leave to like him. You have liked many a stupider person."

"Aye," Jane Austen replied, "I have. And I have not. Remember when I was so young, and I fell in love with the gentleman Tom Lefroy? I wonder if I was smart to like him, or stupid to have done so."

"I find," I coaxed, "that a woman is always both smart and stupid equally for falling in love—yet it's something that can never be helped."

"Aye, but it does make one feel foolish for choosing one who valued the size of his pocketbook over the value of his heart. Money seems to influence every decision, but should it?"

"Aye," Charlotte said, "too much it influences and too little it causes happiness. For people do not understand that comfort and happiness are not two states that always coincide."

"And therefore," Jane Austen said, "if he chooses his desire for money over you, do not think twice of him. That's the only advice I can give."

"Do you still love Tom Lefroy?" Jane asked.

"Always," Jane Austen replied. "Which I suppose makes me a hypocrite, for I cannot follow my own advice."

"Advice is easy to give," Charlotte said, "when you are not the one who has to take it."

"Well, you all sound so dour!" We all turned, and Cassandra Austen was walking up to us, "And I guess I shall give you no choice but to be merry, for Jane." She was speaking to my sister. "Your mother has given me a letter to give to you. And it's from Aginfield Park!"

❧

Jane looked at me and then opened the letter and began reading it.

"My Dear Friend,

If you are not so compassionate as to dine today with Louisa and me, we shall be in danger of hating each other for the rest of our lives, for a whole day's tête-à-tête between two women can never end without a quarrel. Come as soon as you can on the receipt of this. My brother and the gentlemen are to dine with the officers.

Yours ever,
Caroline Bingley."

When she stopped reading, she looked at us.

"Well," I said, "shall you go?"

"Of course, I must, and will," Jane said.

"Of course, she must, and will," Jane Austen echoed. "It would be rude to do so, even though Mr. Bingley's sisters are without doubt the most snobbish women I've ever met."

"Oh, Jane!" Cassandra said, "There are worse women in the world."

"That still doesn't stop me from not liking them."

"Did you not like them?" Jane, my sister, asked.

"No not at all!" The three of us replied.

"Their manners are quite different than their brother's," I said.

"At first, perhaps," Jane said, "certainly not, at first. But they are very pleasing women when you converse with them. Miss Bingley is to live with her brother and keep his house, and I am much mistaken if we shall not find a very charming neighbor in her. Do not you think so?"

"Oh!" I sighed, "You are a great deal too apt you know, to like people in general. You never see a fault in anybody. All the world is good and agreeable in your eyes. I never heard you speak ill of a human being in my life. Even if they deserve it."

"I would wish not to be hasty in censuring any one, but I always speak what I think."

"I know you do, and it is that which makes me wonder. With your good sense, to be so honestly blind to the follies and nonsense of others! To take the good of everybody's character and make it still better and say nothing of the bad—belongs to you alone. By your estimation, you would believe that Mr. Darcy is a kind man."

"He was very wrong to speak so about you," Jane said, "yet I hope that he may improve upon further acquaintance."

"Do you mean that he plans to be in humor to give his attention to ladies who have been slighted by other men?" I laughed, "I dare say he never will. Yet I suppose that I am simply too old for him to think kindly on. Probably in his eyes, I am an old maid."

"Yet I'm sorry, Lizzy," Charlotte said, "to be described as just *tolerable*. He was horrid for saying it."

We exhausted the subject, and I listened in silence as Jane continued to defend the characters of Mr. Bingley's sisters, yet I was not convinced. Their behavior at the assembly had not been calculated to please in general and I was little disposed to approve them. They were in fact very fine ladies, but they seemed proud and conceited, and only quick to be kind to someone when it benefited them in some way.

When Charlotte, Cassandra and Jane Austen left, we went inside and told our parents about Jane's letter. Our mother was happy that Jane had made a good impression on Mr. Bingley's sisters and then turned to me in censure.

"You are lucky that your sister looks after you so," she snapped, "for she has created a connection that you should have done yourself. Lizzy, if Mr. Bingley likes you, then you need to learn how to impress his sisters. I don't require you to care about how Mr. Darcy perceives you, because clearly there is no pleasing that man. You, Jane, must go and do your best to speak well of Elizabeth so that his sisters might invite her to dine with them in the near future."

I didn't argue, because I knew that if I were to tell our mother that Miss Bingley's disgust toward me was probably a jealousy that was sprouted long before now, she would never stop questioning me.

"Then may I have the carriage to go, Father?" Jane asked, where he sat in his armchair.

"Now, Jane," our mother continued, "certainly not! You must go on horseback, for it looks like rain. And if it is so, then you must stay the night, and then the next day we can send Elizabeth to come and fetch you. And that way, she can be thrown in the path of Mr. Bingley, who might just need some further encouragement and get the chance to speak with her in private somewhat."

"Mother!" Jane and I said at the same time.

"Mama, if Mr. Bingley does like me at all," I argued, "which is still not fully proven, I shall meet Mr. Bingley at parties and more assemblies."

"Lizzy! You know nothing of men. There is nothing that they shall like more than to see you in their home. The image of you sitting on his couch will have him wonder if he would like to see you like that always."

"Mother," I began, "I appreciate your wishing to help me, but I cannot use Jane to further my cause in this."

And I was. My mother's sudden desire to help me was quite refreshing and made me feel...loved.

"I am not upset in being helpful," Jane said. "But mother, it will be viewed as inconsiderate of me. And what if they offer me their carriage to take me home? Then I will not have helped Lizzy at all."

"Don't worry about such things," Mrs. Bennet said, "I'm sure they won't think of that."

৩৯৫৩

Unable to persuade her, our mother was resolute. Jane was soon on horseback, riding away from us toward Aginfield Park while we all said goodbye to her.

As she rode on, our mother shouted after her.

"And remember to let them all know that you are engaged to Mr. Brocklehurst of a large estate, for if Mr. Bingley knows that you are marrying into such great status, then it will show him that your sister is worthy of him!"

Jane continued to ride on.

৩৯৫৩

My mother turned out to be correct about the weather, for not twenty minutes after Jane had left, it began to rain hard. She walked around the house, feeling quite satisfied that her plan was in the process of becoming successful.

Yet for Jane, I felt remorse, for not only would she arrive soaked from rainwater and looking chagrinned under the weight of our mother's plans, but it made me feel as if marriage, and all that led up to them, was a maneuvering business, where the people involved were like chess pieces that constantly had to be tossed about.

17

WELCOME TO AGINFIELD

T he next morning, we received a letter from Aginfield Park stating that when Jane arrived there to dine with Mrs. Hurst and Miss Bingley, she had fallen ill from being drowned in rain water. She reported that we should not be alarmed, for excepting a sore throat, fever and headache, there was not the much the matter with her. I felt immediately sorry for her, because when Mr. Bingley returned from dining with the officers, he looked at her state and decided that she could not return home, so he had her stay in their guest room.

When hearing this, my father turned to my mother and smirked.

"Well, my dear, if Jane should die of this fever, it will be a comfort to know that it was in pursuit of Mr. Bingley for her sister."

"Oh, nonsense! People do not die of colds anymore, and this is even better than I had planned. For Lizzy, I was going to have you go and fetch her today, but now that she is ill, you should go and stay with her."

"Mother! I want to go and see her, but if I stay for more than a day, I shall trespass on their hospitality too much and it would make Mr. Bingley regard me even less."

"Oh, that is nonsense."

"I shall go, for I had planned to already, but I shall only stay for the day."

"I suppose that is a hint for me to send for the carriage," Mr. Bennet said.

"Oh, no Father, for I had planned to walk there once we finished our breakfast. It is only three miles to Aginfield, and I shall be back in time for dinner."

"Walk three miles!" Mother said, "You will not be fit to be seen by Mr. Bingley."

"I shall be fit to see Jane, which is all that I am going for. And not for Mr. Bingley."

☙❧

After breakfast, I was off to Aginfield. Along the way, I passed the Austen house, and Cassandra and Jane saw me from their window. When they found out what my plans were, they joined me for a mile of it because they were going to visit Charlotte Lucas, whose house was along the way.

After the first mile, we parted ways and I continued on alone. Walking was one of my favorite pastimes, yet there was fear at the end of my destination. I could stomach the presence of Miss Bingley sneering at me, yet I didn't know if I could face Mr. Darcy.

To be frank, I was still very much bitter toward him and didn't know if I could trust myself to not bestow my rage on him. Yet what anger did I feel that he did not deserve? Not only did he act as if we never had met, but he slighted me in a most unpardonable way.

Yet I knew that Mr. Bingley would not regard my presence as

intrusive and my desire to attend to Jane and see how she fared was enough incentive for me to overcome my apprehensions.

Very soon I came upon Aginfield, and when I approached, the butler let me in.

⚅⚅⚅

I was first attended to by the sisters, who greeted me in their sitting room, and neither of them looked pleased to see me. They smiled, yet it never reached their eyes and was clearly forced. They informed me that Mr. Bingley was coming in from the fields and that Mr. Darcy had to ride into Meryton to buy a sheet of music at a shop for his sister. I politely said that I didn't even know that he had a sister, and then quickly shifted the discussion back to Jane and if I could see to her immediately.

Caroline Bingley escorted me to the guest room, I entered, and Jane was lying on the bed, looking sweaty and very ill. I went to her and immediately began to look after her while Miss Bingley expressed her sadness of Jane's state, and then left us after a few minutes.

I attended to Jane, never leaving her side, and then after half an hour, there was a knock on the door and when I said come in, Mr. Bingley entered.

"Miss Elizabeth, I wish when you came to my home it was under better circumstances, and yet I'm sorry for this all. Yet still, if I may, welcome to Aginfield."

18

HE WOULD DO WHAT HE MUST

"Thank you for the wonderful welcome." I smiled, and added, "And thank you for attending to my sister, for she is in far better comforts than she would have been at home."

"It's a privilege to have her here," he replied, looking at us both. "Though I am not happy that she is ill of course, yet I must confess that if her illness will keep Miss Bennet and her younger sister here, then I am happy for the event." I laughed while Jane smiled.

"Well, then," I said, "I can see that anytime Jane feels the least bit poorly, and every home that we could take refuge in gets swallowed up by an earthquake, then I am happy to know that you shall never forsake us."

"You do say the wittiest things!" Mr. Bingley laughed.

"Holding my tongue has never been a talent."

"And you don't need to," Jane whispered, clearly ill, "for she speaks so well."

"Miss Bennet," Mr. Bingley said, "I have sent for the apothecary and he shall be here within the hour, and hopefully we shall find every way to attend to you."

"Thank you, sir, you are very kind."

"And as I said," Mr. Bingley smiled, "it is very much my pleasure." For a little while he looked at us and then he excused himself. When I knew that we weren't going to be overheard, I turned back to Jane.

"I could not tell which one he was admiring more, me or you."

"I think he was looking at us both," Jane said, "for he looked confused as to which one to gaze at."

We both had a good laugh over that.

"Yet, do not believe that I have forgotten you." She sighed. "I have mentioned to his sisters that I am engaged to Mr. Brocklehurst while you were much admired at Almacks but are still very much free."

"Thank you." I smiled, and added, "Yet I do not come for myself. I think all that we need to focus on is you getting well again."

⊛

As I walked through the hall with an empty pitcher with dirty rags, I was headed to the kitchen of Aginfield to get another one, when a person turned the corner and almost collided into me. I looked up and started.

"Mr. Darcy!"

"Miss Elizabeth!"

Before me, Mr. Darcy stood, and he wore his vest and shirt, but his jacket was missing, which meant that he must've been doing something on his own somewhere in the house.

"I..." I began. "I am here to look after my sister."

"I did not see your carriage or horse outside," he said.

"It's because I walked."

"You walked. On foot?"

"Yes, as I just said that I did," I replied icily.

He only gazed at me and it annoyed me terribly.

"I was told that you were in Meryton."

"Yes. I have returned."

"I can see that as well."

"Aye, you can."

Again, there was another silence, and by this time I was at my wit's end. If he was going to stare at me blankly, then I would not help him with conversation. I had thought to help him once before, and his way of repaying me was running away, as if I had the plague and then accusing me of looking as if I had two noses. Whatever empathy I had for him I now had lost.

"Well then," I said, eyeing him venomously, "excuse me."

I turned around and left him in the hallway while I took the steps. As I walked down them, I could see him looking at me, yet I did not return his gaze that time. And if there was one thing that I promised myself, it was that I would never again stare at Mr. Darcy.

***

Mr. Darcy walked through the halls, his countenance dark. As he walked, he eventually came upon Mr. Bingley who was in the billiards room, playing a game of it with himself.

"Miss Elizabeth is here!" Mr. Darcy stated at once.

"Well," Mr. Bingley replied, surprised with his friend's abrupt declaration, "yes, I know that she is."

"Why is she though?"

"Because she came here to see her sister."

"And she walked?"

"Aye, she did. Caroline and Louisa have been giving her abuse for it all morning. Not to her face of course."

"And we were right to." Darcy and Bingley turned around and Miss Bingley entered. "My goodness, Charles, didn't you see her hem? Six inches deep in mud, I am sure."

"I confess it quite escaped my notice," Mr. Bingley replied, "Caroline, I must say that I thought her to look remarkably well. Now can't you let Mr. Darcy and I have our time for private discussion? That is why god made such things as billiards rooms, so there is a spot that we men can be free from you women in."

"And I have always wanted to learn billiards."

"Don't say such scandalous things."

Caroline Bingley turned to Mr. Darcy. "If you had seen her when she arrived, Mr. Darcy, I'm sure you would have censured her appearance. For walking three miles, her petticoat covered in dirt, it showed an abominable sort of conceited independence. I would have had some cutting words for it."

"It showed an affection for her sister," Mr. Bingley argued, "which is very pleasing."

"So, that is why you are refusing to let Miss Elizabeth return home," Caroline said, "and having her stay here until her sister is well."

"What?" Mr. Darcy asked.

"Aye, Mr. Darcy, my brother has requested that Miss Elizabeth remain here at Aginfield while her sister recovers."

Mr. Darcy inwardly groaned, for the idea of him being in the presence of Elizabeth Bennet for so long would test his resolve, for certain. Not only did he never expect to see her again, but now he was in the same house with her. How could he resist thinking of her when he would encounter her every day?

"Yet, Charles," Mr. Darcy argued, "you shall really have both sisters here for so long?"

"They shall probably be here no longer than a week," Mr. Bingley replied. "Besides, I like their presence. Darcy, call me what you will, yet you know that I love being in the presence of such lovely and artless women."

"I know, yet..."

"And I admit that I am quite taken with both."

"Both?" Mr. Darcy replied, feeling possessive of Elizabeth. "I would have thought that you would have just regarded the eldest Miss Bennet, Jane, as the lovely one."

"A fine concession, but come man, admit it. She's an angel."

"She is beautiful, but she smiles too much."

"Jane Bennet is a sweet girl," Miss Bingley said, "though her mother is the most vulgar and outrageous woman I've ever seen. Her crassness is quite unparalleled. Yet, Mr. Darcy, I heard Eliza Bennet was regarded as another local beauty, and as you see, my brother agrees with them. Yet what do you say to that, Mr. Darcy?"

Not wishing to be found out, as well as hoping that if he bestowed a negative comment on her appearance, it would lessen the chances of Bingley feeling an attraction to her, Mr. Darcy decided that it would be best to be cruel to Elizabeth at present, so he could be kind to his own jealousies later.

"I should as soon call her mother a wit," he replied. Miss Bingley laughed at Mr. Darcy's declaration, for it made her feel content in now knowing that the woman she had been jealous over getting his attention since Almack's meant nothing to him whatsoever. This had the desired effect on her in Darcy's eyes, who hoped that now Miss Bingley would look on Elizabeth as not being a threat, and therefore be nice to her. Yet Mr. Bingley would not be shaken in his belief that Miss Elizabeth was extremely lovely and worthy of his attention. Mr. Darcy then felt an inward anger at not being able to persuade Bingley in the way that he used to. Darcy knew that this was ultimately his fault, for he had always encouraged Bingley to gather more self-confidence in his opinions and beliefs.

Yet Darcy then had another plan, and if he had no choice but to deploy it, then he would do what he must.

❧ 19 ❧

SOME THINGS MUST BE FACED

"Miss Bingley," Mr. Darcy said to her and smiled warmly, "would you excuse your brother and me? I have some counsel to give him that I know would support your argument."

Caroline immediately felt elated at Darcy's warmth to her and willingness to support her opinion. Therefore, she obeyed Darcy with alacrity and left the two men alone. When Darcy closed the door behind her, he turned around and smirked.

"You said that just to get rid of her, didn't you?" Bingley said.

"Of course," Mr. Darcy replied. "Don't say that I never did anything for you."

"You did it just as much for yourself as you did it for me."

"True, you are correct."

"Though I appreciate the gesture. Now what is this hesitation in the presence of the imposing Miss Bennets really about?"

Mr. Darcy thought to tell Bingley about the oath his father told him about the Darcy men and the unknown debt to the Bennet women, yet he knew that it sounded too preposterous, therefore, he decided to keep it to himself.

"I am simply worried," he began, "that they are trying to throw themselves in your path to make you intrigued by them."

"And how is that so different than how we men sometimes throw ourselves in a woman's way, in hopes that they will be intrigued by us?"

"A great difference. With us, we are intended to, yet with them it becomes an art. If you meet a woman with designs on you, then imagine what other designs she may have of which you are unaware."

"Tis true, yet you shall not make me think ill of the Miss Bennets, Darcy."

"Indeed, I should not, for they could very well be very nice women. Yet I must warn you against this pluralistic state as well."

"Pluralistic state? What the devil are you on about?"

"It's not very wise to find two sisters attractive. At least choose the eldest Bennet girl to bestow your affections on and be done with it."

"You have not heard? She is engaged to be married."

"She is?"

"Yes, to a Mr. Brocklehurst of some great estate that I forget the name of. Which makes her beyond my reach."

"Oh, I'm sorry, for she was quite to your tastes."

"My tastes are more complex than they once were, and I am happy for it. When younger, I was foolish, Darcy, and I only had one standard of beauty, yet now that we are a little older, I have improved my mind. Beauty is not a singularity that should only be bestowed on one form of woman. Many of them are lovely. Miss Jane Bennet is an angel... yet Miss Elizabeth... have you spoken with her? She is another form of beauty that I have a hard time looking away from."

Mr. Darcy shifted uncomfortably.

"What do you mean by that, Charles?"

"I mean that she is quick, witty and wise. And she looks as if—

and pardon my words—she looks as if she is the type of woman who a man would love to share intimacy. Jane is the great beauty of that family, but she seems a bit cool and aloof, like loving a statue of perfection, I'd imagine. To be married to a jewel, yet a jewel doesn't have much warmth to it. I want warmth, and Elizabeth seems as if she is the sort that knows how to be loved. She seems passionate, and I want a woman who seems as if she—tastes good."

"Oh, Bingley..." Darcy groaned.

"I sound vulgar, I know."

"I do not judge you, but as you say, she is very smart."

"Do you not think I am smart?"

"You are very much so, but she is smart of a different kind. Do you believe that it would make you happy to pursue her in some way?"

"I do not choose anything at the time," Mr. Bingley said, "for you are correct in worrying. I have fallen in love often, and I don't wish to be fickle anymore. I shall enjoy looking at them both and dreaming of Miss Elizabeth when my mind wanders to her, yet I shall not commit myself."

"That is very good, Bingley," Mr. Darcy said, sighing with happiness at knowing that his friend was not going to pursue the woman upon whom he was secretly dwelling. "And I must say, you really have grown quite wise, Charles."

"It took me a while, yet I got there in the end."

Mr. Darcy clapped him on the shoulder and left Mr. Bingley to finish his game in peace.

❦

Mr. Darcy walked to his bedroom and lay down on the bed instead of sitting in the parlor with everyone else. He knew that it had broken decorum, yet he needed a moment to himself.

As he lay on his bed with his eyes closed, he was in a middle state of slumber. Half-asleep, his mind wandered over to Miss Elizabeth. It was true that her older sister was the great beauty of the set of sisters, but Darcy understood what Bingley meant in regard to his slightly vulgar language about Lizzy.

Elizabeth Bennet appeared to be a woman who might be a good companion, not only as a mistress of a household, but in the bedchamber. She seemed to have a natural, insatiable curiosity about life. Therefore, despite his best efforts to forget about Elizabeth, time and again, she came to the forefront of his mind and he began to dream of her.

It was not the first time, yet it was the most detailed, from him walking into the room and seeing her there. He then walked up to her, lifted her off her feet and kissed her passionately. The feel of her lips against his was intoxicating, and then he raised her up and carried her to his bedroom. As he threw her onto the bed, he turned her over and ripped off her petticoat and undergarments till she lay there in nothing but her knee stockings which were tied by garters.

"You are beautiful, Elizabeth," he had sighed.

"And you, sir," she would sigh in return, "are too far away from me."

Darcy then imagined himself climbing on top of her and kissing her tenderly while he cupped her breasts in his hands. Then he kissed her along the nape of her neck, slid his lips down and began to suckle her. She moaned under his ministrations as he lowered his lips further down. Then she wrapped her legs around his neck and he kissed her between her thighs. Her back arched against the bed and she grabbed his head and hair, moaning in happiness. More and more he kissed her, his lips pressing deeper and deeper until he brought her ecstasy.

Then he raised himself up, kissed her one last time on the lips, then stood up and removed all his clothing. As Elizabeth looked up at him, she smiled.

"Mr. Darcy, you are beautiful," she would say.

"As are you, my dearest and loveliest Elizabeth." When fully nude, Mr. Darcy climbed on top of her. "Lizzy, this will hurt but only for a moment, yet the pain will pass, believe me."

Mr. Darcy inserted himself within her a bit, then, in one thrust he entered her. She cried out and Mr. Darcy slowed his movements until she relaxed in his arms, and he knew her pain had lessened. Then he increased his speed, rocking against her faster and faster, grabbing her hands in his own until he released himself fully inside of her. Feeling spent and content, Mr. Darcy rested his body on top of hers as they lay there.

"So," Elizabeth sighed out, "this is what you wish to do to me?"

"Yes."

"Then, why don't you?"

"Because I shouldn't. I am engaged to my cousin, and I must not allow myself to fall in love with you."

Mr. Darcy's eyes shot up and he was all alone in his bed, fully clothed, as he expected himself to be. Yet looking at the clock, he raised himself up and did his best to appear decent, for now it was the time to dine for lunch.

Some things must be faced, he told himself, and for the moment, his trial would be to go downstairs and face Miss Elizabeth again, after dreaming of her in the most passionate of ways.

❦ 20 ❦

ILL-SUITED

I didn't wish to dine with the Bingley family and chose to remain with Jane to make sure that she ate her food well. Therefore, my dinner was brought to me. The next day, I joined the inhabitants of the house for breakfast, and then returned to Jane. When I thought that she was well, I went to the library to do some reading, and soon I heard footsteps. I looked up to see Mr. Darcy enter. He bowed to me, but he didn't say a word.

My first instinct was to leave immediately, yet I knew that would look rude, therefore I nodded to him and went back to my book. He took one from the shelves, sat down near me and began to read. At first, I withstood the impulse to look at him, yet I couldn't help but steal a glance. I looked over the edge of my book, looked up at him and was startled to see him looking at me.

I looked back down at my book and continued reading. After I read my book for another twenty minutes or so, I decided that I had waited long enough. I stood up, put my book on the shelf and left the library.

That night, Jane had felt better; the apothecary had visited us and was happy to announce that she was improving. Therefore, I had no choice but to get dressed nicely enough, for Mr. Bingley had brought some clothes of mine from Longbourn. Once I saw that Jane was comfortable and ready to sleep, I left her, went down to the drawing room, and then entered.

Mr. Bingley, Miss Bingley, Mrs. Hurst, and Mr. Hurst were all at a table playing cards.

"Miss Bennet." Mr. Bingley stood up and bowed to me. "You look positively well this evening."

"Thank you, Mr. Bingley," I replied, curtsying.

"I trust you do not find your sister worse this day."

"On the contrary, Mr. Bingley," I replied with a smile, "due to your wonderful care and the accurate treatments of the apothecary, she is on the mend."

"That is wonderful to hear."

"Would you like to join us in our game, Miss Bennet?" Mrs. Hurst asked.

"No, thank you, you may resume all that you like," I said. "Yet, Mr. Bingley, would you mind if I were to get a book from your library?"

"Of course, you may! Might I help you?"

"And have me risk you losing a turn in your game?" I laughed. "Never."

"Oh, you are a welcome distraction."

Mr. Bingley escorted me to the library and we made casual and comfortable small conversation along the way. Mr. Bingley was very civil, polite, and attentive, yet I didn't know what to make of him still. Should I have been attracted to him? Or should I have been wary that he might just have been extremely charming?

Yet, as we entered the library, he helped me find a book and did his best to have us linger there, but I was worried to have us remain alone for long. It wasn't just because of propriety, for I trusted Mr. Bingley wholeheartedly. I was worried that his charm might affect me, and I had too many emotional questions within me before I added more to my ponderings.

However, it was undeniable; Mr. Charles Bingley was fascinated by my sister and me. I am aware that such a conclusion might appear as vain to you on my part, yet I am not perfect, and I had no choice but to realize it, for he made it so clear and plain to see.

Eventually we arrived back in the drawing-room and I was surprised when we entered and saw Mr. Darcy sitting at a table and composing a letter.

I halted when seeing him and saw his eyes dart between Mr. Bingley and myself. His eyes grew cold and appeared disdainful, and I could see that he was wondering why Mr. Bingley and I had entered the room together.

"Good evening, Mr. Darcy," I said, curtsying. "Mr. Bingley was just helping me find a book in his library."

"I see." He then stood up and bowed to me. "I hope that your sister is doing well."

"I thank you, for she is doing a little better."

"I am glad to hear it."

I walked over to the sofa and sat down, opening the book I had selected.

"And you are certain that you don't wish to join our game of loo?" Mrs. Hurst questioned.

"I thank you, truly, yet I just wish for some literary stimulus for some reason at the moment."

"And what do you do, sir?" Miss. Bingley asked of Mr. Darcy.

"I am writing to my sister."

Very soon however, the loo game ended. Everyone broke up and began to do their own activities all throughout the room. Mrs. Hurst sat down and just played with her bracelets; Mr. Hurst lay down and decided to do nothing else but fall asleep; Mr. Bingley began to read a book as well, yet what was most curious of all was Miss Bingley. Upon my word, some women try too hard and don't know that they are, which was the unfortunately entertaining case of Miss Bingley. She walked over to Mr. Darcy and began to watch him as he composed his letter.

"How delighted Miss Darcy will be to receive such a letter!" she said.

Mr. Darcy did not reply.

"You write uncommonly fast."

"You are mistaken. I write rather slowly," was his only reply.

"How many letters you must have occasion to write in the course of the year! Letters of business too! How odious I should think them!"

"It is fortunate, then, that it's my burden to write them, and not yours."

"Pray tell your sister that I long to see her."

"I have already told her so…a couple of times now."

At this point, I wanted to burst out laughing. My goodness, did she never know that trying too hard to get someone's attentions never shows one to the best advantage? It was clear that she was infatuated with Mr. Darcy, yet he displayed the same indifference he showed to everyone. I found her to be quite mad to be pursuing someone who never showed any affection or consideration for her presence.

"How can you contrive to write so even?" she pursued.

Mr. Darcy was silent again and did not reply.

"Tell your sister I am delighted to hear of her improvement on the harp and pray let her know that I am quite in raptures with her beautiful little design for a table, and I think it infinitely superior to Miss Whitby's."

"Will you give me leave to defer your raptures till I write again? At present I have not room to do them justice."

"Oh! It is of no consequence. I shall see her in March. But do you always write such eloquent, long letters to her, Mr. Darcy?"

"I am very much long-winded in my writing, but I believe they are almost never eloquent, for eloquence is not something in which I am proficient."

"It is a rule with me that a person who can write a long letter, with ease, cannot help but be eloquent in some way."

"That will not do for a compliment to Darcy, Caroline," cried her brother, "because he does not write with ease. He studies too much for words of five syllables. Eh, Darcy?"

"You and I do have very different writing styles and speeds."

"Oh!" cried Miss Bingley, "Charles has the worst handwriting ever."

"My ideas flow so quickly that I get them jumbled easily when transmitting them on paper—as a sad result my letters sometimes convey no ideas at all to my correspondents."

"Your humility, Mr. Bingley," I said, "must disarm reproof. Also, I cannot boast of having the best handwriting myself, for I do very much sometimes write something, then scratch it out, leave out words, and blot out some others."

"You echo my flaws within yourself." Mr. Bingley smiled. "Be careful, Miss Elizabeth, or I shall wish to have you with me always as my advocate."

"While I wish to be of service, I am not proficient enough a debater to save myself often enough, therefore I would feel ashamed if I were to take up the charge and not save you in one instance."

"You save me at the moment," he said and smiled at me. "And that, at present, is reward enough for having you near me."

"Then I am happy to know," I said, and smiled in return, "that you and I possess the same flaws and have the humility to recognize our imperfections."

"Nothing is more deceitful," Darcy said, "than the appearance of humility. It is often only carelessness of opinion, and sometimes an indirect boast."

I looked at Mr. Darcy sharply, for if I was correct, he was angry that I complimented Mr. Bingley—and tried to spitefully turn the conversation in his favor.

"And which of the two do you call Mr. Bingley's little recent piece of modesty?"

"The indirect boast," Mr. Darcy said, putting down his pen and looking at me directly, "for Bingley is really proud of his defects in writing, because he considers them as proceeding from quick thinking. You would have no choice but to admire him for it. The power of doing anything with quickness makes the possessor believe it is an impulse of their wit, and if the side effect of their speed is inaccuracy, then so be it."

"Darcy," Bingley said, "you do know that I am in the room right now and that I can hear you."

"He apologizes," I said for Mr. Darcy.

Mr. Darcy turned to me in shock that I had spoken for him.

"It is so late," I exclaimed to the room, "and I make it a rule that no one should begin a strong argument so late in the day, but rather he should do it early in the morning so that both sides have time to argue their point, then get mad at each other over it, then realize that it was needless to argue in the first place, and then resolve their differences and become friends once more by dinner time."

"That is a wonderful plan, Miss Elizabeth," Mr. Bingley said, smiling at me.

"I am happy to be of service, Mr. Bingley."

"And I am exceedingly gratified, by your converting what my friend says into a fun situation, when he made it to be one of censure."

"I see your design, Bingley," Mr. Darcy said. "You dislike an argument and want to silence this."

"Perhaps I do. Arguments upset my emotional digestion."

"Your desire to let peace reign," I said, "is no sacrifice on my side. Especially if your emotional digestion will feel a philosophical disturbance due to it. I have a book to read, and Mr. Darcy has a letter to finish."

Mr. Darcy then took my advice and finished his letter. He may have been ill-suited to speak with me for long, yet he at least had the understanding to listen to me when the time came to do so.

❧ 21 ❧

THE JOYS OF DISAGREEING

The next day, Jane had been feeling a little better and she could sit in the drawing-room and converse with everyone for a short duration of time.

While we sat there, the conversation had taken a turn about the residents in Hampshire. Mrs. Hurst and Miss Bingley asked about the Austens and the Lucases.

"Ah," Jane said, "both families are the best of people. We sometimes get together and put on home theatricals, where only our families are invited to play the audience of course."

"A home theatrical?" Mr. Bingley smiled. "That sounds like very much fun."

"Yes," I added, "it is, and while we sometimes do popular plays, we do plays that are written by one of their daughters, Jane Austen."

This announcement seemed to cause quite a stir and it was not a positive one.

"Miss Jane Austen?" Mr. Darcy says, "She is a writer?"

"Yes,"

"Of what?" Mr. Hurst asked.

"Of novels and short plays."

"Novels? A female writer?"

"Aye."

He looked around as if I could not have said anything worse.

"The times," he groaned, "the times indeed."

"Well, it is a noble profession," I added, "and a wonderful way to occupy one's time."

"Tis true," Mr. Bingley said, "Writing, I can see it being a fun pastime. If I had any talent myself, I would undertake it."

"As would I," I agreed, "yet I lack the talent as well."

"Then we have even more in common."

"And I," Jane added, "which is why I can't help but be amazed at her, for I can't even profess myself to be a great reader. I wish that I read more, but there always seems like the day gets filled so quickly with other obligations and duties."

"I have the same sentiment," Mr. Bingley agreed, eyeing Jane fondly. And it was moments like those where Mr. Bingley made me so confused, for his charm did seem to make his attentions very vague, though I did enjoy him tremendously.

There was a silence for a while and then Mr. Darcy began speaking.

"So, Miss Bennet and Miss Elizabeth, you truly support this Miss Austen and her writing?"

"She is quite accomplished at it," I argued, "and she is so much so that her father, our rector, even buys her paper because he believes in her talents."

"To support such a woman in such an endeavor would make you an idealist."

"I wish that I could be so, yet I simply believe that we humans should never sneer at others for wishing to have some occupation of some kind to find a shed of importance. Wouldn't you find some happiness in having something to fill up your time?"

"Of course not," he objected, "That is a very strange and un-gentlemanlike notion."

"And how so?"

"Because of the status of aristocracy of our society, it is a position in life, our role is to be seen as always being unoccupied."

"You suggest that it is attractive that we always should sit around and be motionless, like statues, and then and only then, can we be considered beautiful or of good breeding."

"That is a very accurate description of good breeding in its own right."

"And I can support that the assertion is Mr. Darcy's views," Mr. Bingley interjected, "for he considers any sudden movement as a sign of ill-breeding: walking briskly, running, or even rising precipitously from a chair. Therefore, if this friend of yours, Miss Austen, writes her words for her novels quickly, Darcy would be affronted."

"Then forgive me," I said, "yet I wish to disagree with you, Mr. Darcy, and it is within my rights to do so."

"Why is that, Miss Elizabeth?"

"Because it is still the morning, therefore we have the right to argue, then the evening to realize that we were foolish for arguing to begin with, and then by dinner time we will have resolved our differences and sat down as friends again."

Mr. Bingley laughed. Jane looked confused of what I said. Mr. Hurst didn't care what I said. Mrs. Hurst pretended to comprehend what I said, and Miss Bingley looked at me with pure venom for taking hold of Mr. Darcy's attention once more.

Yet Mr. Darcy himself was silent and I was content in knowing that I had fully partaken in the joys of disagreeing and silencing my foe as a result.

22

OUR LAST NIGHT AT AGINFIELD

Later that day, my mother and my two youngest sisters arrived to inquire after Jane. When they saw that she was doing better, my mother sighed out and allowed herself to be relieved. Then, when she was just alone with us, she turned to me.

"So, Lizzy, tell me," she huffed, "have you found a way to make Mr. Bingley fall in love with you yet?"

"Mama..." I groaned.

"Lizzy has made a lot of progress, Mama," Jane said, "and Mr. Bingley loves to show her around his library."

Our mother was all a flutter when Jane had told her this, so she met with the rest of the family, declared that Jane was still too ill to be moved, and therefore Jane and I would have to remain for a couple more days. I knew that she did this to keep me there for longer in hopes that Mr. Bingley might propose to me. Yet I didn't believe that Mr. Bingley, with all his desires for swift actions and decision making, would propose to a woman who had stayed in his home for only seven days.

Later, when my mother and sisters left, I went back to stay with

Jane, yet the day soon ended, and I found myself once more going back down to dine with the residents of Aginfield.

Once more we were all assembled in the drawing room. Mrs. Hurst and Mr. Bingley were playing backgammon while Mr. Darcy read, and I did some needlework and sewing. And Mr. Hurst was sleeping—again. Though to be honest, I preferred him that way as opposed to being awake, for when so, he was very much a waste of air.

The most curious in action was Miss Bingley again. She had begun with reading a book as well, but very much eyeing Mr. Darcy over the edge of it. It was made very clear that she only decided to read that night just to impress him, and it was even clearer, from looking at her book, that she chose it only because it was the second volume to the book that Mr. Darcy had.

"How pleasant it is to spend an evening in this way!" she said, clearly trying to get attention. "I declare that of all the amusements there are in the world, there is no enjoyment like reading!"

No one made a reply. Then she yawned, threw the book aside and cast her eyes around the room. Suddenly her eyes darted between Mr. Darcy and me. I pretended not to notice however until she got up and walked towards me. When she approached, I looked up to see her smiling down at me.

"Miss Eliza Bennet, let me persuade you to follow my example, and take a turn about the room. I assure you it is very refreshing."

I was surprised by this but agreed to it to be polite. We stood up and began to pace around the room, and I could easily see that Miss Bingley's objective had been achieved, for Mr. Darcy had lowered his book and looked up at us.

"Would you like to join us, Mr. Darcy?" Miss Bingley asked.

"That would defeat the object."

"What could he mean? Miss Eliza, what do you think Mr. Darcy is on about?"

"I do not comprehend," I replied, "for Mr. Darcy's mind is like a safe and asking to open it is dangerous."

"Nay, I am incapable of letting curiosity be curbed," Miss Bingley said, "so do tell us, Mr. Darcy, what you mean by your statement?"

"I welcome talking of my theories behind your intentions," Mr. Darcy replied, "You are either wishing to walk together because you are in each other's confidence and wish to converse alone, or because you are conscious that your figures appear to the greatest advantage in walking—if the first, I should be completely in your way. And if the second, I can admire you much better as I sit by the fire."

"Oh! Shocking!" cried Miss Bingley. "I never heard anything so abominable. How shall we punish him for such a speech?"

"Nothing so easy," I replied "We can all hurt and vex one another. Tease him—call him names or mock him. Surely that would be the best and only way."

"What? Tease a man who lacks vices or vanities, including petty imperfections? No, no. For to laugh at him must mean that he should be ridiculed, and being ridiculed implies that he was at fault, which he never is."

"Mr. Darcy is not to be laughed at!" I gasped in pretend surprise. "That is an uncommon talent, though everyone wishes they possessed it—though I have my doubts. Or at the very least, I wish to question. Mr. Darcy is a man who is never at fault? I never knew such a man existed before."

"Miss Bingley," Mr. Darcy added, "has given me too much credit. The wisest and the best of men, nay, the wisest and best of their actions, may be rendered ridiculous by a person whose first object in life is a joke."

"Certainly, there are such people, but I hope I am not one of them. I hope I never ridicule what is right and moral, though I do love to laugh at the foolish. But it's implied that you don't have vices?"

"To be perfect is impossible. But it has been the study of my life to avoid those weaknesses which often expose a strong understanding to ridicule."

"Would you count pride amongst those weaknesses?"

"Yes, depending on the possessor. It all must do with the mind of the person, the will of the person and the soul of them. Pride—where there is a real superiority of mind and soul, pride will be always under good regulation. Yet where there is no superiority of mind, will, or soul, pride then becomes a flaw, a plague upon its possessor, in which they wield it to hurt others—or oppress them with it."

"And you believe yourself to have good regulation?"

"I believe so."

"Then pray tell, what is your fault?"

"I suppose it should not be spoken of."

"A fault in a conversation about faults can always be spoken of."

"I have one that I know of."

"But no others?"

"Then I shall correct myself. I have one that I shall willingly speak of."

"Then you are in a room of people who will not despise you for your confession. Or perhaps I should speak for myself."

"Perhaps you already are."

"Then...proceed, at no one's risk, even your own."

"I...it's my temper. It is something I dare not vouch for. I cannot forget the follies and vices of others as soon as I ought, nor their offences against myself. My feelings are not puffed about with every attempt to move them. My temper would perhaps be called resentful. My good opinion once lost is lost forever."

"That is a failing indeed! Implacable resentment is a shade in a character. And yet you are not safe from me yet, for tell me, what stands your belief on forgetfulness?"

"Forgetfulness?"

"Sometimes one is struck by a tragedy of forgetting those that they shouldn't." I thought then that it would be harmless to remind him of our past and see how his composure took it. "Do you always remember those that you should?"

"I always remember everyone who is worthy of remembering," he said staring blatantly at me. "Everyone."

What did he mean? Did he mean that I wasn't worth remembering, or that he did remember me, but just didn't show it?

"Do let us have a little music," Miss Bingley interrupted, tired of a conversation in which she clearly had no share. She walked over to the piano and began playing.

When the night had ended, I went to visit Jane and retired for the evening. And I was too happy to do so, for I had learned the dangers of giving Mr. Darcy a little too much attention.

❧

The next day, I took refuge in the library and was surprised to hear the footsteps of someone. I didn't know how, but I could tell that those footsteps belonged to a man, and sensing that if it was Mr. Darcy, I wouldn't want to see him, so I then hid behind some shelves.

I had been correct, for Mr. Darcy had entered and he walked up to where I'd been sitting. I felt sad in seeing that I left my opened book there on the table. He picked it up and I began to silently tiptoe out of the room, but I was stopped by his voice.

"Miss Elizabeth," he said, still looking at my book. "I know that you are in here. And I also know that you are hiding behind the bookshelf now. Hiding does not become you, so please step from out of the shadows."

I bit my lip, then walked around the shelves and faced him.

"I was leaving just now."

"Without your book?" Mr. Darcy said, "Are you lying to me, Miss Elizabeth?"

"Mr. Darcy!"

"It is only a question with no intention of offence behind it."

"Fine then," I said boldly, "I was lying just now."

"You were avoiding me."

"Yes, Mr. Darcy I was."

"Is avoiding people a defect of yours?"

"Unlike your defect, which is a propensity to hate everyone."

"While yours is to willfully misunderstand them."

"I do not misunderstand the fact that you acted as if we have never met."

"Yet we didn't officially."

"You almost kissed me."

Mr. Darcy flinched and looked away from me.

"I apologize for that."

"Then you might as well apologize for when you would not dance with me at the assembly and then called me only tolerable."

"You overheard that?"

"You were standing near me, Mr. Darcy. How could you say such a thing? What did I do to deserve such a comment?"

"You intrigue me."

🙰

I was startled.

"What?"

"Why do you think that I almost kissed you? You, Miss Elizabeth, you fascinate me."

"Then..." I did not know what to say to that and I turned away. "Mr. Darcy, I did not expect you to confess such a thing."

"Nor did I. On the contrary, this admission is very much not like me."

"Then why would you hurt me so?"

"Because I don't want to be fascinated with you."

"And why not?"

"We should end this conversation now."

"You told me to stay, therefore if I heard you out and answered your questions, then you ought to answer mine." I was so much driven by his revelations that I could not obey propriety and cease my tongue. I had to know what way Mr. Darcy's mind worked. "Why do you wish to avoid me?"

"Because I—you are not good for me."

I felt as if he had hurt me completely.

"I..." I gasped, backing away from him. "How could you say such a thing?"

"Miss Elizabeth, believe me I didn't mean to offend you. I meant it in the highest praise of you."

"Don't speak to me, don't say anything!"

"No, I do respect you very much. I just can't tell you everything."

"And why not?"

"Because, as I said...I do not want to feel bound to you. I will not!"

"You disgust me. You are worthless!"

I tried to run from him, but he grabbed my arm and spun me around.

"Miss Elizabeth, forgive me! I am being cruel!"

"You are, and I don't wish to ever see you! Let go of me!"

"I will not." He then leaned down and kissed me passionately. I went from beating my arms against his chest to falling into his embrace. I could not understand why I gave into him so easily, yet I could not help but do so. We continued to kiss, and then Mr. Darcy stopped abruptly. He released me, walked to the door, and didn't look at me.

"I know that I have been horrible. I'm not worth forgiving and I see that now. We can never do that again, for you deserve better," he said, and then he walked out.

The whole night, we did not speak. I was too heartbroken, and I would never forgive him. Between my sister and me, we spent our last night in Aginfield in two different attitudes. Jane spent it fully recovering, and I spent it weeping.

23

OUR COUSIN

The next morning, the occupants of Aginfield saw us off in our carriage and I had never been happier to leave a place in my life.

We journeyed homeward and we were greeted by a most unwelcome sight. As our carriage pulled into Longbourn, we were greeted by Lydia and Kitty who ran up to our carriage.

"Lizzy and Jane!" Kitty cried, "Here you are at last! The most perplexing thing has happened. And you shall never guess, so we shall just tell you."

"Our cousin Mr. Collins is here!" Lydia said, "And he is ghastly!"

"Lower your voice," Jane said as we stepped down from the carriage, "and tell us what you are talking about."

"Oh, you remember our cousin, don't you?" Lydia said.

We had a cousin named Mr. William Collins, who was the son of our father's brother. My father and his brother had a falling out years ago and stopped talking to each other since even before I was born. Mr. Collins, however, was not just the son of our uncle who we never knew, but he was also guilty of the crime of being our father's heir to Longbourn. Unfortunately, our father's estate was arranged in such a way that it was entailed to a male heir. Because our father had only daughters, none of us would inherit Longbourn. Therefore, the only way that we had a future for ourselves was if we married, or at least a couple of us had to save us from the rocks of harsh fortune.

"Well, it turns out that our father didn't tell any of us that he had been communicating with Mr. Collins through letters. Mr. Collins was the first to do it. He wrote to our father, hoping to yield the breach that existed between our father and his. Basically, he wanted peace in the family and asked to visit to make amends to us for him being the inheritor of Longbourn."

"Yet, the entail is not his fault," I said, "therefore how could he repay us?"

"I have an idea," Lydia said, "and it's a frightening one."

"And you said that he is here now!"

"Yes, Father, being one to always love a prank, didn't tell mama until three days before Mr. Collins arrived. That didn't even give us time to warn you all, because you have all been at Aginfield."

While I appreciated my father's sense of amusement, this was a joke that he had taken too far.

Jane and I looked at each other and then turned to Lydia and Kitty.

"And what is he like, our cousin?" Jane asked.

"And like I said before," Lydia said.

"Ghastly!" they both said together.

Ghastly turned out not to be a sufficient enough definition of Mr. Collins' character.

We followed our sisters inside. Our parents were sitting with Mr. Collins and Mary, who then stood up and turned to us.

"Ah!" Mr. Collins said, "These fine creatures must be my eldest cousins, Miss Jane and Miss Elizabeth."

We bowed to him, he smiled at us and it was the most frightening thing that I had ever seen. He was not an ugly man, yet nor was he handsome, his face just seemed—strange, and made one feel very uncomfortable. Yet, I was hesitant to judge him from his outward appearance and waited for him to speak—but that proved to not be his strong suit either.

"Mr. Bennet..." and here Mr. Collins made a very strange sound with his voice, a wheezing sound that almost seemed as if he was beginning to have a seizure, yet the seizure never came. "You must gaze like a king on your magnificent beauties that are your daughters."

"I do, Mr. Collins," our father said, much amused at our cousin's absurdities. "I even have a crown when I feel especially a part of the occasion."

"Yet I heard that you were ill, Miss Bennet," Mr. Collins said to Jane.

"Aye sir, I am well now though."

"And yet I heard that you fell ill riding a horse in the rain. Oh dear, we shall not tell Lady Catherine about that, for she objects greatly to ladies riding, especially during this season."

"What makes this season different than any other?" I asked, but our mother looked at me in a way that bade me to be quiet.

"And pray tell," Jane asked, "Who is Lady Catherine?"

Behind Mr. Collins, our father rubbed his eyes, which clearly showed me that he had heard this subject already in full—to the point where he really didn't want to hear it again.

"Ah, you have not heard?" Mr. Collins said, puffing out his chest. "Then I shall be happy to fill in your ignorance on the matter, and I must remember that young ladies don't always have such skills at memory retention."

I could feel my lips tightening in one straight line. Did he honestly just say that?

Mr. Collins began his explanation of his profession and the history that he was fortunate enough to have in it.

"I, my fair cousins, am a clergyman, and received my ordination at Easter. I have been so fortunate as to be distinguished by the patronage of the Right Honorable Lady Catherine de Bourgh, widow of Sir Lewis de Bourgh, whose bounty and beneficence has preferred me to the valuable rectory of this parish, where it shall be my earnest endeavor to demean myself with grateful respect towards her Ladyship and be ever ready to perform those rites and ceremonies which are instituted by the Church of England. I very much do wish to baptize and bury my parishioners with equal amount of care all the way around. As a clergyman, moreover, I feel it my duty to promote and establish the blessing of peace in all families within the reach of my influence; and on these grounds, I flatter myself that my present overtures of good-will are highly commendable, and that the circumstance of my being next in the entail of Longbourn estate, will be kindly overlooked, and I am staying here for a fortnight to yield the breach between our families.

My stay shall not be an inconvenience to my patroness, as Lady Catherine is far from objecting to my occasional absence on a Sunday, provided that some other clergyman is engaged to do the duty of the day. Therefore, now you know the history, and are fortunate in seeing that my position in life, my connection to a noble family, has made me the most fortunate of men, and I flatter myself, will suit me in full, for I am up to the task."

"Oh," was Jane and my reply.

"Well," Jane said, "I am happy that you are so fortunate in your choice of patroness."

"Oh, Lady Catherine! I have never been treated with such affability. I have been invited to dine four times at Rosings. And she had sent for me only the Saturday before, to play backgammon in the evening. Lady Catherine has been reckoned proud by many people, but I have never seen anything but affability in her. She has always spoken to me as she would to any other gentleman and made not the smallest objection to me joining in the society of the neighborhood, or to me leaving the parish occasionally for a week or two, to visit relations. She has even advised me to marry as soon as I was able, provided I choose with discretion, of course, and had once paid me a visit in my humble parsonage, where she has perfectly approved all the alterations I was making to the home, and had even vouchsafed to suggest some things as well. For example, she advised that I put some rugs in the bedrooms upstairs."

"Rugs in the bedrooms?" I asked. "That is a very fortunate suggestion on her part."

"It was indeed."

Rugs in a bedroom was a very customary thing, therefore I did not know why it fazed him so.

"Well!" Mr. Bennet said, clapping his hands together and clearly observing the stupidity of Mr. Collins. "That is all very proper and civil, I am sure, and I daresay she is a very agreeable woman. It is a pity that great ladies in general are not more like her."

Mr. Collins was a heavy-looking man who was late in his twenties. He smiled often, yet his air was stately, and his manners were formal without appearing graceful. I could not explain it, yet he appeared...awkward. He then went on to say that rumors he heard of our beauty truly had fallen short of actuality, and then he told our mother that no doubt she would see us disposed in marriage very soon. As you could imagine, this form of gallantry was not much to my taste, but our mother enjoyed the compliment.

Unfortunately, his gaze lingered on us for too long and I very soon had the assumption of what he meant when he wished to make up to us his inheriting our home. I believed, looking on him now, that his intention was to marry one of us so that when he inherited Longbourn, it would remain in the family. While this was a very noble and honorable intention, and it very much should have endeared him to me, I could not help but very quickly find him ridiculous.

❧

And my first impulse would prove to be correct. Mr. Collins turned out to be an obsequious and odious man. At dinner, he continually spoke about Lady Catherine De Bourgh and his position as a clergyman of her parish at Hunsford.

Then we went into our sitting room and sat by the fire, and he continued to speak of Lady Catherine De Bourgh and his position as a clergyman of her parish at Hunsford.

Then he read us an excerpt from the book 'Fordyce's Sermons' which as he put it 'spoke very eloquently of everything that was moral', and then when done, he continued to speak of Lady Catherine De Bourgh and his position as a clergyman.

When he began to speak of the largeness of Lady Catherine's estate, Rosing's Park, and went on to talk about how her wealth was so large that a statue in one of her rooms alone cost 600 pounds, I was done pretending to listen to his lectures.

I let my mind wander. Yet before I had done so I noticed that Mr. Collins's eyes were darting over to Jane every now and again. Thank god Jane was safe from him!

❧

The next day, I walked downstairs for it was nearing time for dinner and I came up to a doorway where I heard our mother talking to Mr. Collins. Eavesdropping was a bad habit that ran through our family and I had inherited that flaw, therefore I stayed where I was and overheard everything.

"Mrs. Bennet," Mr. Collins began, "you do know that, due to the good graces of our Father, that I have been bestowed a parsonage of sufficient size."

"Mr. Collins, you have spoken so of it often."

"Yes, well, as I spoke to you about this before, I have been bestowed this grace also by the benevolence of Lady Catherine De Bourgh, who is a most pleasing and admirable woman, whose bounty and beneficence had recommended to my most lucky seat..."

I could not believe how long it was taking him to get to his point, for he continued on and on in this way for quite some time. Then eventually, he changed the course of his action and got back to the point he was trying to make.

"Well, as she has often said, 'Mr. Collins, you must marry', and she is quite correct, for it is one of the holiest of sacraments, and surely, if I wish to set the right example in my own life for my parishioners."

And then he strayed from his course of subject again. *Good god, Mr. Collins, get to the point!* After another minute of speaking about the holiness of matrimony, he got to the point.

"Yet, regarding her advising me to marry, I have come to Hampshire expressly for that purpose. And I am quite struck by the charms of your daughters."

"Oh, thank you sir, they are excellent girls, though I say it myself."

"Well, I am in hopes of seeking a mistress for my estate and I must say that the eldest Miss Bennet has caught my particular attentions. She seems like the perfect sort of woman to suit the needs of a humble clergyman."

"Oh, Mr. Collins, it is incumbent upon me to tell you that she is engaged to be married to a Mr. Brocklehurst from London. The wedding shall take place in a month's time—or sooner."

"Oh, engaged," Mr. Collins sighed, "well, then, how about her younger sister, Miss Elizabeth?"

"And I am sorry again, sir, but it is very likely that Lizzy will be soon engaged herself as well. Yet as to my three youngest daughters, well they are all not attached in any way at all."

"Thank you. For with three alternatives still left, I'm sure that I could find something to suit my preferences."

I chuckled to myself and then quietly went into the sitting room. A man such as Mr. Collins had no right to have any preferences whatsoever, for whoever chose him would be resigning themselves to a very unfortunate fate. For indeed, to spend a moment with him felt as if one was spending an eternity.

As I sat down, I felt happy in knowing that some good could come from stubbornness of opinion. My mother was so set on Mr. Bingley being in love with me, that it convinced her that I was not available, and as such, I was free from Mr. Collins' gaze.

Yet my youngest sisters were not. On the contrary, I was not worried about them at all. For Lydia would never appeal to him. She was lovely, yes, just as Kitty was, but she was very high-spirited, never paid attention to Mr. Collins and her form of conversation never suited him. And since it is the nature of man to not find what ignores them as beautiful, she was free as well. Kitty was nice enough to him, but she always followed wherever Lydia led, even though she was the older one, and therefore Mr. Collins would naturally not regard her. Yet, Mary, who was known for being the plainest of us, did pay much attention to Mr. Collins, partook in discussions with him on Fordyce's Sermon's and was regarded as being accomplished. Therefore, she should and would be the perfect choice for our cousin who came to stay.

24

WRONG CHOICE

As I readied myself for bed, there was a knock on my door and then Jane entered.

"I was worried that you would be in bed already," she said, coming in and closing the door behind her.

"No, I am not sleepy at all."

"Lizzy, I... I must ask you something. Are you in love with Mr. Bingley?"

I sighed and decided that now was as good of a time as any to tell the truth.

"Jane, you shall think me cold, for Mr. Bingley is wonderful, honorable, and quite charming. He has shown interest in me, yet there is the first problem. He shows interest in every woman it seems, and I wonder if he is kind and warm to all womankind in general. That is a noble trait, yet it makes his affections hard to see truly. I feel as if he could love any woman that he looks on. And yet, I might do the same thing as well, for him and I are both lively in nature. Yet, in truth, I am not at all in love with him. I know I should be, and honestly, my not being so makes me wonder if love is something that I could ever truly feel for any man, yet I don't."

"It's fine. I knew that you didn't."

"You did?"

"Yes, you received his attentions with pleasure, yet I never found any particular regard. I had known that if you felt something more, then you would have displayed it."

"I know that I am strange for not feeling anything deeper."

"One cannot dictate who one naturally feels for. Yet our mother is determined to see your happy event."

"Well, she shall have to content herself with your happy ending."

"I have received a letter from Mr. Brocklehurst." Jane smiled, and added, "He spoke of how much he loves me. It fills me with assurance. I do so love him."

⊗⊱⊚

The next day, I was just returning home from taking a walk among the trees when Kitty had run to me from the direction of our home.

"Lizzy, please don't tell me that you wish to return home yet."

"I was."

"No, you cannot. You must let me walk with you further along the path, at least for another twenty minutes or so."

She grabbed my arm and pulled me along.

"Why what is it?"

"I need some peace!" she said.

"Peace, from what?"

"From him of course."

"From who?"

"Mr. Collins."

"What has he annoyed you with now?" I laughed as I said, "Did he threaten you with another reading of Fordyce's Sermons?"

"Well, yes, but more than that. He keeps following me everywhere."

"What?"

"Yes. When I was tossing horseshoes with Lydia, he offered to throw mine for me, and then he wished to read to me, and then asked me what I liked to do. When I walk places, he decides to always join me. The only reason I was able to get away was because I told father where I was headed, but no one else."

I was startled by this news and none of it made sense logically.

"No," I sighed, "it cannot be..."

"What cannot be?" Kitty asked. "What could he mean by annoying me so?"

"He's not annoying you in his eyes. He's courting you."

"I beg your pardon?"

I then told Kitty about all that I had overheard and how Mr. Collins came to Longbourn to seek a wife. At the end of my revealing, Kitty looked at me and gasped.

"Mr. Collins is in love with me? No!"

Over the next couple of days, it had proven to be so. Mr. Collins chose to escort Kitty places, compliment her often, even go so far as to hold her thread if she were sewing, and agreed to dance with her at the next assembly we had at The Red Lion Assembly Room.

I could not understand how he could have been so erroneous in his choice. Our sister Mary was the one who gave him attention and shared many common interests with him—and failed to always see how ridiculous he could be. Why did he not choose her? Also, Mary was the older one and therefore should have followed his respect for seniority.

Yet it all came down to appearances, and Kitty was the fairer of the two.

Poor Kitty!

And foolish Mr. Collins!

He had made the wrong choice. And it was almost as comical as the potential idea of him choosing me.

25

THE LADY IN BLUE

Watching the continual pursuit of Kitty on Mr. Collin's part was comical and tragic, for our mother encouraged the match and Kitty was at a loss of what to do. She did respect our mother's opinion to an extent, but every proper feeling within her detested the idea of a marriage to Mr. Collins. Yet our mother was a most determined woman, our Aunt Phillips's support of it was a most determined influence, and our father's indifference to the whole situation was a most determined loss of support from his side.

I hoped that Kitty would not ask me for my advice ever, for I would honestly not be able to hold my tongue and tell her to reject his attentions if he ever made an offer—for she did not love him.

Yet the most surprising and disturbing thing to occur was not the pleasing attentions of Mr. Collins on Kitty, but rather it came in the form of a lady in blue who came to our doorstep and requested an entrance to speak to a Miss Jane Bennet.

She was granted entry and was led into our sitting room where

Jane and I sat together. Luckily our mother was out visiting our Aunt Phillips and our father didn't care to leave his library.

We stood when she entered, and she was a nicely dressed woman, clearly of some wealth and had a keen sense of fashion as well. Her skin was olive in complexion and it gave me the sense of her being a foreigner. Then she opened her mouth and I was proven to be correct.

"Good day, Miss Bennet and..."

"I am her younger sister, Miss Elizabeth."

"Oh." She curtsied to us and we responded in kind.

"I am Signora Rosa Bramante," she said.

"It is a pleasure to make your acquaintance," Jane began, "and you are from Italy?"

"Indeed, I am, yet at present I come from London. I come in regards to a man with whom we are both acquainted. A Mr. Brocklehurst."

"Oh, yes, we are engaged to be married. Is he well? Has something happened to him?"

"He is quite well, just simply confused." Signora Bramante's eyes darted to me. "I would prefer it if we spoke in private."

"My sister is safe to remain with us."

"I trust she is, yet this next news is delicate, and will be difficult for you to hear."

Impatient to get to the point, I decided simply to be pertinent.

"Forgive me, signora, yet she is my sister. Whatever you tell me, she shall tell me afterwards anyway."

"I never had any sisters," Signora Bramante said, "therefore, I am unaware of such intimacy, yet you are correct, therefore I shall begin."

We all sat down, and Signora Bramante began speaking.

"I come regarding your engagement to Mr. Brocklehurst. I urge you now not to marry him."

"But—" Jane started, "how dare you..."

"You can't marry him. Because he is married to me."

⚜

"What?" I gasped.

"Well, we are not legally married. Yet I am his mistress and we have three children together. We share a house in London, yet we also have a house in Italy. We are not able to marry because I don't fit within the society of his that has obliged him to marry a gentlewoman, whether he loves her or not. I love him, Miss Bennet, and I know that you must hate me for coming."

"It is not only that!" Jane gasped, heartbroken, "But how can I trust that you are even telling me the truth?"

"Indeed," I argued with her, "you could be lying."

"I could be, but I am not. What would I have to gain from coming here from London merely to pull a trick on you? Indeed, I am in earnest, I am his mistress, we have three wonderful children, and if you marry him, then you will marry a man who will only give you half of his life. For the other half of it he will spend with me. By the looks of you, Miss Bennet, you are not a woman who has not felt the power of love. It is strong, and I would never reject him, and he will never reject me. Therefore, you must accept the fact that if you marry him, you will be marrying a man who likes you, but is not in love with you and never will be."

I looked toward Jane. She was frozen in place, and then she stood up and walked to the fireplace and looked into it.

"I know you must hate me for coming here, and I know you must still doubt me," she added.

"You have to understand," I said, "that it is not wise to believe everyone who simply comes to your door and professes to be something."

"And that's why I offer your sister proof."

Jane turned around.

"Proof?" she said, "Of what kind?"

"Proof from Mr. Brocklehurst's own lips. He doesn't know that I am here, yet he will come. In two days' time, he plans to visit you to put your plans of marriage forward. Ask him about me. And about our children. Then tell him that I came to see you. Mark his answer, and then make your decision accordingly."

Signora Rosa stood up and curtsied to us.

"I am very sorry to have caused you pain, Miss Bennet, for I can see that you deserve better."

Signora Rosa quitted the house immediately, got back into her carriage and drove off.

Jane and I were both fortunate that our parents were not present for such a scene, and with any luck, they would never learn about or hear about the lady who came to visit...of the lady in blue.

❦ 26 ❦

THE LIE THAT WOULD SAVE US ALL

In two days, Mr. Brocklehurst did arrive, and our mother was in all happiness to see him again. Jane was subdued, and I was somber, for his coming in two days proved Signora Rosa's accuracy. She definitely did know him.

When he arrived, and our mother finished making a show, Jane humbly and gently asked us all to leave them alone so that they would be within each other's confidence. Though this was breaching propriety, our mother was only too happy to satisfy the couple, and I unfortunately could not listen in.

Yet it turns out that I did not need to, for not ten minutes later, I saw Mr. Brocklehurst quit our house immediately, rush into his carriage and had his driver ride him off with alacrity.

After I saw that, I went downstairs to see Jane sitting on the floor, crying. I rushed up to her and held her, then our mother entered, saw the state Jane was in and had only one thing to shout— even though she still did not know what had occurred.

"That fiend!"

Knowing that this was a story the whole family—except for Mr.

Collins—needed to hear, I took Jane and our mother to my father's study and entered without knocking first. He looked up at us over his book, wondering why we invaded his privacy. Yet taking one look at Jane's face made his apathy soften to empathy. He stood up, closed the door behind us and asked for the full story of what had happened.

Jane told them everything; from the report Signora Rosa gave her to Mr. Brocklehurst's confession of the whole truth. When Jane had confronted him, Mr. Brocklehurst still believed that they should go through with the marriage and Jane was against it in full. He still claimed to love Jane terribly, despite his previous actions or present course. Thinking her stubborn, Mr. Brocklehurst quitted the house as soon as he realized that she could not be moved on the subject.

After I got over my anger at the prospect of him being the one angry with her for being rational, I only then could take in our mother's reaction.

"What a horrid man!" she cried, "Wicked and false! Oh, if he were only here now!"

"Mama," I whispered, "you must lower your voice."

"And, why should I? Let the whole world hear me!"

"Yet I do not want the whole world to hear it, Mother," Jane said softly.

"Precisely," our father said, falling back into his indifferent ways, and sounding practical and nothing more. "If you shout about this, then Mr. Collins will find out, and how shall it make our family look in his eyes? Then it shall reach the whole house and the maids, who will then tell other maids in other households and very soon all of Hampshire shall know of what Jane has gone through."

"Precisely," I said, "And Mother, don't expose Jane to the world in that way."

"Oh well!" Our mother snapped. "I suppose that it must be if you put it like that. Yet what are we to do? This has ruined everything!"

"And me most of all." Jane sighed once more, turned to me and said, "For when I saw him again, I did remember my love for him. I did love him, Lizzy!"

"I know that you did."

We were at a loss of what to do for a while. And we didn't know how to tell Mary, Kitty and Lydia. It is a terrible thing when one does not think one can trust one's own family, yet it was the case at present. If we told Mary, she would more than likely do some moralizing and then accidentally let it slip to Mr. Collins.

If we told Kitty, then we could persuade her of silence, I was sure, yet there was the problem of Lydia. Lydia would want to tell everyone that she knew about it, and even if we made her swear to keep the secret, she would still let her tongue wag.

Therefore, we decided that at present, it would be best not to tell them.

Yet we had to tell them something, and we did not know what.

At first, we wondered if the best course of action were to just say that Mr. Brocklehurst needed to postpone the marriage further, but it didn't answer any of our problems. Our mother eventually sat down, complained about how this news had destroyed her poor nerves, it was too much for her to bear, and that she felt as if she would die. At that announcement, our father's head shot up.

"Wait, that's it!"

"What is it? Me dying?"

"My dear you have never died of your nerves, and I'm wondering if they shall ever fully get the better of you." With vitality that I had never seen him move with before, our father went to the window of his study, rolled up the window and began to hail one of the farmers on our estate.

"Hullo there, Andrews!"

"Good day, sir," Andrews replied while tending to our garden, "how are you this morning?"

"Oh, it goes very ill, Andrews! Would you believe the tragedy of this? The man that our dear Jane was to marry, Mr. Brocklehurst. Well it turns out that he has met the worst carriage accident while travelling from London to the country and he has died!"

"Mr. Bennet!" Our mother gasped.

"Be quiet, woman!" Mr. Bennet hissed, "Can't you see? I'm saving the day."

Then he turned to Andrews and continued to speak.

"Yes, the poor man is dead."

"Oh, I am sorry," Andrews cried, "that is horrible. And poor Miss Bennet, to lose the man that she loves at such a wonderful time in her life."

"Yes, yes, yes, she is heartbroken. Very heartbroken. Yet do me a favor, for you know how my dear Jane is, she is such a sweet thing. She wants you to tell all the farmers and have them tell everyone they know about his poor accident and pray for him."

"I can do that, sir."

"Thank you, Andrews. Good man."

Mr. Bennet then closed the window and looked at us with extreme self-satisfaction.

"Problem solved."

"It is not solved, you fool!" Our mother exclaimed. "What happens when they find out that he is alive?"

"First, very rarely do people go up to London from Hampshire. Second, no one in Hampshire ever really met him so they don't know what he looks like. Only our maid does, but she doesn't even know the particulars, therefore no one will think she is much of an authority. And the last thing Mr. Brocklehurst will do is ever come back to the village that has a woman who refused him in it. And thirdly—well, in truth, fourthly, Edmund Brocklehurst, I'm sure is a very common name. Therefore, there are probably many of them in the world, which means that if we were to invent one and have the invented one die, then suppose someone met the real one. They would just simply think that we were referencing two different Mr. Brocklehursts."

"And about his estate? We told everyone what estate he owned."

"Oh, that tiny detail that no one probably remembered? Hold on for one moment, Mrs. Bennet." Our dad walked over to the window again, raised it and called out once more to the farmers. "Hullo, Andrews and the rest of you lot, do you remember the name of the estate Mr. Brocklehurst had?"

"Not really, sir, no!" Were pretty much all their replies.

"Perfect answer!" Our dad said, "Now carry on." He closed the window and turned back to us. "See the answer to all of our woes. Mr. Brocklehurst is now dead, and we should keep it that way. Jane, I know the traditional mourning period, but you only need wear your black gown for a couple days, and I daresay no one will think any less of you. Now, if you all would be so kind as to leave my study as I like it—in perfect peace and solitude—I would be most appreciative." He sat down and continued to read his book.

Mr. Brocklehurst's demise spread all over Hampshire and Jane received many visitors who offered their condolences for her loss. She wore her black gown for four days, shed it on the fifth, and was available once more. It turned out that our dad's scheme had worked, and it was the lie that would save us all.

27

A NEW ARRIVAL

Later that evening, Jane had told me the full conversation that she had had with Mr. Brocklehurst. After she told me how it had gone, I could understand why she was torn between her desire for him and her strong choice for relinquishing any hopes of being his wife. For it had gone as such…

"So, it is all true, then?" Jane gasped after she had reported the coming of Signora Bramante. "You really are promised to her."

"Jane…" Mr. Brocklehurst sighed.

"Please, Samuel," Jane pleaded, taking his hand. "Look me in the eye and tell me that it is not true."

When seeing her imploring look, Mr. Brocklehurst buckled.

"Jane, I am so sorry. Indeed, I do have a family with Signora Bramante."

"And you have…children?"

"I confess that I do."

Jane moved away from him, but Mr. Brocklehurst grabbed her hands.

"Jane, please don't think on it."

"Don't think on it!" Jane cried, "How can I not think on it?"

"Because it changes nothing between us."

"How can it not?"

"Because it doesn't change how I feel toward you."

"How you feel toward me? How can you feel anything toward me? You have a wife."

"Jane, she and I are not married. Yet you and I shall be."

"Does her marital status with you change the alliance between you both? You have another family."

Mr. Brocklehurst ran his hand through his hair and turned away. When he had collected himself, he turned back to Jane.

"And this is the even-handed dealing of the world," he scoffed, "We attend church where we are taught to forgive one another, but in this world, a simple mistake destroys us for life. I was younger when I met Signora Bramante. I was in fact in love with her, but due to our different upbringings and positions in society, it was impossible for us both to marry. Indeed, both of our families were against it. Yet she was—with child—I confess that I didn't control myself as I ought to have. That is my shame, I do not deny it. And I was able to set up a house for her and see her privately. Yet time does what it does to us all."

"And what is that?"

"It changes our heart. I did love her, very much so. But over time, well, my heart has grown."

"And you are going to tell me that you love me?"

"At first when we met, I was hoping it was a passing fancy of mine, which is why I didn't seek you out and visit your home. But over time, your memory gnawed at me. Every time I discovered that you were in London, I could not help but see you. And then over time, the impulse grew, and I could not resist you. Yes, I fell in love with you. Jane, you must believe that. I have spent these last couple of months trying to arrange everything so that you would be happy, that my past with her would not collide with the present I would have with you. But—sometimes one must understand that it is possible, and very likely, that we people can have more than one love in our lives."

"But not more than one at the same time," Jane cried. "I love you, unlike any other man I have ever met. Indeed, no man compares to you in my eyes. So how can I trust your words?"

"If you love me, then stay with me."

"You think I ought to let my love for you have me commit to such an act? I cannot do it. Besides, look what you have shown me? You loved her. Now you do not love her as much. You say you love me now. But what about in a few years when we have a family? Will you turn to another woman?"

"I would not."

"But you have. Besides, if we marry, what about your other family? They will still be in your life, won't they?"

Mr. Brocklehurst was silent.

"Yes, they shall. Jane, no man should forsake his children. No matter how he conceived them and how illegitimate they are."

"And that is very good of you, but can you look me in the eye and tell me that when you would visit her, you won't feel any desire for her?"

Mr. Brocklehurst was silent at this, and it gave Jane all the confirmation that she needed.

"Of course, you would," she finalized, "for I would not have chosen a man who could forsake a woman forever. But I don't want to share any man I choose with another woman. I want him and him alone."

"Jane, please," Mr. Brocklehurst pleaded, "are you about to withdraw yourself from me?"

Mr. Brocklehurst pulled Jane close to him, leaned down, and

kissed her passionately. Having never been kissed before, Jane was overwhelmed. Mr. Brocklehurst took this as encouragement, and he lifted her up, twirled her around, then lay her on the seat, kissing her continuously.

"Would you not have me?" He whispered, kissing her neck, "When I feel this deeply for you?"

He ran his hands over and under her dress, grabbing her thighs as he pulled down the front of her dress and began to kiss her breasts. Jane was enraptured, but before he could fully raise her dress with his other hand, Jane came to her senses.

"No, stop!" She cried, rising, and moving away from him. He pursued her, attempting to persuade her.

"You could have me as your companion every night," he assured her. "I will always make you feel special. I just cannot forsake that part of my life."

"And I would never ask you to," Jane swore. "I would never want to be the woman who came between you and the woman who deserves to have you in full. And so, this is my sacrifice." Jane turned to Mr. Brocklehurst. "Edmund, I am in love with you."

"And I am in love with you," he whispered desperately.

"And so is she, or she would not have come."

"No, Jane," he cried, taking her face in his hands, and pressing her face against his. "Please, don't do this. Don't be an angel just now."

"I will, if it helps us both make the right decision. Samuel, I will always love you, but we cannot get married. I cannot marry you."

Mr. Brocklehurst looked at her, bitter.

"You break my heart, Jane. And I will never forgive you."

With that, he quitted the house.

After Jane had told me everything, I knew her heart was deeply affected and always would be. For your last memory of the man you loved to be a look of bitterness was hard. And despite her having done right, a part of Jane's heart would always regret her decision. Sometimes, with love, it can often feel as if there is no right or wrong—it only is about what feels good. But Jane had the strength to resist it. She deserved praise, but a part of her heart would always regret the strength she had to do so.

☙❧

Jane's news of lost love was the talk of the neighborhood for quite some time, yet only one thing can eclipse the news of a death, and that is the rumor of a ball.

Mr. Bingley, who had gained quite a lot of popularity amongst Hampshire and had become quite a favorite, had announced that he would be giving a ball in a little over a month's time. He thought this was a sufficient enough time for everyone who might have been doing something else to change their plans and attend.

If Mr. Bingley had not already been liked in the neighborhood, now he was. The offering of giving a ball was news that warmed the hearts of many of the people and was the talk on every woman's tongue for days. Especially our mother and that of Aunt Phillips.

While I was excited at the prospect, I didn't really have much to look forward to, in regard to seeing anyone, for Mr. Darcy was going to be there. And yet, there were many other enjoyments that could be found, for dancing was always one of my favorite activities. Also now that Jane was at liberty, there was the chance that she would be able to enjoy herself at a ball as we used to: light and free.

And I would be in a whole roomful of people, making Mr. Darcy's appearance of little matter. If anything, I might be able to pass the whole night without ever speaking with him once. Such was my hope, for I could not deny his hold on me. He made me hate him. Yet he also made me admire him. He made me wish that I could hit him. Then he also made me powerless to his kissing me.

Could it have been in life's plan all along to make the lines between love and hate so very thin?

Yet there was always one flaw in every plan we made through the days, and it was Mr. Collins. Somehow, when he heard the mention of the ball, and was gratified when the invitation had been extended to him, he wrote to Lady Catherine De Bourgh to extend his visit with us.

His pride at having been invited to a ball by such a noted gentleman as Mr. Bingley had puffed him up and his whole air and manner of walking showed it. Kitty, on the other hand, was not inwardly satisfied with this, for it not only elongated his stay, but also meant that she couldn't enjoy herself amongst the officers whom she had come to befriend with Lydia.

Therefore, when she found an argument that she thought would suffice, she began her attack.

"But," Kitty said to Mr. Collins, regarding his invitation, "should you accept, sir? It is a dance after all, would your bishop approve of it? Also, would Lady Catherine enjoy your elongated stay, for you'll be here for another month complete, and I don't want Lady Catherine to be upset with you in any way."

"Your thoughtfulness does you credit, cousin," he said, impressed with her, "yet I am certain, since Mr. Bingley is such a refined gentleman, that there can be no objection of my taking part in it. And I have just heard from Lady Catherine today that she is perfectly satisfied with me staying another month."

I wondered why Lady Catherine De Bourgh did not object to his lengthy visit. It made me wonder if she truly liked him fully as her clergyman, or if she simply liked moving people around like they were chess pieces on a chess board.

"And," Mr. Collins continued, "I am so very fond of dancing

myself, and even her ladyship has complimented me often on my lightness of foot. Yes, I enjoy dancing so much that I shall take this opportunity of soliciting your hand, right now, Miss Kitty. Please, may I engage you for the first two dances? Afterwards, I shall like to dance with all my fair cousins."

Kitty looked shocked, and Mr. Collins took it as feminine delicacy, yet I knew that it was a look of horror. Over Mr. Collins's shoulder, our mother encouraged Kitty to say yes, and Kitty acquiesced.

Poor Kitty! The very argument she presented to keep Mr. Collins away from her only drew him to her more.

⚜

One day, Jane, Lydia, Kitty, Charlotte, Cassandra Austen with her sister Jane and I, were walking to the marketplace in Hampshire, and Mr. Collins was escorting us. He kept mostly to Kitty at first, yet Charlotte and Cassandra did their best to engage him in conversation and eventually he was distracted. Jane Austen was highly diverted at the situation and Jane and I were left to talk of trivialities alone.

Eventually we reached Meryton and we were in the process of looking at some bonnets in a shop window when Lydia noticed some officers walking down the street.

"Oh, Kitty! Look! It's Denny and Captain Carter."

We both looked up and saw the two soldiers, yet there was a third person there who was exquisitely handsome—so much so that it was disarming.

"Who is that with them though?" Jane Austen asked.

"I haven't the slightest idea."

"He is handsome though," Charlotte Lucas said.

"He would be if he were in regimentals. I think a man nothing without wearing regimentals."

I rolled my eyes at Lydia's comment. The soldiers, dressed in their uniforms, did render them handsome, yes, but I did wish that she thought of more than just soldiers all the time.

Lydia and Kitty waved to them, and the soldiers waved back, then they began to walk toward us.

When the three men accosted us, they bowed, and we curtsied to them.

"Good day, ladies," Denny said.

"And good day," Carter said as well.

"Hello, Denny and Carter," Cassandra said. "We were told that you were still in town."

"There was nothing that was amusing enough to hold us there," Captain Carter replied.

"Though might we be so fortunate as to introduce you to our friend?" Denny asked, gesturing to the gentleman who was next to him, "Ladies, this is our good friend, Mr. Wickham."

"Ladies," Mr. Wickham said, tipping his hat to us. "It is a pleasure to make your acquaintance."

We all bowed to him as Mr. Denny told him all our names.

"And it is our turn to introduce you," Jane said, for she was the oldest of us Bennets and it was her due. "This is our cousin, Mr. Collins."

Mr. Collins bowed as well, yet I could tell that he was dismayed at no longer being the only man in our group. Up until then, he had the good fortune to be the center of attention and now the entrance of three more men, and two of them being in regimentals, would force him into the background.

I could not help but look at Mr. Wickham in admiration, for much of nature was greatly in his favor. He had all the best part of beauty, a fine countenance, a good figure, and very pleasing address.

"Welcome to Hampshire, Mr. Wickham," I said.

"Thank you, Miss Elizabeth. I look forward to my stay here."

"And how long do you intend to stay?"

"All winter, I am happy to say. I have taken up a position in Colonel Forster's regiment, and therefore have gone into the army. Which means, that though I am dressed as the gentleman at present, I shall very soon be in regimentals myself."

"And render them much distinction, I daresay," Captain Carter said, "be more becoming in red than the rest of us, huh Wickham?"

"Denny, you puff me up, yet in truth I shall be next to not important, and yet I shall enjoy the employment, for I cannot bear to be idle."

"Well then," Cassandra said, "I hope you shall enjoy your stay in Hampshire."

"I believe that I shall. Thank you, Miss Austen, for what little I have seen so far, I am more than pleased to be posted here. For I am in the very best of society and have been met with manner, ease of attitude, and lovely ladies."

He looked at us with ease but also with meaning, and every woman felt his influence most acutely.

We were torn from the power of his gaze when Kitty cried out.

"Jane and Lizzy! Look, it's Mr. Darcy and Mr. Bingley."

We all turned, and Mr. Darcy and Mr. Bingley were riding toward us on horseback.

When they approached us, Kitty turned to Mr. Collins and decided to be kind.

"Mr. Collins, that there is Mr. Bingley, who has invited you to his ball at Aginfield, and along with him is his good friend, Mr. Darcy of Pemberly in Kent."

"I am delighted to meet them," Mr. Collins said proudly.

The men reached us, and Mr. Bingley got down from his horse and bowed to us.

"Ladies, it is fortunate, for we were riding towards Longbourn to inquire after you all and visit."

"Are you happy that you don't have to go so far?" I smiled.

"Very, for I have missed the company of you all."

"My sister is looking quite well, and she is fully recovered."

"Yes, she is," Mr. Bingley said, taken aback that I had turned the conversation toward Jane so suddenly, especially since she was right there. "Miss Bennet, I believe you look remarkably well, but then you always do."

"Thank you for both compliments, Mr. Bingley," Jane said, "for in a manner of speaking you have just given me two of them. One in my ability to have a speedy recovery and the other in my appearance."

I was quite proud of Jane just then! For she had said something witty, which was usually never her way. Mr. Bingley noted the difference and began to feel more ease toward her. They then began to talk together, and I tore my attention away from them and focused it on Mr. Darcy.

And that was the surprise. Mr. Darcy was looking at Mr. Wickham with rage and animosity. I looked toward Mr. Wickham, who looked red in the face when he beheld Mr. Darcy. If I was not mistaken, both men knew each other and there was a history to their story that was not pleasant. Then Mr. Wickham turned toward me and began to speak, but he was interrupted by Mr. Darcy.

"Miss Elizabeth," Mr. Darcy said, dismounting from his horse, "I must ask you for a favor. I am shopping for my sister and I would like to buy her some ribbon, yet I don't know what would please her. Would you mind saving me from my ignorance and showing me what are the best ribbons for a woman to wish in her hair?"

I could not deny such a request, and I must admit to being curious about what he would want of me. I also wanted to know the history behind the look that he gave Mr. Wickham, and for my part, I believed that I was most likely to get an answer from Mr. Darcy, despite our tempestuous past.

"Sir, I would be delighted to help you."

I took his arm and walked onward with him while he led his horse beside us.

"Well," I began, "Good afternoon, Mr. Darcy."

"Good afternoon, Miss Bennet. I trust you are well?"

"I am. And you?"

"I am well also, thank you."

"Tell me the truth, Mr. Darcy. Does your sister truly need ribbon?"

"Of course not. She has tons of ribbons."

"Then what is the reason for why you have taken me away from the presence of the new arrival, Mr. Wickham?"

"Expressly for that reason. There is nothing good about that new arrival."

28

THE TRUTH

"Then," I began, "what is the truth about him?"

"I'm afraid that I cannot tell you," Mr. Darcy said, tying up his horse and walking into the shop with me to keep up the pretense that we were looking for ribbon, "Yet you must trust me that Mr. George Wickham is the worst of men."

"Anyone can be claimed to be so by someone who doesn't like them," I argued. "I am not liked by some people. Therefore, you must forgive me for hesitating to trust you. You must give me names, facts of the circumstances, and proof of his villainy, or I will have no choice but to call you the villain of this group."

"Me the villain?"

"Aye, for you have given me nothing but a foul feeling and have not told me the reason behind why you slander someone that I had just met."

"You are quick to defend someone that you just met? Over someone that you already know?"

"I don't know you, Mr. Darcy, for you will not let me. And you hurt me often."

"I know and I'm sorry for it."

"A part of me will never forgive you."

"A part of you never should."

Mr. Darcy was silent at that and I took the time to look at some ribbon. I handed it to him and said that it was a lovely piece.

"Yes, it is," he said. "Very well. Miss Elizabeth, I will tell you everything, yet we are in too public of a place for such confessions. Where can I meet you privately?"

"That is inappropriate."

"What is necessary is never inappropriate."

"Yet we are not safe from each other in private. Therefore, I will only agree to meet you in a public place that is private enough. I walk along the Green Path that borders Mr. Long's estate. If you do not agree to that place, then I shall never meet with you."

"Very well then, agreed. But what time?"

❦

It was eleven o'clock in the morning of the next day and I was standing on the Green Path, waiting for Mr. Darcy. I didn't have to wait long, for he appeared on his horse a couple minutes after I had come. He dismounted and approached me. When introductions were finished, we began walking alongside each other down the path.

"Mr. Darcy," I began, "you had something to tell me."

"I know, I'm just losing my nerve."

"You are safe with me, you know this. And if you like, I shall swear to not ever tell anyone this—except for Jane, of course. You have to accept that I tell her everything, as she does with me."

"Can you keep it between yourselves?"

"Without a doubt. What you say will not go past either of us."

"Very well then, here it is. Mr. Wickham and I have known each other for our entire lives. His father was my father's steward and was the very best of men. Since we were always so close, George Wickham and I grew up together, played with each other as children, and my father was very fond of him. As you could see for yourself, Mr. Wickham is a man who was blessed with such happy manners that it endears him to anyone, though whether he is capable of keeping friends is less certain. My father paid his way through university at Cambridge, yet by that point, Mr. Wickham's habits were as dissolute as his manners were engaging. Miss Elizabeth, he gambled often, partook in the worst parts of society, and he would bring women back to our room—and by that, I mean women whose reputations were at risk by him seducing them, yet he did not care."

I felt disturbed at such an image.

"However, my father's attachment to him was so steadfast that he left him the living of Acton on our estate and planned for his future to be a clergyman for the church. When my own excellent father died, Mr. Wickham pronounced that he had no intention of taking holy orders and being ordained, and therefore granted, and was given the sum of 3,000 pounds instead of the living. He said that he intended to study the law, yet I wished rather than believed him to be sincere. How he lived, I know not, yet I do know that he gambled most of the money away. After that, I thought all connections between us had ceased, but I was forced to see him again, and this time it was under the most painful of circumstances.

My sister, Georgiana, who was nineteen years old at the time, was staying at Ramsgate under the gaze of a chaperone and companion named Mrs. Younge, in whose character we were unhappily deceived. There Mr. Wickham went by design."

"Yet how did he know that your sister was in Ramsgate?" I asked, thoroughly engaged in his narrative.

"I can only assume that Mrs. Younge had let him know of it somehow, yet he pretended to meet Georgiana by mere chance. He began to visit her every day, and Mr. Wickham did everything in his power to seduce her, and eventually she was led to believe herself in love. So much so, Miss Bennet, that she agreed to an elopement.

Yet, fortune does truly live amongst us, for I visited her two days before their intended elopement and I came upon them as they were walking about. Not wishing to cause me any pain, my sister then told me the whole plan at once. You can imagine how I acted. However, I coerced Mr. Wickham to see me alone and told him that if he married my sister, he would not get any of her dowry, which was his intention all along. She had a dowry of 50,000 pounds."

"Dear god!" I gasped, "That is just monstrous!"

"Yes. Needless to say, he quitted the house immediately and I never saw him again, until this day. Georgiana was heartbroken, and her spirits have never been the same since."

"Mr. Darcy, I am so sorry."

"And if you still doubt me, then if Mr. Wickham ever chooses to bring up our history, which I'm sure that he will, you can always present him with the truth, from which he will not be able to deny. He always starts out with lies, yet he doesn't know how to continue them ever. They always catch up to him eventually."

"Thank you for telling me. I know what pains it must be putting you through right now to confess such a thing to me."

"It does cause me pain, indeed, yet this is something you must know. He is a man not to be trusted, and I would then be a villain if I didn't warn you."

"Your warning will be heeded."

❦

We walked on a little further in silence and I wondered at all that had been told to me.

"Miss Elizabeth?" he said.

"Yes."

"You must forgive me for everything else."

"Everything else?"

"For when I said that you were tolerable. I was angry about many things at the time, and I took it out on you."

"What were you angry at?"

"Myself mostly. And some recent decisions that I have made. Or rather one decision in particular."

"And what decision is this?"

"It is...not important."

"You must not be afraid to open up to me. For you always try and you never succeed. And then you lose in the end anyway, yet no harm comes to it."

"I know that you don't love Mr. Bingley," he said suddenly. I was too startled to realize that he had changed the subject.

"How did you know?"

"For when I kissed you, you did not exclaim about how I had no right to, seeing as how you loved my friend. And Mr. Bingley does not deserve a woman that doesn't love him."

"And I didn't mean to give him the impression that I encouraged his suit, nor did I believe that he was serious in his pursuit of me. He is so charming to all women, and I never thought his feelings toward me went further than that."

"They don't," Mr. Darcy sighed happily. "You are right, he is very charming, yet doesn't feel anything for anyone at present. He likes you terribly, is very fond of you, yet it is not love."

"I could tell straight away."

"You are a smart one, Miss Elizabeth." His eyes softened even more.

"Thank you, and when you set your heart to it, you can be a very good talker."

"Am I?"

"Yes, very. Now I must be off, or my mother will have a fit."

"But now that you know the truth, promise that you won't reveal it to anyone past your sister?"

"Yes, Mr. Darcy. I now know the truth, and it shall rest just between she and I."

"As for my abominable treatment toward you..."

"I still cannot forgive you."

"I know, and I admire you for it."

29

A VILLAIN DISCOVERED

After I had told Jane about everything Mr. Darcy disclosed to me, she was distressed, and she could not make out the contradiction of Mr. Wickham's outward appearance of fairness to his inward attitude of sordidness.

"Poor Mr. Darcy," she said, "and poor Mr. Wickham, there is such an expression of goodness in his character."

"Yes," I said and laughed. "In between Mr. Darcy, one has all the goodness and the other all the appearance of it."

"But I cannot think Mr. Darcy would invent such a history, so it all must be true. Yet maybe there is some terrible mistake, maybe both have been slandered by other interested parties who wanted to see both men at odds with each other."

"Oh, Jane that will not do. You cannot absolve them both, for in this tale, there is only room for one good sort of man, and for my part, I am inclined to think it all Mr. Darcy's. Yet there is one thing I need your opinion on. I promised Mr. Darcy so faithfully that I would not tell another soul, but are we right to do so? We don't have to disclose all the details and can keep out the ones that have to do with Mr. Darcy, but we can still expose Mr. Wickham for being a man not worthy to be trusted. I don't know what to do."

"Perhaps we should not, though. Perhaps Mr. Wickham repents his past actions, and is eager to re-establish his character, which is why he has decided to come here. We must not ruin his chances."

"You are correct, for I did promise Mr. Darcy so faithfully that I would say nothing."

"Then we both have to honor that."

"True, true."

One night we went to a dinner party that our Aunt Phillips had put on for the introduction of the soldiers in Hampshire. Naturally Mr. Bingley and his party did not attend—and I'm quite sure Mr. Darcy did not wish to be near Wickham.

Yet naturally, my whole family attended, so did the Lucases, the Austens, the Longs, the Pratts and quite a few of the militia. The head of the militia attended with his very young wife, Colonel Forster and Mrs. Forster. And yet, despite the age difference, they both seemed quite content with each other therefore no one could argue that they weren't particularly suited for one another.

Among the soldiers was Mr. Wickham, who our youngest sisters took to immediately. Kitty could attend to him as well as the other soldiers because Mr. Collins was occupied at the moment by sitting down and playing a game of Whist with a few others. This made her free of him for a few moments of the evening. I realized that I had to make it a point to suggest to my Aunt to hold him for another game just so that Kitty could be free a little longer, when I was surprised to see Mr. Wickham sit down right beside me and began speaking.

"I must confess," he began, "that I never thought that I would be able to make my way through the sea of elegant females to you, Miss Elizabeth, for I have wished to further our acquaintance."

"Well," I said with a laugh, willing to play along and see if he was hoping to deceive me in any way, "congratulations, for I see that you have not sunk, and stay perfectly afloat."

"And have managed to swim all the way to this seat," Mr. Wickham said, happy with my easy reception of him. "This gives me leave to ask you any manner of question I please that is a safe subject of a drawing room."

"What do you wish to know?"

"Well, for starters, I have noticed that I am not the only new addition to this neighborhood. I was told that Mr. Bingley is new to Hampshire."

"He is, he originally comes from the North."

"And how far is his estate Aginfield from Steventon?"

"About three miles."

"Oh, therefore you live close enough to him?"

"Close enough to say that we don't live too far."

He chuckled charmingly.

"And how long has Mr. Darcy been staying at Aginfield?"

"About a month. He is a man of a very large property in Kent."

"Yes, his estate there is a noble one. A clear 10,000 pounds per annum. You could not have met with a person more capable of giving you certain information on that head than me...for I have been connected with his family in a particular manner from my infancy. You may well be surprised, Miss Bennet, at such an assertion, after seeing, as you probably might, the very cold manner of our meeting yesterday. Are you much acquainted with Mr. Darcy?"

I decided to play along just to see what form of falsehood he was preparing to give me, for it was very apparent that he was preparing to tell me a lie.

"As much as I ever wish to be," I replied. "I have spent seven days in the same house with him, and I know very little of him."

"I have no right to give my opinion," said Wickham, "as to his being agreeable or otherwise. I am not qualified to form one. I have known him too long and too well to be a fair judge. It is impossible for me to be impartial. The world is blinded by his fortune and consequence, or frightened by his high and imposing manners, and sees him only as he chooses to be seen."

Ah, so that was his game! Mr. Wickham was at first going to attack Mr. Darcy's character and then was probably going to build up from there. Well, I was curious to see just how far he was going to take this.

"Do not think I will allow myself to be driven away, no," Mr. Wickham said, "I am not so easily frightened."

And now he was playing the hero.

"We are not on friendly terms," he continued, "and it always gives me pain to meet him, but I have no reason for avoiding him but what I might proclaim to all the world; a sense of very great ill usage, and he has quite ruined my life."

At this point, I gave him encouragement, and he sensed it. Yet I could see that he was not used to a woman not hanging on his every word of self-pity, and maybe at one point, that might've been me, yet I had been warned already. Yet, still wishing to see him continue this fabrication, I leaned forward and pretended to be shocked and sorry for him.

"Oh no!" I acted, "What did he do to you?"

"Well, Miss Elizabeth, it is a long story, and it hurts me to remember it. His father, Miss Bennet, the late Mr. Darcy, was one of the best men that ever breathed, and the truest friend I ever had, and I can never be in company with this Mr. Darcy without being grieved to the soul by a thousand tender recollections. His behavior to myself has been scandalous. Yet do not mistake my sadness for a somber eternity, for I very much am happy, for I now am in a very good neighborhood of excellent community. Society, I own, is necessary to me. I have been a disappointed man, and my spirits will not bear solitude. I must have employment and society. A military life is not what I was intended for, but circumstances have now made it eligible. The church ought to have been my profession. I was brought up for the church, and I should at this time have been in possession of a most valuable living, had it pleased the gentleman we were speaking of just now."

"Indeed!"

"Yes...the late Mr. Darcy bequeathed me the position as a clergyman. He was my godfather, and excessively attached to me. He meant to provide for me amply, but when he died, and the living was offered, it was given elsewhere."

"Good heavens!" I cried, faking surprise and anguish. Honestly! I felt as if I was an actress on a stage at that point. "But how could that be? How could his will be disregarded? Why did not you seek legal redress?"

"There was just such an informality in the terms of the bequest as to give me no hope from the law. A man of honor could not have doubted the intention, but Mr. Darcy chose to ignore or defy it—or to treat it as if I was granted the living on condition only. Certain it is, that the living became vacant two years ago, exactly as I was of an age to hold it, and that it was given to another man. But the fact is, that we are very different sort of men, and that he hates me. And it pains me still, when I think of how close we were as children, and now to experience what Mr. Darcy has done to me. Yet as I said, I still hold the memory of his father as dear to me."

Unbelievable! I knew that when he began his story, he was going to lie in the most extreme ways, yet I had no idea it was going to begin to have no sense to it. Did he honestly expect me so unintelligent that I would not see all the holes in his tale? If the will was properly written and said that he was to inherit the living, then he could never have lost it—unless it was by his choosing. And he had chosen.

"This is quite shocking!" I said. "He deserves to be publicly disgraced."

"Some time or other he will be, but it shall not be by me. Till I can forget his father, I can never defy or expose him."

And that was where I had to draw the lie to a close.

"Except," I began, "that you did just expose him, which makes your last sentence a contradiction to your actions."

"Oh..." Mr. Wickham said, confused at my willingness to call him out on his own hypocrisy. "Well, I suppose I did."

"And your story would have been one to have invoked a great deal of pity out of me, if it were true."

Mr. Wickham then looked at me, shocked.

"Yet, from what I hear, preaching sermons was not as palatable to your tastes as you seem to think so now. The living was left to you, I heard, yet you declined the living and in recompense, you requested and was granted the sum of the living, which was 3,000 pounds and the late Mr. Darcy was still alive. And now that you are employed in the militia, it could only mean that you have spent all the money on gambling, frivolous activities, and pleasant company —and by that, I mean fancy ladies."

Mr. Wickham's expression went from warm to shock and embarrassment at being discovered. He no longer had any control over the situation or lies to puff himself up, and therefore there was nothing left but his pretty face and empty sentiments.

"You see, Mr. Wickham?" I smiled, "I have stories of my own."

"Yes...well, your sister needs my help, so if you will excuse me."

"Yes go, go. For I see that you are a man who is often needed in many places, as long as those places can believe your stories."

As he stood up, I felt compelled to say one last thing.

"And Mr. Wickham?"

He turned to me.

"Yes, Miss Elizabeth?"

"Remember to be good. And stay away from the ladies in this neighborhood, for I will always be watching."

He nodded to me coldly and walked away.

***

The whole evening passed in a most amusing manner. Every now and again, I stared very fixedly at Mr. Wickham, just to scare him, and I could see that it was quite effective. On his side, must've been an aggravated feeling, for his lies could not even be spread. For if they were, then I would be there to correct him. As such, Mr. Darcy had made himself not very well-liked in Hampshire, yet Mr. Wickham could not feed on that.

And on my side, I contented myself with knowing that I made him very aware that he was a villain discovered for what he was.

❦ 30 ❦

ALL THAT COULD BE EXPECTED

The evening of the ball soon arrived, and our carriage was quite cramped, for there were eight of us: my parents, us sisters and Mr. Collins.

When we arrived in the ballroom at Aginfield, it was already filled up with everyone who had been invited, which were many. Yet despite all who were there, including the militia, I was happy in knowing that Mr. Wickham had made himself scarce and did not attend. Then again, he was too much of a coward to do so.

When we entered, Mr. Bingley took me and my sister's arm and walked with us around the room. He requested the first dance for me, then the next with Jane, and wondered if Mary would be willing to dance as well, for he wished to dance with all of us Bennet girls that night.

My first dance with Mr. Bingley was fun and invigorating. We talked of nothing and everything all at the same time, which was wonderful, for I did not wish to undertake a dance with any serious intention in mind in regard to affection. By the end of our set it became even clearer to me that Mr. Bingley was attracted to me, just as he was attracted to Jane, yet it was one of enjoyment and loose attachment than that of anything serious or substantial.

I liked him, yet I did not love him at all.

He liked me, yet did not love me in any way, shape or form. I would not have preferred it in any other way.

Kitty however, had no choice but to dance the first dance with Mr. Collins, who danced so terribly that it embarrassed her greatly. Not wishing for her to undergo such a sadness once more, I asked Mr. Collins if Kitty could have a break while I danced with him in her stead. Kitty mouthed her thanks to me behind Mr. Collins's back and Mr. Collins felt gratified beyond all words and kept bobbing his head up and down, nodding his enjoyment of such a plan. Therefore, for the next set, I went onto the dance floor with him and joined the rest of the dancers. Mr. Collins started out well enough, but one time stepped on my foot, then bumped into another man, then a woman, and I had to whisper the correct movements to him.

He apologized over and over, yet it didn't stop the sadness of the situation. As I danced, I saw Mr. Darcy standing amongst the crowd and watching me most acutely. He probably was enjoying the spectacle of Mr. Collins and me and finding it quite amusing.

Yet as Mr. Collins danced with me, he continued to talk to me about Kitty.

"Your sister is more delicate than I realized," he began.

"Is she?" I replied.

"Yes. For when I told her that it was my express desire to remain close to her the entire evening, she practically tripped on the hem of her dress."

I had to hold in my laughter.

"My goodness, she had been so surprised. I thought my attentions toward her had been too marked to be mistaken, yet she had been unaware of my suit the whole time, which makes her more modest than I had expected. Yet modesty is the perfect virtue for one of my position—for as you know, me being the clergyman of the right Honorable Lady Catherine De Bourgh—who's kindness, yet desire for me to find a woman who is modest, economical and not foolish in any way..."

He went on and on in this way for quite some time until he got to the end of his remarks on Lady Catherine De Bourgh. Then he got back on subject.

"And your sister is such a woman."

"Such a woman for what, sir?"

"To marry," he said to me obviously, "Which is what we were speaking of."

"Oh," I said, surprised. "I, in truth, had not known that your will leant its way toward that so soon."

"I don't have all the time in the world, and yet, I feel as if the time I have reflected on it and have given Kitty was time enough. Yes, I'm sure it is. Ah...she will be most pleased, and, I flatter myself, that she will take great pleasure in when I finally offer myself."

On that note, the dance ended, and I knew that Kitty would eventually be made a very unhappy woman.

While I was talking to Charlotte Lucas, I saw Mr. Collins approach Kitty, but this time Jane Austen appeared and began to engage Mr. Collins in conversation long enough for Kitty to run and hide behind some curtains.

At ease, I turned to Charlotte Lucas, but our attention was seized by Mr. Darcy, who appeared at our side and bowed.

"Miss Elizabeth," he began, "I was wondering if you would dance this next set with me?"

"Oh! I thank you, yes."

Mr. Darcy bowed and walked off toward the dance floor, ready to expect me.

"Lizzy, tell me in earnest," Charlotte said. "Is Mr. Darcy in love with you?"

"I have no idea," I confessed, "One moment he seems to care for me, then the next he forgets my very existence. All he leaves me with is a certainty of being confused. Also, I both like and hate him equally. I have told him so often enough to say that I have kept my dignity, despite sometimes forgetting my self-control."

I left Charlotte and walked toward the dance floor where the music was struck, and Mr. Darcy and I began to dance together. As we did so, at first, he said nothing, and I did not know what for. Surely, he should know to abandon his silent nature in such moments.

"Mr. Darcy, does dancing make you silent?" I asked.

"No, it is not dancing, but something else."

"Pray tell, what is the truth?"

"I am simply wondering if I might ask you something."

"You want to know if I told my sister?"

"Yes, I do."

"Aye, I did. And I promise you, that you have nothing to fear. Your secret shall die within us."

"Very good, forgive me for doubting you."

"I understand your suspicion. For it is a hard thing that you have revealed. Yet what I wonder is why did you tell it to me in the first place?"

"I should have thought it were obvious."

"No, you are never obvious."

"I shall take that as a compliment. Well, you were in danger."

"Was I?"

"Wickham is nefarious, yet he is also persuasive. I did not want him to work his schemes on you, for he does so often, and men like him sicken me to the core. There are too many people like him in this world, for they can turn the minds of rational people with their words and warp reality. Their charm makes them powerful. As well as dangerous."

"Then you care for my welfare."

"I do."

"Then I have no choice but to think you a good man now."

Mr. Darcy looked at me sharply.

"Did you not want to think of me as a good man before?"

"I admit that it was easier."

"Why?"

"I don't know."

"Surely you must know."

"Not liking you is easier than liking you."

"I should be upset with you."

"Are you?"

"I don't know."

"Surely you must know."

"I do know. But I am afraid to say."

"I am strong enough for your anger now."

"Yes, but not for my adoration."

"Are you saying that you adore me?" I whispered.

"I should not say."

"No, you should not. And I should not ask. Yet I did."

"Yes, you did."

"And now I will help you."

"How so?"

"I will change the subject."

"Thank you."

"How is your sister, Miss Darcy? Is she recovering? Or is she still in pain over her heartache?"

Mr. Darcy looked sad. "I believe that she truly did love Wickham."

"It's not her fault. As you say, his charms make him persuasive.

And she is in her early twenties? That makes her at the perfect place to fall in love."

"I thought the teens were so?"

"Our lifestyle gets it wrong all too often. A person's teens are the time to become obsessed over the opposite sex. Yet it's not the time to understand true love. When one reaches their twenties, that's when one begins to understand, and our nerves become less tense, we begin to understand ourselves. Then as our age progresses and we reach our mid to late twenties, we begin to learn what it means to love for the right reasons as opposed to the wrong ones. And Miss Darcy is in the right time to do so, yet you need not worry, for she shall recover. That's the one good thing about pain. Eventually it does leave us."

All throughout my speech I didn't notice the somber but attentive mood that had overcome Mr. Darcy.

"Mr. Darcy? Is everything all right?"

"When the next dance is to take place, I should like you to dance with me again."

"Very well."

During the next dance, Mr. Darcy and I danced once more, and I was happy to see Jane and Mr. Bingley dancing again. For though Jane was still shaken by Mr. Brocklehurst's deception, Mr. Bingley would be a good distraction to help her overcome her heartache— for he could be very funny and charming, which was enough to divert anyone back into good spirits.

Mr. Darcy and I didn't speak much when we danced the second set. Yet his silence was heavy and strong. I didn't know what to make of him by the end, for nothing had truly been resolved between us, and no understanding had been reached.

Our fate seemed to be that we would feel a significant curiosity about each other, but nothing more. I still, strangely enough, could not be disgusted by his kissing me, and at that point I had quite forgiven him. My first kiss should have gone to the man who would eventually become my husband, yet more and more I was resolving myself to the fact that I might never marry. Therefore, maybe that is why I didn't hate Darcy. He didn't steal any precious moments from me, but gave me one, however temporary that it might be. I should have felt pain and weak for not caring that decorum and propriety had been breached all too often. Yet, I was not perfect.

The dance ended and all around the room there were many sights. My sister Mary was playing on the piano-forte and singing, but her voice was poor and she was embarrassing herself. Lydia was exposing herself to ridicule by flirting terribly with some officers, Kitty was still running from Mr. Collins, Jane and Mr. Bingley were talking, my father looked bored, and my mother very loudly was talking about how she expected two of her daughters to be very soon married, and Jane would quickly find another to replace the *late Mr. Brocklehurst.*

Wishing to get away from them all, I ducked out of the ballroom and into the darkness of the hallway. I leaned against the wall, and breathed out and in evenly, trying to steady myself. I closed my eyes for a while, and then heard footsteps. I opened them slowly, thinking it was Mr. Bingley.

"Oh, I only need a moment to—"

I was utterly surprised when I found that it was Mr. Darcy!

"I..." I began, "I can explain."

"I didn't come here for that," was his only reply. Suddenly he grabbed my hand and led me down the hallway and into another room, closing the door behind us. It all happened so fast that I didn't even have time to object.

After he realized that the door was closed, he turned to me slowly. I barely saw him through the darkness, yet I saw him well enough.

"Mr. Darcy please...we mustn't do this."

"I know, but...so help me, Miss Elizabeth."

He rushed to me and kissed me once more. At first, I did my

best to push him off, yet very quickly, I found myself wrapping my hands around his neck and leaning into him desperately. I did not know why I could not resist him by any means, and why I welcomed his attentions, yet for some reason, all rationality had abandoned me, and I could not define nor excuse my actions. Then again, Mr. Darcy, due to possessing too much will or too little will, had been the one to start the beginning, then the middle and then the end.

He lifted me up, laid me down on a couch and sat beside me, kissing me again. His hands travelled along the top of my dress, slid his fingers beneath my modest neckline and started pulling it down before I could think on our actions.

"Mr. Darcy, please..."

"I cannot..."

"You will ruin me."

Somehow that one admission broke the trance that fell over him and his eyes darted open. He looked up and gazed seriously into my eyes.

"I am horrible," he said stoically. He removed his form from beside me and then stood up. He took my hand, helped me up as well and then made sure that I looked presentable.

"I shall walk in first, and then wait for ten minutes, then appear yourself."

"Yes," I sighed, not understanding how to act.

"I will not ask for your forgiveness, because what I have done was unforgiveable."

"Yes," I replied softly, my voice trembling.

There was a silence between us for a while before he spoke again.

"I will make sure that we shall never be near each other, I shall do everything in my power to keep you free of me and I shall separate myself from this, to keep you away from me and out of danger. I will not be the ruin of you. I promise to hurt you no more.

You are the best woman that I know. Therefore, you deserve better than a man such as I."

He left the room and I was alone.

Eventually, the ball ended and in the early hours of the morning, our party left Aginfield. Mr. Bingley saw us off and our mother declared the night a success and it was all that could be expected—for she did not know that everything did not go at all how she expected.

31

DISAPPOINTED HOPES

The next morning, we all were tired when we wakened. When we went down to breakfast however, Mr. Collins entered and soon accosted our mother.

"Mrs. Bennet," he began, "I wondered if I might request a private audience with Miss Kitty in the course of the morning."

We all sat there frozen, but Kitty was the most distressed. Our mother eagerly said yes and ordered everyone out of the room except for Kitty. Kitty at first stood up and objected, stating that there should be no need for everyone to leave them alone, but our mother didn't heed her request and ordered her to remain.

We all left them and sat either on the steps, in the neighboring room or kitchen. I worried for Kitty as did Jane, Mary only looked jealous, our mother looked excited and anxious, and Lydia laughed, happy that it wasn't her that was forced into the situation. I then waited on the porch of our home, yet not two minutes after we all had left the room, Kitty came bursting from the room, ran down the front steps and began running through our field.

"Kitty!" I cried, running after her, "Kitty!"

"I won't do it!" She shrieked and kept running. "I'd rather run away first."

"Kitty!" Our mother cried, running after us.

"Kitty!" Jane shouted, running at first, and then realizing that she was already getting out of breath and stopped. I looked behind me and Mr. Collins had come to the porch and stood next to Lydia and Mary, amazed that Kitty had run from him. I kept chasing Kitty, however she proved to be a greater runner than I, which I had never known, for I loved to run.

Eventually, enjoying the whole situation and out of breath, I stopped, collapsed on the ground, and began to laugh uncontrollably. My mother eventually caught up with us and was out of breath as well.

"Well!" She gasped, "Why did you not keep running after her?"

"Good God, Mother, can't you see? I can't run because I'm laughing!"

My mother groaned and then stood there, trying to catch her breath.

"I have not the nerves for this! Or the corset!"

Lydia eventually walked up to us, eating an apple.

"I do believe that I know where she has gone," she said.

"Then why did you not tell us before?" Our mother cried.

"Because I found this all quite amusing. And would you believe that Mr. Collins still regards her 'no' as a yes. He just thinks that she ran off because of her *feminine delicacy*."

"Oh, good God," I moaned, "why must it always be something. All right Lydia... tell us where she went."

◈

After Lydia told us everything, we went to the house to get the carriage, yet our mother felt that she needed a rest. The rest of them were feeling perfectly up for the task, therefore we offered to ride to where she was, send our driver and carriage back to Longbourn and have them pick up our parents and take them to the spot where Kitty was.

This was all agreed upon and very soon, the four remaining Bennet girls were heading off toward the Winding Path in our carriage. Yet before I had done so, I turned to Mr. Collins...

"Just in case Kitty's refusal does in fact turn out to be a refusal...Mary is very nice. Think on that."

I got into the carriage and we were off.

After a little bit of a drive, we picked up the Austen sisters, because we knew that if our mother would try to pressure Kitty, she would be less inclined to do it if some of our neighbors were watching, especially if those neighbors were daughters of our church clergyman.

After a quarter of an hour, we arrived at the tree that Lydia told us Kitty liked to climb and sure enough, Kitty was sitting at the top of it. We exited the carriage and called up to her.

"I will not come down!" Kitty cried, "And I will not marry him! You cannot make me!"

"We're not making you do anything, Kitty," Jane said. "We just came to give you some water because you must be thirsty."

"Really?" Kitty leaned forward. "I am thirsty."

We produced a jug of water from the carriage, allowed our driver to ride back to Longbourn to get our parents and climbed the tree to hand the jug to Kitty. She took it and drank it greedily.

"Kitty," Lydia began, "just to warn you, our parents will be coming soon."

"I know, and I don't know what to say to them when they do come. I know mother will be furious, but I trust father won't care."

"No, he won't," I said, "yet mama will care enough for the both of them."

We all kept her company and soon enough we heard a carriage rolling by.

Soon it appeared, it was ours and our parents climbed down from it. One looked furious and the other looked amused.

"Kitty!" Our mother cried, "I am shocked and appalled at you! I would have expected this sort of behavior from Lizzy, but not from you."

"Thanks, Mother!" I sneered.

"I can't help it, Lizzy. Honestly, you still have not even let Mr. Bingley stay around you long enough to bind him to a proposal."

"That's not Lizzy's fault!" Jane Austen said, standing up.

"And what are you and your sister doing here?"

"We had them come with us," I said.

"Aye," Jane added, "for we thought they could help us in our search."

"Well then," our mother groaned, then looked at the tree. "Kitty! You shall climb down that tree this instant, come back to Longbourn and agree to marry Mr. Collins, and then we shall all sit down to pudding."

"Pudding is not needed right now, my dear," our father said.

"Yet still, Kitty, you will stop disobliging your family. If you marry Mr. Collins now, you will have our house and save our family from being destitute if anything happens to your father," Mother said.

"I can't marry him! I won't and I'm sorry, but I never shall."

"If you don't then I shall never see you again, Miss Kitty!"

"Well," our father interrupted, "just so that I can make sure I am clear on all of this, Mr. Collins has proposed to you Kitty, you have said no, your mother wants you to say yes, but you won't and now she threatens you with isolation. Is this true?"

"It is!" Kitty cried from the branches.

"Well, then," Mr. Bennet said, "an unhappy alternative is before you. Your mother will never see you again if you do not marry Mr. Collins and I shall never see you again, if you do."

We all turned to him, amazed and happy at his stance in supporting Kitty.

"But, Mr. Bennet!" Our mother cried.

"My dear, Mrs. Bennet," Mr. Bennet said, "I and my foolishness, along with yours, has left our children virtually penniless. Yet here and now, I have decided that our children will not suffer for it in such a cruel way to be forced into an unhappy marriage, for that is a painful fate to push on anyone. A person cannot find happiness in an eternity if their partner is not worthy of them. And Mr. Collins, though his actions were noble, he is not worthy of Kitty, the way that he was never worthy of Lizzy, Jane, Mary, or Lydia. All our daughters deserve better, and it is time that we saw that. Let Kitty find her love. She deserves to have that chance. Let them all have it. Let that be our legacy."

We all stood there, amazed.

"Mr. Bennet," Cassandra Austen professed.

"Yes," he said, "let it be known once, that there was some good in Mr. Bennet."

He went to the carriage and our mother, who looked flabbergasted, had no choice but to join him. Soon, after watching them speak, they drove off.

By the time we all returned, our father had let Mr. Collins know that Kitty was sincere, and therefore, Mr. Collins retreated into his room, disappointed.

❧ 32 ❧

DESPERATE MEASURES

Mr. Collins's pride was affected in the worst way when Kitty had rejected him. He felt ill-used, not appreciated and as if he had offered her all that could be sought in happiness of marriage through his holy person and his position as being the clergyman to nobility. He could not believe her rejection of him!

While I had hoped that he would heed my advice of looking toward Mary, who had been more to his taste as well as liking him all along, this did not suit him. Because Kitty had rejected him, we all were tainted in his eyes and could not be forgiven.

I mentioned his skulking around the house in such a manner to Charlotte Lucas, who immediately offered to have him dine and stay at Lucas Lodge for a time so that we would be free of him. I thought her actions were that of a good and true friend, until her real design had shown itself.

It turned out that my dear friend, Charlotte, who was a creature of rationality and reason, could use those same talents and lean herself towards scheming and self-advancement.

When Mr. Collins had dined at her home, she had paid much

attention to him and took heed to his every word. This fed Mr. Collins's pride and made him feel of great importance—yet it fed his vanity as well. She made him feel special and worthy of being loved. And the more that she showed it, the more he fed off her pleasing attentions.

He kept returning to Lucas Lodge, and we all assumed that Charlotte simply was wishing to alleviate our woes. Yet on the fourth day of this, Mr. Collins left our house early, had went and proposed to her, to which he was met with an acceptance, and the man who had been wooing my sister a week ago, was now engaged to one of my closest friends.

Mr. Collins made the announcement to us all one morning and we all were met with surprise and shock. At first, I thought Mr. Collins had lost the little bit of sanity that he had left. Yet when my sisters and I went to visit the Lucases to confirm this, Charlotte Lucas had echoed Mr. Collins news.

Very soon, the Austen sisters also arrived, for news had spread of the engagement quite quickly. Cassandra was pretending to be happy, yet Jane Austen was livid.

"Charlotte?" she said when we were alone with her, "How could you?"

"Well," I said, "and I thought I was going to be the one to object in the most spirited way."

"No," Jane Austen said, "I have beaten you to it. Charlotte, Mr. Collins had just been pursuing Kitty up and down the countryside not even a week ago."

"Precisely," I agreed. "How can you expect him to have directed his feelings truthfully to you so quickly?"

"I don't expect him to have," Charlotte said, "and I'm not foolish enough to ever think so."

"Charlotte?" Lydia said, "I never really knew how your brain works, so can you please tell me now exactly how it functions?"

"Do you all think," Charlotte continued, "that Mr. Collins could not win anyone's affections because he was not fortunate with Kitty?"

"That is not what we mean," I said. "We simply mean that his feelings for you may be false and felt out of vanity."

"Because it is," Charlotte said. "I'm not a romantic, you all know. All I ask is for a comfortable home. And considering Mr. Collins's character and situation in life, I believe that I shall be content in my choice."

"You do not care that you will not marry for love?" Cassandra asked.

"As I say, I am not a romantic. And besides...you are all my closest and dearest friends. Yet I am twenty-nine years old, and this is a most fortunate chance for me. I—in truth, do want something to stabilize and support myself."

We all were silenced by her admission.

"Well then," Jane said, "if it be so, then we are happy for you both."

"Thank you."

❧

When we left, we began talking about it amongst ourselves.

"I had never known being unattached had such an effect on her," Kitty said.

"Nor I," I admitted, "and it makes me feel as if I had never known Charlotte as well as I thought I had."

"Aye, but we do know her," Jane Austen said. "I daresay that she has always been like that, yet we just didn't want to see it. You must all tell me now, am I foolish for letting my writing be of such importance to me?"

"No," we all said, "not at all."

"Thank you," Jane Austen said, "for it is, so much so that I don't even think of the prospect of having to marry out of obligation any longer. The idea would repulse me."

"It would repulse all of us at our ages," Cassandra said. "We've reached that stage where a perfect marriage would be enjoyable, yet it is not necessary to our happiness in full. We have found other ways, taken other paths. Charlotte however, is not on the path that we are on, yet we must support her."

"Support her," I echoed, yet it was hard for me to feel that way.

❦

The marriage between Mr. Collins and Charlotte Lucas took place quite swiftly, and I still couldn't warm up to the idea of it happening even after it did.

However, what was certain was that our mother was now in pure panic and agony of knowing that Charlotte Lucas would now be the future mistress of Longbourn and take her place in it once our father passed away and the estate fell into the hands of Mr. Collins.

Needing an outlet for her frustration, she hurled it at the one person who she felt was responsible—Kitty. She began to attack her verbally for it all the time, so much so, that Kitty was often running from a room in tears. My heart went out to Kitty, as did Jane's and we then begin to think of some desperate measures to find a way to rescue her from her situation.

❧ 33 ❧

THE GARDINERS TO THE RESCUE

It was Mary's idea. She had felt bad for being jealous of Kitty when Kitty had never done anything to seek Mr. Collins's attention. Mary also realized that by rejecting Mr. Collins, Kitty had spared her a lot of pain. Therefore, seeing Kitty being treated cruelly by our mother, Mary felt obliged to Kitty and therefore suggested to us that we should ask Aunt and Uncle Gardiner to let us stay in Cheapside with them for a while, in hopes that the distance would make our mother's love for Kitty forgive her for not marrying our cousin.

Our father sent the letter, and we received a reply a week later. Our uncle said yes, and they were willing to take on two of us again. I offered to go with Kitty. Our plans were put into motion very quickly, and soon Kitty and I traveled by carriage to London and arrived on Gracechurch Street.

Our aunt and uncle were glad to see me once more, and Kitty was happy to be there, for distance from Hampshire was exactly what she had needed.

As we stayed with them, I was surprised in seeing that Kitty had a very good sort of nature to her. Yet she had just been always linking herself to our youngest sister, Lydia, who was—though I loved her—a bad influence. Yet now that Kitty was removed from that, she seemed to adapt herself well to the quiet lifestyle of our aunt and uncle with ease, which meant that there was chance for improvement of her mind, as long as she had the right influences.

Our aunt and uncle noted this marked change and were happy in knowing that they were a part of it, and to make a note to themselves to invite Kitty to Gracechurch Street more often, in hopes that it would broaden her mind and spirit.

Kitty surprisingly was a very good companion for me in London as well, for when I took an interest in going with our uncle to his factory to look at textiles and fabrics, Kitty also attended, and she loved it. She inquired our uncle on many things and wanted to know how the trade worked. We spent our days there often, wishing to learn what the other workers did, and for one second, we indulged the idea of being allowed to work and find significance to our lives outside of the prospect of who we would marry. We knew that we could not do so in full, yet it was nice to dream about it. To have a choice, a hope of something that was ours and could not be taken—and yet, we all knew that it was a dream.

Yet while we felt as if the Gardiners had come to the rescue of not just Kitty, but of the peace of our household, it proved also to be a chance for fate to play a joke one day. While we accompanied our uncle to his factory one day and prepared to work there while he promised not to tell anyone, we entered his work place with him and came face to face with Mr. Bingley—who was accompanied by Mr. Darcy.

❧ 34 ❧

A PARTING OF THE WAYS

"M r. Darcy!" I gasped, "And Mr. Bingley!"

"Miss Bennet and Miss Kitty," Mr. Bingley said, taking off his hat. "It is a wonderful surprise to see you both here."

"And we could say the same," Kitty said.

I looked toward my uncle and assumed that I should introduce them.

"Oh, if you haven't met, this is our uncle, Mr. Gardiner. Uncle Gardiner, this is Mr. Bingley of Aginfield in Hampshire and Mr. Darcy of Pemberly in Kent."

Our uncle and the two gentlemen bowed to each other and made proper introductions. It turned out that Mr. Bingley had been wishing to pursue trade once more, even though his father worked so that his son could be regarded as a gentleman. Kitty and I supported the idea, yet Mr. Bingley hinted that we should not tell anyone of it, however, for it would not be most beneficial to him. To make him feel more comfortable and knowing that he could trust us, Kitty told them about how we worked at our uncle's factory sometimes in secret just to occupy ourselves. Mr. Bingley reveled at the idea, and Mr. Darcy didn't seem to know what to make of us.

Mr. Bingley followed my uncle into his office to discuss taking stock in our Uncle Gardiner's factory, for he heard that our uncle was a very good businessman. Kitty and I then went off to be taught something by a factory worker, and Mr. Darcy asked to attend to us as we did so. When the factory worker was showing something to Kitty, Mr. Darcy leaned in toward me.

"Are you in earnest?" He asked, "Are you truly meaning to work?"

"It helps us to pass our time, and we like being close to our uncle, for he and my aunt have helped us tremendously."

"Yes, yet how can you pay that back by such actions? No gentlewoman works."

"I have kept your secrets, then why would you not keep mine?"

"I would keep yours, and I promise, yet still..."

"Do you have something to define your life, Mr. Darcy? Do you have a hope, a choice of some occupation of some kind?"

"I take pleasure in looking after my estate in Pemberly, yes, for it takes much work."

"Yes, and you define yourself probably through the success you have with your lands and your tenants on it. Now take all that away and strip yourself away from no choice or hope of any occupation to pass the time. Imagine going from day to day and never saying you did anything with your year that truly marked a difference. You were just there to sit, sew and play the piano-forte, yet no more. How would you feel?"

Mr. Darcy did not respond at first.

"Do I appear as less to you?" I asked.

"No, Miss Bennet, you could never appear so. I am just—I still regret how I treat you."

"As you should. You forget about me one moment and then desire me in the next. I can get used to either attitude if you are consistent in them. If you want to forget about me, then do so. If you want to desire me, then do so. I can overcome you, if you let me. And I can learn to love you terribly if you will let me do that."

"You acknowledge so much? And yet you are not afraid in saying these things."

"I am working, Mr. Darcy. Work makes me bolder I daresay."

"You've always been bold." Mr. Darcy smiled.

"Did I just make you smile?"

"Yes, and I promise that you shall never do that again."

"Mr. Darcy, what do you want from me?"

"I want... I want you to not have such a hold over me. I want... I want to not wake up and be thinking of you. I want to be able to move about life and be free of you and your fine eyes. And yet, I do not want to be away from you."

"Then don't be. And when you are ready to not be afraid of your feelings, then I am here."

"You are not of this world, Miss Bennet."

"I suppose you are right. Perhaps I should have been born in a different time and place. Yet I was not. I was born here and now."

⚜

Mr. Bingley came looking for Mr. Darcy and found him with us as we were working.

"I must confess, Misses Bennets," Mr. Bingley said, "that you make work appear as a lovely labor."

"For it is," Kitty said, "or sometimes I find it to be so."

"Miss Kitty," Mr. Bingley said, "I must say that you are looking even lovelier of late."

"Thank you, Mr. Bingley, that's a wonderful compliment."

Mr. Bingley showed just how much he enjoyed women all around and only solidified my first impression of him which was that he loved to please all and be pleased by all women he enjoyed. Yet he meant no harm and was a very good man.

"And I shall miss getting to enjoy London with both of you."

"Why, are you going somewhere?"

"Aye, I must away to America."

"America?" We said, shocked. "What for?"

"And wouldn't that be dangerous," I said. "Due to the impressment of sailors by our navy, America and England are at odds with each other and the threat of war is on everyone's tongues these days."

"That is why I must go," Mr. Bingley said. "One of my father's factories was in America and I wish to go there to sell it before war breaks out. The currency that I can make from the sale can help me invest in your uncle's factory as well as buy products for my own."

"Then," I asked Mr. Darcy, "are you going as well, for you are quite bosom friends."

"I had wanted to," Mr. Darcy said, "yet I cannot be so far from my sister at present. To be separated by a couple of towns is fine, yet to be separated by an entire ocean is not something that I should burden her with. I have made mistakes with her in the past, and I don't wish to make any more."

"Well then," I said, "be careful, Mr. Bingley."

Kitty echoed my sentiments and both men left us in warm spirits.

When we got back home, there was a letter from Jane, telling us about how Mr. Bingley and his whole family had left Aginfield and Mr. Bingley would be traveling to America.

By the ending of the next week, Mr. Bingley had boarded a ship that was headed for America, and there was a parting of the ways. Mr. Bingley was off to America, while Mr. Darcy remained in London. It was a strange thing, for I was so used to seeing both together that I could not fathom them being separated by an entire ocean.

❦ 35 ❦

A CHANGED MAN

The next day, we received a visitor. Mr. Darcy had come with the express desire to see if we would dine at his townhouse the next evening and then join him for a night at the theatre where we were going to see a production of *A Midsummer Night's Dream.* This was incentive enough to join even if we didn't enjoy Mr. Darcy's company—which we did.

My aunt, uncle and Kitty were delighted. We arrived at his townhouse the next day, our father had gotten us new gowns to wear—from which I believed that he did more so because of our love at joining him at the factory as opposed to just impressing Mr. Darcy—and we arrived at Mr. Darcy's house. He met us in his sitting room and took us into tea. The dinner began a little awkward, yet when Kitty confessed that she was looking forward to seeing the play that night because she had never seen it before, Mr. Darcy then began to open up and tell us about all the plays that he had seen as well as all the ones that he had read.

I was delighted that two of his favorite Shakespeare comedies were *Much Ado About Nothing* and *Merry Wives of Windsor.* I was equally happy in knowing that he no longer scoffed at the fact that my sisters and I did some home theatricals with the Austens and one of the plays we did was *Merry Wives at Windsor*.

Having never undergone one, he was curious as to how they were performed.

"They become fun, if you know that they are supposed to be fun," I said, "yet the moment that you begin to take it too seriously, then all the fun is gone. You have to be willing to understand that sometimes you all will forget your lines, that the set will fall, that many things can go wrong, yet never get angry with each other, never lose your temper and just..."

"Forgive one another," Mr. Darcy finished for me.

"Precisely."

We all finished eating and then went to the theatre. The first half of the show occurred, and we were enjoying ourselves tremendously. Kitty was giddy, yet in a very good way, for she never had the chance to undertake something such as that, and she seemed to sense that everything that was occurring around her was special.

During the intermission, Mr. Darcy and I began to talk in between ourselves while Kitty told our Aunt and Uncle Gardiner about which actors that she favored.

"I was quite surprised," I said.

"At what?" he replied, "at me inviting you?"

"Well, yes, that as well, yet I was surprised at your enjoying the concept of our home theatricals. After all, you are a man who is described as looking on sudden movement of any kind as a sign of bad breeding, including rising precipitously from a chair."

"You tease me."

"Yes, I do. Yet I still want an answer."

"Well," Mr. Darcy said with a smile, "I have been... re-defining my concepts of good breeding and of what is acceptable."

"And this includes our theatricals?"

"It has included many things."

"Such as?"

"Well, to be honest, when Mr. Bingley told me that he wished to continue his father's business, I viewed it a foolish idea, for it would have set him backwards, for being of profession makes him unable to be considered a gentleman."

"True, yes, but I will never accept the concept of a profession being erroneous for a man. The world turns by the force of those who toil, and many a man has found definition to his life by having some occupation of some kind."

"I am beginning to see that. Mr. Bingley is becoming a more solid man because of his pursuits. He has more aim in his direction at life, and there was a time when he relied on my advice all too often, and while I enjoyed it, I now see that he must become his own man, and I must as well myself. In truth, Miss Bennet, I am beginning to understand that my pride is not always under good regulation, or that I mix it with vanity. Seeing you yesterday with your sister, working under your uncle has shown me that."

"Well…" I sighed, a little speechless. "While the idea of my actions affecting you so has made me feel quite insecure, I am happy if it has enhanced your idea of who to regard as acceptable. And thank you for inviting my family, for my aunt and uncle are good people. And Kitty—well, for too long she has been forced to walk in the footsteps of the wrong influences. Therefore, it is nice for her to see the fruits she gains from walking in the right footsteps."

"You are welcome, and yet you need not thank me. It was nice for you all to join me. Bingley is gone, and I won't see him for quite some time. I daresay that you have saved me from loneliness."

"Oh," I said archly, "that is why we are here? As a substitute? For if that is the case, then we have no choice but to fall short as well, for substitutes always do so eventually."

"You need not worry," Mr. Darcy laughed, "though that is a natural concern." We stood in silence for a while.

"Miss Bennet?" he said at last.

"Yes?"

"I once said before that I would do my best to avoid you. Yet, I shall now be honest with myself. I don't wish to avoid you. And I don't think that I even have the power to."

"Then don't."

Mr. Darcy looked at me with intensity.

"Then... you are offering me encouragement?"

"Mr. Darcy, are you so thick? I've offered you encouragement before."

"I know, but... I thought I ruined my chances."

"And you haven't."

Intermission had ended, and we went back to our seats. As the show commenced, Mr. Darcy stealthily snuck his hand over to mine and embraced it. I had allowed him such a liberty—for at that point, I learned that I could deny him nothing.

◈

The next evening, Mr. Darcy invited us to dine with him again. Yet Kitty wished to remain home, for she said that she had a headache, and would rather have spent the evening with her cousins while my aunt, uncle and I went to Mr. Darcy's home once more.

When we arrived, Mr. Darcy introduced me to his sister, Georgiana Darcy and his cousin was there, named Colonel Fitzwilliam. Colonel Fitzwilliam proved to be a very entertaining man, and at first, I could not help but think him a good match for Jane or Kitty. However, it was made very apparent to me rather quickly that he was the second son of an earl, his older brother was the sole inheritor of his father's fortune, and therefore Colonel Fitzwilliam had to make his way in the world as well as marry a woman of a significant dowry—which was something my sisters and I didn't have. Therefore, in that regard, I was happy that Kitty didn't come that evening, for she and Colonel Fitzwilliam might've been very well-suited for each other—their souls were very much the same.

What struck me however most was Mr. Darcy's sister, Georgiana. She was extremely shy, yet I did not hold that against her, for she must not have known how to receive me. She also didn't know what to make of me, that was clear, and was doing her best to play the hostess, and I did my best to make her comfortable. Her brother did so as well, and I could see the affection and paternal nature that he had over her, and it made me like him all the more.

By the end of the evening, Miss Georgiana had asked me if I would like to go out with her the next day and go shopping. I accepted yet asked her if she would mind if I brought Kitty along, for they were closer to being the same age. At first Georgiana clearly was frightened at the idea of me inviting another person, and I immediately rejected my original idea. However, encouraged by Mr. Darcy, she accepted my original plan, and my party left for Gracechurch Street at the end.

෴

When we had returned home, we found Kitty putting the pieces of a puzzle together with our aunt and uncle's children, and she looked positively recovered.

"How was the dinner?" Kitty asked, jumping up. "I trust it went well."

Aunt and Uncle Gardiner gave her positive reviews of the evening, yet when alone, I told Kitty about our outing with Georgiana. Kitty, wanting to make a good impression, inquired about Miss Darcy's character, for she wanted to know how to act. I told her about her shyness, but also told Kitty that I wanted her very much to just be herself, for I thought Kitty had the natural disposition to draw Georgiana out of her shell.

"So," Kitty said after we exhausted the conversation on Miss Darcy, "I am assuming that Mr. Darcy hasn't proposed to you yet?"

"No, wait, no! What are you talking about?"

"I could see that he is in love with you. Do not think me a fool, Lizzy. For you now know that I am not."

"Yes, but...wait, you didn't really have a headache, did you?"

"Of course not. I just thought it would be best if I was not there so that he could have more intimate conversations with you."

"Well, you succeeded in that way. Yet, while one can wish that there were no obstacles to him growing a permanent attachment to me, the truth is, Kitty, I am worried. There are many things that are going to keep him from attaching himself to me fully. There's our lack of a dowry for one, our family's lack of prestige for another—and I am not sure that he is in love with me."

"Yet are you in love with him?"

"I...I... I should not say. It is not wise."

"What is necessary to say is always wise."

"You have grown smart."

"I have been allowed to. Now do be serious, do you love him?"

"Yes, Kitty. Not at first, yet time has proven to make him quite the model of perfection in my eyes. Even when he is not perfect, even when I should run from him, I cannot. For he is quite a changed man in my eyes. And his faults are nothing compared to his virtues. I suppose that I do love him."

❧ 36 ❧

CAN HAPPINESS BE FOUND SO
EASILY?

Our outing with Georgiana began and ended well, thank goodness. I was happy to see that I had been right to have invited Kitty. Kitty, whose natural energy, and brightness was always augmented when going shopping, therefore, Georgiana was able to simply take to her.

The day proved quite lovely and one day Georgiana, Kitty and I were looking at some fabric when Georgiana laughed energetically at something I said.

"I declare, I never had such fun shopping before!" She exclaimed.

"Have you not? It's our favorite activity at home," Kitty said. "Indeed, we might even say that we do it too often."

"What makes one happy that is not harmful at all can never be done too much," Georgiana said with a smile.

"Our sister Lydia would love that statement," I said. "Shopping becomes a vice when one is one of five sisters."

"I should have loved to have had a sister," Georgiana confessed.

"I can see such a desire," I said, "yet we also should have loved to have had a brother. Therefore, we both have reasons to be jealous of one another."

"I suppose you are right."

"Annoying, isn't it?" Kitty laughed. "That one cannot have everything? Though I suppose that it's best that we don't."

"It very well might be best," I said. "For if so, then we would all grow puffy from being spoiled. Yet one thing that we can have is that wonderful fabric over there!"

They all turned to where I pointed and we all walked toward the fabric, and it turned out to be everything that we hoped it would be.

As we left the store, there was a general restlessness amongst the people walking among the street, and we soon discovered why. The Prince Regent was riding along with the royal guards and all had to stop and curtsy or bow when he passed.

Georgiana, Kitty, and I placed our parcels on the ground and curtsied in his presence. When we looked up, however, the Prince Regent's head turned to us and he stopped his horse. His attention focused on Miss Darcy and then narrowed its attention on my sister and me.

"You three," he said, "come forward."

We three approached, and I felt everyone's eyes on us. The Prince Regent got off his horse and faced us as we curtsied.

"Miss Darcy," he said, "I believe that it is you."

"It is, your highness," Miss Darcy said, standing up, "it is... nice to see you again."

"I know your brother, so I know that you don't really mean that," he whispered, smirking, "Yet you are looking well. And you have grown much since I last saw you."

"Thank you, sir, for your compliment. Might I... introduce you to my friends?"

"I would be delighted. For they are pretty sorts."

Kitty and I stood up as Georgiana introduced us. When hearing our names, the Prince's eyes perked up.

"Bennet? Well, Miss Elizabeth and Kitty Bennet. So, you are the one that Mr. Darcy had me look for?"

"I—" I replied, not knowing what to say, "I don't understand of what you are speaking."

"Oh, he hasn't told you? I suppose that it was meant to be a secret. He was looking for you, and he used my services. Well then, since I am a curious sort, tomorrow there is a celebration in honor of my father's returning sanity—however temporary it may be—in the royal gardens. Miss Darcy, you will receive two express invitations. One for yourself and your brother, and another to keep for the Miss Bennets here. For I wish to see for myself why Mr. Darcy was so taken with you."

He soon parted ways with us, climbed back onto his horse and left with his guards.

When we told our Aunt and Uncle Gardiner, they were delighted, and they felt the good fortune of our stay even more-so now. Our uncle allowed us to go and accompany Miss Darcy and Mr. Darcy as well, and our Aunt went to her writing table to compose a letter to our parents of our invitation to the royal celebration by the Prince himself.

I was surprised at how our fortune had changed so utterly, yet one thing was certain: there was no way that our mother could be angry with Kitty now, for the Prince of England surely wasn't, and I daresay that his actions would greatly overwhelm her sensibilities.

"Well," Kitty said, "the answer is simple now. Mr. Darcy is in love with you!"

Mr. Darcy arrived the next morning in his carriage, accompanied by Miss Darcy, to escort us to the royal gardens. Before we set off, however, I was able to get Mr. Darcy alone for a moment to ask him about what the Prince meant by looking for me under his express wishes.

"It's true," Mr. Darcy replied simply. "Um, after I saw you at the ball, I wanted to know your name and whereabouts."

"You could have asked me when I saw you in the park," I replied.

"I know, and I should have, but you remember me back then, for I was lost."

"'Tis true, yet I found you eventually. And it does make me feel nice that you apparently sent out a royal quest just to discover my identity."

"Yes, I can see how flattering that must be now."

He kissed my hand and then we were met by the others and took off to the gardens. When we arrived, many families of the aristocracy were already there, and the gardens were full. As we walked around, I found many people staring at us as we walked. I was self-conscious at first, because it was very apparent that Kitty and I were the center of their curiosity, for we must've been on everyone's tongues after the Prince had spoken to us in public.

Mr. Darcy began to introduce us to other acquaintances of his, and once he did, many others began to accost us as well with an express wish to get to know us. Among them were a few well-known poets, Lord Byron being amongst them. His charm was infectious, and Mr. Darcy tried to steer Kitty away from him as soon as it was polite to do so.

King George and his Queen presented themselves to the multitude where their son, the Prince Regent, accompanied them. They walked through the crowd and spoke to some, then the Prince Regent saw us and soon approached us.

"Mr. Darcy?"

"Your highness." He bowed to the Prince and we curtsied to him. The Prince's eyes rested on me and then turned to Kitty. "Might I have your arm, my lady?"

"Why thank you, your highness," Kitty said, taking his arm.

"Come," the Prince Regent said, "let us walk together now. For there is a particular part of the gardens that I believe you will like."

Mr. Darcy had me on one arm, Miss Darcy on the other, and we walked together where the Prince led us. I could sense Mr. Darcy's back stiffen and he looked at the Prince Regent with antipathy.

"Lovely day, isn't it?" the Prince said.

"It is," Kitty answered, "a lovely day has shined on your father's celebration."

"And what if it doesn't last? What if the storm clouds arrive? Will it be looked at as our Holy Father not blessing my father's health?"

"I would say that when the weather is lovely," Kitty said, "it is a blessing, yet when it is not, it is less so. Nor more and no less."

"An excellent belief, Miss Kitty, and what do you think of that, Miss Bennet?"

"Well," I began, "I would regard bad weather as a great nuisance if it weren't necessary, yet it is, therefore I shall call a sunny day beautiful, and a cloudy day less so, but I'll still smile during it. It will help pass the time."

"Both very good answers," the Prince replied, "I could see a man falling in love with you both and then being torn about which one to choose. And then there is Miss Darcy over there, who is a silent intrigue, and would make the choice even more complicated."

"I have a voice, your highness," Miss Darcy said simply, "and it comes when you least expect it."

"Was that just a spirited reply, Miss Darcy?" The Prince smiled, "You surprise me!"

"My sister has her own sense of wit," Mr. Darcy said, "and it is a wonderful one."

"Yes, it is, and I am quite surprised. To be around such wonderful women, it makes me quite beside myself, yet marriage is the inevitable outcome to such desires, and some men pursue it better than me. Which reminds me, Mr. Darcy, I must congratulate you, for I have just heard all the rumors that have been spreading around London for weeks, about your engagement to your cousin, Miss Anne De Bourgh."

My head darted back towards Mr. Darcy, as did my sister and as did Georgiana. Both looked on Mr. Darcy with shock and alarm, and I felt as if my chest had frozen over.

"For I did hear correctly?" The Prince questioned, "And I hope that I am not wrong, for that would mean that much of London is in error. Are you not engaged to your cousin?"

Mr. Darcy's eyes shot around in discomfort.

"Well yes...yet the matter is not fully..."

"I heard that it was fully settled, and Lady Catherine De Bourgh has been telling all who would listen of how you proposed to her daughter in your townhouse, she accepted and now all is well. For both Pemberly and Rosing's Park estates will now remain in your families. Such a smart move."

"I..."

"Well, I must be off now. As you can see, here is the area that I have loved so much in the garden, and I'm sorry that you shall have to enjoy it yourselves. Yet my mother is requesting my presence beside them now, so you must excuse me at present. Yet again, Mr. Darcy, I commend you on your engagement. To find happiness with

Miss De Bourgh, for when all of mankind asks the question of can happiness be found so easily, you show them that it can."

The Prince Regent left us on that part of the garden where we were alone and looking at a lovely spot that none of us was fully gazing upon.

A BROKEN IMAGE

"Lizzy," Mr. Darcy whispered.

"Is it true?" I asked, desperate. "And do not lie to me in any way. Are you engaged to another?"

"Allow me to explain—"

"I said, don't lie to me!"

"It is complicated—"

"I said, don't lie to me!"

Mr. Darcy sighed and looked down at the ground.

"Yes," he whispered, "I am currently engaged to our cousin, Anne De Bourgh."

"Oh, but that is not real!" Georgiana said, "Lizzy, our aunt has been wishing my brother to marry our cousin since they were children, but it's all just lies. She just tells everyone that it is so."

"Georgiana..." her brother said, "I told Anne myself that I would marry her."

"What?" Georgiana gasped, "Why did I not hear of this?"

"You were in the country for so long and the news has just been circulating around town."

"But...you don't love her."

"I was in despair, Georgiana. Our father had just died, he wanted me to marry Anne, and I wanted to please him. Our mother wanted it too."

"No, she didn't!" Georgiana gasped. "She never wanted it, and she told me so often."

"What?" Mr. Darcy gasped.

"Yes, she just went along with it because it pleased our aunt and father. Yes, he might have wanted it from an economical state, yet I know that he also wanted you to be happy. I know this! He would never have forced you into this as you have done now. And now you are trapped."

"No, I am not."

"Yes, you are," I hissed. "You made a promise to this woman, and you have not broken it. How long have you remained attached to her?"

"I—"

"How long, Fitzwilliam!"

He started at hearing me say his first name.

"Over five months now."

"Five months! You led me on all this time?"

"I meant it all, and I do love you! I just made a mistake before, and I tried to avoid hurting you, but I could not resist you."

"You should have told me from the beginning."

"I know, but you would have turned on me."

"I'm turning on you now!"

"You cannot."

"You are engaged! You have a wife, already."

"But I love you!"

"And your love has ruined me! It's made me not care about anything but you, devote myself to you, and forgive every pain that you have caused me because I saw something in you that wasn't there. You have deceived me!"

"Mr. Darcy," Kitty said, "enough words have been spoken in public, and my sister has lost enough as it is, so please call your carriage and take us back home."

"I must—"

"Mr. Darcy!" Kitty said sharply, "I was not asking. You will take my sister home, and please, just do the right thing."

Mr. Darcy was silent for a moment and I was too heartbroken to care about his apprehensions—which was fine, for he did little to care about my sensibilities.

⚜

We walked to the front of the gardens, our carriage was brought, and we entered it and rode off in silence. Very soon we reached Gracechurch Street and Kitty looked at me.

"Kitty," I whispered, "please give me a moment with Mr. Darcy."

"Aye."

Kitty exited the carriage and waited for me on the steps.

"Miss Darcy," I said, "please look away for a moment."

Georgiana nodded and turned away.

"I will not ruin this woman's life by begging you to choose me," I said firmly. "You promised yourself to her and you will stick to it."

"I didn't mean for this," Mr. Darcy replied, "and I did love you—"

I slapped him.

"Now you are Mr. Wickham," I hissed, "for you have filled me with empty promises and you broke my heart. No more of me forgiving you for every offense you have committed. No more of me giving in to your sudden empty acts of affection. Never come here again, and never will I ever want to see your face in the course of my life—for you are the last man in the world whom I ever wish to know."

I exited the carriage and it drove off immediately.

When I entered my Uncle's home, I could not hold back my tears and I rushed to my room. Everyone scurried to me but was stopped by Kitty. As I cried in my room, Kitty must've told our aunt and uncle everything, for very soon, Aunt Gardiner entered and began to hold me. I wept as if I was a little girl and pressed my head into her neck, wishing that I could just disappear.

Kitty entered and sat in a chair, looking hopeless and helpless. Then our uncle entered and looked at me with sorrow and empathy.

"Lizzy," he said, "I am so sorry. Would you wish me to do something about this, to call him out?"

"No..." I whispered desperately, "he may have broken my heart, yet I can't have anything happen to him, or you. I wouldn't want it."

"I know, I just figured that would...I just feel so helpless," he said. "And I hate not being able to do anything for you."

"You can tell me... what was he thinking? What did he expect to get from me? To get out of it all? How long did he expect to live this lie?"

"For as long as he could probably," he replied, "Men can be foolish when it comes to love, and if this marriage is not as he wishes, then he looked at you as his last great chance, his last moment to find happiness, however temporary."

"He was selfish!"

"Yes, he was. And I'm sorry, for I had believed him to be the best of men."

"The best of men..."

I closed my eyes, aware of the image that I had of Mr. Darcy, and that image had now been broken.

❧ 38 ❧

WHAT WAS LOST WOULD BE FOUND
AGAIN

I did not succumb to my grief, though it never left me. I continued to go to the factory with my uncle and Kitty, yet after a month, my Uncle wanted to do something that would cheer us up, and he knew that I didn't wish to go home just yet.

Our mother had forgiven Kitty utterly, for news spread even into Hampshire of how Kitty and I walked with the Prince Regent in the gardens. Yet now her focus would be on wondering why we returned when we should have stayed in London to use the Prince's acknowledgement of us to have someone think we were worth marrying.

She sent news to us that Lydia had been invited by Colonel Forster's wife, Mrs. Forster, to join her at Brighton where they were to stay with the militia. I did not like this plan whatsoever, for Lydia was quite possibly the most foolish and thoughtless girl ever. Yet our mother assured us that she would be safe there, and that Mrs. Forster would look after her. However, being away, there was nothing I could do to influence them against letting her go to Brighton with her friends and the soldiers, and all I could do was remain in London and enjoy the quietness and sense that reigned over Gracechurch Street.

My uncle then decided that, since business was extremely successful for him, it would be wonderful for us to go on holiday, and while we could not travel to the Lake District for it was too far, we could go to Derbyshire and see the beauty of the Peaks. Kitty and I were amazed with this and thanked them for allowing us to not only stay with them for so long, but also to treat us to such a wonderful escape.

We made the plans to have Jane travel to London where she would keep house for the Gardiners and look after their children while we were away.

She came in a months' time, and Kitty and I embraced her with much energy—to the point where we almost pushed her over.

After she was settled for a day, my aunt, uncle, Kitty and I prepared our luggage, carriage and were off to Derbyshire. Leaving London behind was beautiful to me at the time, because this would put me far and away from Mr. Darcy's townhouse, and even further from his estate of Pemberly in Kent.

❦

Derbyshire was a lovely spot, the Peaks were a pleasure to see, and we visited some lovely houses and estates as well, including Blenheim.

What was an incredible surprise, while we were traveling through the countryside and were staying at an inn in Lambton, was that we came upon Colonel Fitzwilliam.

"Miss Bennet!" He said, "It is wonderful to see you again."

"Colonel Fitzwilliam!" I gasped, "Well, isn't this a wonderful surprise? My aunt and uncle are here, but I do wish that you had gotten to see my sister, Kitty. She came down with a cold while we were traveling, and she can't leave her bed."

"Oh, I do hope she recovers."

"Thank you, though I find it quite comical how you always miss her. For some reason, it's as if fortune does not want you to meet Kitty."

"Forces working against me?" Colonel Fitzwilliam laughed. "Well, whatever did I do to offend fate so? And if I did do something, I sure hope that one day it shall get over it and let me meet this sister of yours."

"Well, my aunt and uncle will have to do." We all re-met and he ate dinner with us. He made sure also not to mention Mr. Darcy in my presence, which was nice, but he mentioned Miss Darcy to me, and I felt bad that her last memory of me was hitting her brother— yet that could not be helped.

Colonel Fitzwilliam inquired after our trip and wondered how much longer we were going to stay in Lambton. When I let him know that we were staying for a week there, he asked if he could call on us sometimes and let him show us some of his favorite rural areas.

My aunt and uncle agreed immediately, as did I, and we parted ways for the day.

The next day, my aunt, uncle and I were preparing to leave when I received two letters from Mary.

"A letter from Mary, at last," I said. "I was wondering why I did not hear back from Longbourn when I had sent them my first missive. Never mind, no wonder for on this one Mary wrote the address of the letter very ill indeed. Would you mind if I were to postpone our outing?"

"Of course, you want to read your letters," Aunt Gardiner said, "We shall walk to the church, and you can meet us when you are ready."

They left me alone to read them and I was quiet, for Kitty was still sleeping in the other room as I sat down and began reading:

Dearest Lizzy and Kitty,

The worst has happened! And I do not hide my anger for Lydia has done some foolish things in her day, yet this one I offer no sympathies for her plight and I am very vexed with her. I shall pray for her, yet I have no hope for her spirit at this point.

Lizzy and Kitty, as you know, Lydia was invited to go to Brighton with Mrs. Forster where she could indulge herself in such stupid activities such as going to balls and parties and all such things that are not moral in any way.

While there, she suddenly disappeared, and Mrs. Forster found a note that she left her. The note said that she had gone to Scotland, to Gretna Green and had fled Brighton with one of the officers. She said that she had gone there with Mr. Wickham! Yes, the very same Mr. Wickham who everyone here thought was all that was good in the world. Lydia believes that he will take her to elope and that they shall return man and wife. Our mother, when hearing this news, lost control of all her nerves—though she always does—our father grew quiet and felt quite foolish for ever letting Lydia go to begin with. He has left for London to look for her as well and visits Jane at Gracechurch Street. I shall hope that all is not lost, yet I have given up all hope of our sister ever returning, for she has thrown herself away and has fallen terribly.

I shall write to you when I have more news,

Etc.

Shocked, I ripped open the next letter and read.

"Lizzy and Kitty! It all has gotten worse, for we know that the wedding must not have taken place, for they have not been traced passed London, which means that they still must be there. In other words, they are living together, and are not married. I cannot believe the scandal. Now, desperate to look for them, we ask that you all return home to help us search for her.

We have sent a letter to Jane at Gracechurch Street as well,
and she also awaits your return.
Yours etc.
Mary

I closed the next letter, and though angry and sad, I was not shocked. The second I read that Lydia had run away with Mr. Wickham was the same second that I knew that he did not intend to marry her. For it was all too clear to me; I was no longer there, but my family was, and Mr. Wickham would naturally want to take revenge out on me for siding with Mr. Darcy and threatening to expose him if he hurt my family in any way. It was all in retaliation.

I began to weep silently, yet as I stood up to leave, the door opened, and the maid showed in Colonel Fitzwilliam, who bowed but then took one look at my face and saw distress.

"Miss Bennet," he said, "dear me, are you all right?"

"Sorry, excuse me sir, I have to find my aunt and uncle and have not a moment to lose."

"Good god, what is the matter? Well, never mind that, let me go after them or send someone to go in your place, for you cannot go yourself."

"I must, for I have just received some news that I must let them know immediately."

"Then I shall send the maid to go." I told him that my aunt and uncle went to the church, he told the maid to bring them there and then he saw to me. "Miss Bennet, please tell me what is wrong?"

"It is the worst of news, Colonel."

"Is there anything that I can do to give you present relief?"

"No, it is not the matter with me, but it is the news. It is so terrible that I suppose cannot be hidden. It—my youngest sister, Lydia, has left her friends in Brighton, has eloped and has thrown herself into the powers of Mr. Wickham."

Colonel Fitzwilliam looked stunned.

"Yes," I sighed, "I know the history he has with your family. And the same scandalous behavior he pulled on your cousin, he is now pulling on my sister, and he has succeeded. There is no possible hope, for you know Mr. Wickham, Colonel, for how is such a man to be worked on?"

"I am aware of his habits, yes. Yet it never stops it from being disturbing to me. What has been done to recover your sister?"

"My father has gone to London where he knows that they are there, yet London is large, and I fear that she is lost forever."

Colonel Fitzwilliam grabbed my hand without fear of breaking decorum.

"Don't worry, Miss Bennet, all is not lost. Trust me. Now, I believe that you have long been desiring my absence."

He stood up and I didn't know if I was right to have confided in him, or wrong to have done so. Yet he was a comfort at the present.

"I am very sorry for this occurrence," he said, "and I wish you all the luck in retrieving her. Yet Miss Bennet, truly, do not despair."

He then left me alone.

Suddenly the door to the next room opened and Kitty, in a nightgown, entered.

"So, all of that is true?"

"You were listening in?" I asked.

"I heard you speaking to someone, yet I only heard his voice and didn't see him. Yet, was all of that true?"

"Yes, Lydia has eloped, and we must leave here immediately."

Kitty groaned out and punched the wall.

"Darn you, Lydia!"

Our aunt and uncle returned, and we set off immediately for London. After a few days, we arrived back on Gracechurch Street where Jane was eager to see us. Later that night, our father came to Cheapside, and he looked awful, for he had no idea still where Lydia was.

He was at first ashamed to look at Jane, Kitty and I, for Lydia's plight had cemented the flaw our father had of always not being a proper father and being cautious.

When we all sat down together, he began to confess his feelings.

"I am heartily ashamed of myself," he began. "I should have taken better care of you all, yet I didn't. Yet I suppose, if a lesson needs to be learned, then I have learned mine too late. They always say better late than never. Yet this is one circumstance where never would have been preferable. Lydia and Wickham are definitely still here, yet I have no hope in finding them, and it makes me feel so weak, so useless..."

When he was done with his confession, we all hugged him, and he exclaimed that Kitty did in fact look quite different than how he remembered her. He therefore decided that the next day, he would return home, for Uncle Gardiner had offered to take up the search of finding her.

As we all went to bed, our aunt coaxed us, trying to ease our woes.

"Remember, hope never should forsake anyone," she advised, "and what was lost would be found again."

Kitty, Jane, and I went to bed, feeling forsaken in regard to hope.

❧ 39 ☙

WAKING UP THE SAVIOR

Colonel Fitzwilliam, once he left Elizabeth in the inn, immediately planned to leave for London. Always a man of action, he was able to pack and prepare in less than an hour's time.

Always feeling as if he was a man on the move, who never had the chance to relax even when he was on leave, he travelled to London. However, this mission was a necessary one, for Wickham was the man who hurt his cousin, Georgiana, and had now hurt the Bennet girls. This, Colonel Fitzwilliam declared, was a vicious cycle that must end and would end by his will and by Darcy's.

He drove his carriage to Grosvenor Square and was seen into Mr. Darcy's home where his cousin met him immediately.

"Richard?" Mr. Darcy said.

"Darcy, where is Georgiana?"

"She is upstairs."

"Good, let her stay there and don't tell her why I have come. She has gone through enough pain already."

"Richard, what are you on about?"

"It's the worst of things. Darcy, Wickham has struck again."

Colonel Fitzwilliam told Mr. Darcy everything and Mr. Darcy wanted to slam his hand against the desk.

"I cannot believe it!" He cried.

"It's true." Colonel Fitzwilliam sighed. "You know Wickham and it's something he would do. And now it's time for you to act. And you shall."

"I know. As much as I wish to admit that his choosing Lydia was a random choice, I know that it wasn't. He deliberately wanted to wound me, because Miss Elizabeth chose to trust me over him, and therefore he is taking revenge on her as well."

"Aye, making this something that we have to fix. And a chance to redeem yourself."

"Redeem myself?"

"I know about what you have done to Miss Bennet. I always did."

"Well...she will never forgive me."

"It doesn't matter if she does or doesn't. You owe this to her. If you are going to destroy her life one moment, then you damn well better be the one to fix it again."

Mr. Darcy looked at the fireplace.

"You and I both know Mr. Wickham's habits and where he shall go," Mr. Darcy professed, "He will have visited Mrs. Younge, for she is now in the business of renting rooms in London. I need you to go to her and find a way to convince her to tell you where Wickham is, for I bet that he went to her for assistance. And take my valet, Jefferson, with you, for he is very good on that score."

"What will you do?"

"I am going to make sure that when you find him, he will have no means of escape. I am going to call in a favor."

Mr. Darcy found himself being led along a house of nobility by a few guards. He was angry that he had to be reduced to this yet again, but there was nothing for it. And besides—Elizabeth deserved it.

He was led into a room where the Prince Regent was sitting amongst some of the aristocracy—and Mr. Darcy knew them to all be the Prince's personal sycophants. When he entered, the Prince smiled at him and told everyone in the room to leave.

When alone, the Prince drank some wine and stood up.

"So, have you come to thank me yet?"

"Thank you? You have ruined my life."

"No, you did that one, Darcy. I merely woke you up to the concept that you can't have everything."

"Well, I am here to ask for your help."

"My help?"

"Yes."

The Prince gasped sarcastically.

"Proud Mr. Darcy is asking me for his help this time? After all that I have done for you already?"

"And what do you mean by that? I have been the one helping you in the past."

"But my last deed trumped all those things."

"How so? You ruined my happiness and now Miss Bennet doesn't wish to see me again."

"Wait, what?"

"You seem surprised."

"I am! You are not marrying her now?"

"No, she—wait, what did you mean by that you had helped me?"

"Well, despite all my flaws, I thought I could do you one good deed, which was force you to make the right decision. It was clear that you proposed to your cousin because of familial obligation, not love. Just as it was clear that Miss Bennet was with you at the gardens because you loved her but could not propose. Therefore, I figured, that if I presented you with the truth, it would force you to finally wake up, and make the right choice. And yet I see now that you have not. Why didn't you break off your marriage to Anne immediately and then propose to Miss Bennet?"

"Because I made a promise to Anne."

"Which needs to be broken! For everyone's sake."

"And why do you care, your highness?"

"Because for one second, one moment, I thought that I was doing a good deed. We royalty very rarely ever get to do those, so it's nice when it's within our power to do so. Fine then, I shall make another deal with you. Do you want to marry this Miss Bennet, Darcy?"

"More than anything."

"If free of Anne, but not having to suffer the side effects of breaking your oath to her, will you marry this woman?"

"I will, yet now I don't even care what the world thinks. I will do as I wish, for I am sick of decorum."

"Finally, Mr. Darcy learns that he, like the rest of us, is human. And that was all the payment I needed. Now what do you need?"

"I, your highness, need to borrow some of your personal guards."

❊

With the Prince's personal guards watching every exit, Colonel Fitzwilliam turned to Darcy and smiled.

"You look good as being a hero," he said, "and it's nice to see that it takes extreme action sometimes to successfully accomplish waking up the savior."

"You are correct," he replied. "I have been not living up to the man that I should be for so long. Now let us finish this."

Colonel Fitzwilliam entered with Darcy, and they walked up the steps to the door of a room and knocked. The door was opened by Lydia Bennet, who looked shocked to see Mr. Darcy, yet her shock was not nearly as immense as the look on Wickham's face when he beheld them.

They pushed past Lydia and entered.

"Hello, Wickham," Mr. Darcy said. Wickham backed up against the wall and started to inch toward the window.

"Oh, there is no point," Colonel Fitzwilliam said, sitting down, "we have the Prince's best guards all posted outside, just hoping for you to attempt to make an escape."

Wickham looked out of the window and sure enough, he saw the red-coated guards.

"So, tell me Wickham," Mr. Darcy said, "What do you think we have come here to talk about?"

✺ 40 ✺

AMENDS HAVE BEEN MADE

At Longbourn, three weeks had gone by before we received a letter from London. Jane, Kitty, and I returned there to help Mary look after our mother. All the time we sat in between agony, expectation, and willingness to accept our fate, for it wasn't just Lydia who would be ruined by her disgrace, but all of us. Her elopement would reflect on the family and we would all have to partake in her infamy—we would become a family with whom no one would want to connect or associate.

Naturally when we arrived, our mother was full of hysterics, the house was in confusion, Mary was at a loss as to what to do, and our mother's voluble nature made it so that our hired help knew about it and therefore spread it throughout Steventon.

Lady Lucas, Charlotte's mother, came by to offer her services, yet I was too angry to care. What was most annoying was the sudden arrival of Mr. Collins, who could not have been least wanted. He came to tell us of how we were a family in distress who were greatly to be pitied for we were, as his patroness, Lady Catherine De Bourgh said, 'a family who no one would want to

242

connect with after such an incident'. And that the Christian and moral thing to do would be to reject our dear sister forever, and if she had died, it would have been better news than what she had done instead. Literally, that was his phrasing and intent. When he left the house, I was never happier than to see a person leave our domicile.

⚜

However, when the letter came from my Uncle Gardiner, it came bearing good news—or as good of news as could be expected.

Our father read the letter to all of us; our uncle had found Lydia and Wickham in a questionable area of London. They were not married, and were in no position to become so, yet he was forcing them to marry very soon. By the end of the month, Lydia and Mr. Wickham would offer their nuptials and be man and wife. There were other bits of information, such as Mr. Wickham only asked for 100 pounds per annum for her dowry, which was very little. When I asked our father how Mr. Wickham could be persuaded to take on Lydia with so little, he acknowledged that he would owe our uncle tremendously. For the only way Mr. Wickham would marry Lydia under so slight a temptation was if Uncle Gardiner had given him at least 10,000 pounds. That sum startled all of us, yet we didn't wish to think on it, for it was all out of our hands and in between the grasp of our father and uncle alone.

We went upstairs to tell our mother, who was sick with worry all that time. When she heard that Lydia would marry, she jumped out of her bed, overjoyed, but halted when Kitty, Mary, Jane, and I both looked at her in anger.

"A daughter married!" She cried. "Isn't it wonderful?"

"It would be if it weren't for the fact that she is marrying the worst man in England."

"Lizzy, all that matters is that she is married, and I'm sure there are much worse men, and Mr. Wickham was always greatly misunderstood."

"No, he wasn't, Mama," Kitty said. "He is a foul git."

"And a man who placed his own desires," Mary said, "before our own."

"All that matters," our mother said, "is that it has been made right by the end. And Jane, tell the servants that in honor of her marriage, they can have a glass of punch."

"I will tell them no such thing!" Jane snapped, and it shocked us all. Even our mother stopped fluttering here and there and faced her, stiff as a board. "I will not let them celebrate something that has only been brought out through our uncle having to bribe such a despicable man as Mr. Wickham to marry our sister. I will not have them celebrate the fruits of my sister who was spoiled rotten by my parents. Mama, you must see that what Lydia has done was awful and she is to blame for it. Just as you are to see that Wickham is awful. And we gained nothing by this, for he would shun us all in a moment if we came to his door in need. And I beg of you, for once mother, see the situation for what it is, become more objective about the things you ought to, and stop excusing Lydia's behavior. Become a better parent, I beg you now."

"But I..."

"And do you know the worst thing about it?" Jane said, beginning to cry, "is that all my life I have hoped that you would become the mother I always dreamed you would be."

Our mother sat down, disturbed, and feeling as if till then she had never known herself.

"Well," Mary said, "what she said."

Then we all left our mother alone to realize what she would.

When alone, I touched Jane's shoulder.

"Jane." I smiled at her. "That was brilliant!"

"Thank you," she said, then laughed, and added, "and it felt good to say."

News reached us through our uncle that Lydia and Wickham got married, he was given a position in the militia at Southampton, and before they were to go there, they wished to break their journey at Longbourn.

Our father, however, was against it for the moment and told them to go to Southampton, for he would risk being made fun of by all of Hampshire rather than let them in his home at that time. He granted them to come at Christmas, because he assumed that the holidays would put him in a giving mood. Our mother didn't even try to argue with him, and Mr. and Mrs. Wickham did not come to Longbourn as they might have hoped. Only years later would I learn that our father's severity had a lasting impression on Lydia and was the beginning of her learning that her actions did in fact have consequences.

Yet at Longbourn, the rumor was spread of Lydia and Wickham marrying, for it was in the newspapers, and therefore any reports of us being a fallen family had ended and our lives could go back to what they once were.

The Austens were the only ones who had been consistently nice to us throughout the terrible ordeal. But after it was all resolved, only then did Jane Austen fold her arms and exclaim 'amends have been made, now let's go do something scandalous like climb another tree'.

❧ 41 ❧

THINGS FALLING BACK
INTO PLACE

O ur Aunt Phillips came by one day and told us all some exciting news.

"Wonderful!" she exclaimed, "for the neighborhood is all abuzz. Aginfield Park has been opened once more because Mr. Bingley has returned from America."

This roused our spirits because Mr. Bingley was always a neighbor in whom we took great interest. Yet our mother had ceased teasing me and hinting at trying to get me to warm up to him, for she could tell that there was no hope on that score, just as she realized that Kitty had avoided a terrible fate in refusing to marry Mr. Collins. For even she could now see that he was ridiculous.

"Oh, and I almost forgot to mention," Aunt Phillips said, "Mr. Darcy has come with him."

"What?" I gasped. Everyone looked at me with surprise, except for Kitty, who knew my reasons.

"Well," Aunt Phillips continued, "Yes, but Mr. Bingley's sisters shall remain in town."

"Oh," I said, trying to remain calm. "Well, if they bring no ladies with them, then that means that we shall not see them, for they must just be a shooting party."

❦

I wondered what Mr. Darcy could be doing here! If he came in regard to trying to soften me towards him, I was afraid that I would not have the strength to repel him again. I could not deny my love for him any longer, and I thought of him often. Yet it didn't change the fact that it was not wise for me to be in his company.

Why did his hold on me have to be so strong? And why could I never resist it? Even love should not make me that compliant, for my nature usually did not lean so. Yet I promised myself to maintain composure and not let my temper flare if I did see him, for scenes might arise that were unpleasant to more than myself.

❦

One day, I was returning to Longbourn from visiting the Austens, for Henry Austen, who was Jane and Cassandra's brother, had returned from a life as a captain at sea, and he brought his wife with him. I always both did and did not like Henry, for he was charming —in both harmless and harmful sort of ways all at the same time. Yet I always got along well with him enough.

When I returned home, I was met with the news that I had just missed Mr. Darcy and Mr. Bingley, who had come to visit and take tea with us. I exhaled, happy that I had not seen Mr. Darcy just yet.

Jane, however, filled me in on all the details. Mr. Bingley had returned from America with sad news, for now it was made clear that America and England were threatening war, and America was not a place that he could set up his trade with.

Jane, Mary, and I sat there for a while, talking about this crisis, for we had hoped that both our countries could find resolution. Yet conflict had become imminent, especially since Mr. Bingley himself had met a man who lost his brother due to the impressment of sailors along British vessels. Therefore, dark times might be ahead.

We were all sorry for the potential fate of both our countries and hoped the threat of war would be resolved quickly after it began, and the crisis would be averted.

Jane and Cassandra Austen had a different outlook on the situation, however.

"Resolution could occur between our countries quite easily," Cassandra observed, "if only the monarchy would recognize that we have no claims to take their sailors any longer, if we ever did. And if America would leave our Canadian brethren well enough alone."

"The Prince Regent could put an end to it easily," Jane Austen always said, "by just illegalizing impressment. Yet he does not. I will always wonder if he has it within him to ever do a good deed, for I do find him to be quite a waste of space!"

❦

Mr. Bingley and Mr. Darcy would not return to Longbourn till four days after their initial visit, for they promised to dine at the Lucases one night, the Longs on another, the Austens for another, and the Prices after.

Therefore, in the meantime, I had time to gather my own strength and ready myself to meet Mr. Darcy when the moment came. I knew that my heart would break when I saw him, and I would hate knowing once more that we could never be together. Yet it could not be helped.

I was thinking of this subject when an extraordinary carriage pulled before our house and an older but clearly prestigious lady stepped down and marched to our front door, where Hill let her in. I saw this woman from the window and went downstairs to see her for myself up close and then I came face to face with her in the doorway.

"Are you one of the Bennet girls?" she said with venom.

"I am, yet I have not made your acquaintance."

"I," she swelled, "am Lady Catherine De Bourgh, and I am looking for a Miss Elizabeth Bennet."

◈

Hill asked her to remain there so that she could announce her, yet Lady Catherine De Bourgh demanded to be let into the sitting room at once so that she could meet the head of the household, Mrs. Bennet. Kitty and Mary were behind me and we all went down to the sitting room to see this extreme woman. We entered, and Lady Catherine had entered the room and plopped down on the best-looking couch we had. Then she looked up at us as if we were intruding on her space.

"Ma'am," Hill said, "this is Lady Catherine De Bourgh of Rosing's Park."

"So," Lady Catherine said to our mother, "you are Mrs. Bennet?"

"I am," our mother said, "and I am pleased to make your acquaintance."

"Hmm."

Lady Catherine then looked at us.

"And these are your daughters?"

"All but one, your ladyship. My youngest is lately married."

"To Mr. Wickham? Yes, my clergyman, Mr. Collins, has told me all about that. As well as the fact that he came here to marry one of your daughters, and she rejected him." Lady Catherine raised her cane and pointed it at us. "So, which of you did the rejecting?"

"I..." Kitty said, "I did."

"Well," Lady Catherine sneered, "you would never have done. Charlotte Lucas was a better choice for him on the whole."

"What do you mean by that?" Our mother said. "My daughters are as good as any other, and better often."

Lady Catherine, to my surprise, did not say anything in retaliation, yet looked back at us.

"And which one of you is Elizabeth?"

"I am," I said, "your ladyship. Yet I do not believe that we are acquainted."

"We are not!" She snapped, "yet I know your name and history well," she said standing up, "for you are the one who has seduced my nephew."

"I beg your pardon?"

"You are the woman with whom he has been walking all around London with, in hopes of drawing him in with your arts and allurements."

"I do not even know who your nephew is."

"Mr. Fitzwilliam Darcy!"

The name hung in the air for a bit before any of us spoke again.

"For in London," Lady Catherine hissed, "an alarming report has reached me, that you, Miss Elizabeth, have formed an attachment with my nephew, Mr. Fitzwilliam Darcy of Pemberly."

"Your ladyship is mistaken," my mother said, "for she is not attached to him whatsoever."

"Mama..." I whispered. My mother turned to me and read my expression.

"Then there is some truth to this scandalous falsehood? For I tell you now that it cannot be so because Mr. Darcy is engaged to my daughter, Anne!"

"Your ladyship says truth and scandalous falsehood of the same thing," I argued. "It cannot be both."

"Are these reports true?"

"When last I heard," I argued, "Mr. Darcy was said to be engaged to your daughter, Anne De Bourgh."

"That is as it should be so."

"Then why do you come all this way if this is fact? What could your ladyship mean by it?"

"I came instantly to make my sentiments known and to make sure that it is not true, yet do not pretend to be ignorant of what I speak."

"Of what are you speaking?"

"You wish to play ignorant of this? Don't lie to me. You know how Mr. Darcy has written a letter, breaking off his engagement."

"He what?" I gasped, almost falling down. "He broke off his engagement?"

"Then this is your fault?" She hissed. "Your arts and allurements, you have drawn him in. Is this to be endured—it shall not be—if you marry Mr. Darcy, your alliance will be a disgrace, your name will never be mentioned by any of his family members."

"And what is so terrible with her name?" Our mother interrupted. "What is wrong with any of my daughters that makes them lower than yours? Nothing."

"My daughter is of noble blood," Lady Catherine argued, "but you, woman, who are you?"

"I have married a gentleman."

"But you were not born a gentlewoman, you are the daughter of a lowly man who was in trade."

"Don't speak like that to my mother," I cried.

"And don't speak like that to any of my daughters, you prig!" Our mother cried.

"How dare you?" Lady Catherine hissed.

"I dare easily. My daughter is of as much value as any that you could produce, and probably more-so because anything that could come from a woman such as you must not have been born well."

"How dare you, you idiotic woman! You all refuse to lay to the claims of honor and credit of my nephew, and what about your youngest daughter's infamous elopement? I know it all. Are the shades of Pemberly to be thus polluted?"

"That is enough!" Our mother cried, "And you need to shut up, you old hag! You have insulted my children and me in every possible way, and I tell you this now, my children are worth more than you complete, and if this nephew of yours wishes to marry my daughter, then he is right to do so!"

"How dare you call me such names! I am of noble blood!"

"And I am her mother! Take a hint of which one should mean more to her. I shall tell you now, that you shall quit this house immediately or I shall stick you with every sewing needle we have in this household, for you clearly are filled with hot air."

"I take my leave of you, you banshee!" Lady Catherine cried. "And I have never been thus treated in my entire life."

On that last line, Lady Catherine quitted the house, never to be seen under the shades of Longbourn again.

I turned to my mother and laughed. "Mother, that was incredible of you!"

"Yes, well," she sighed, amazed at her courage, "no one speaks like that about my daughters." She breathed in and out, and then sat down.

"And," she said, "now what is this nonsense about you being in love with Mr. Darcy?"

❦

I had told my mother everything and she was very surprised at how everything had worked out, even though nothing in full had worked out yet. Mr. Darcy had not proposed to me, Lydia was married to the most worthless man in Britain, Kitty was not married to Mr. Collins and Jane was not married to Mr. Brocklehurst.

And yet, by the end of it, she still felt as if she had gained something. It truly was quite extraordinary.

Later during the day, I stared out the window and saw the day grow cloudy. Mr. Darcy had called off his engagement, which took much strength, and he was unattached—he was free. Ever since I learned this, I had thought of nothing but him, yet thought was just not enough. I had to go to him, I had to see him, and I could not wait another three days till he dined with us.

Gathering up my nerves, I put on my coat, jacket and scarf and then slipped out of the back of the house. I began to walk the three mile walk toward Aginfield.

Two miles into my journey, it began to rain. I was soaked through, yet I could not turn back then. If I were to go to him, wet and ugly, I would still go to him. After the rest of the mile of the walk, I reached Aginfield and I began to walk toward the front of the house. As I did so, the front door opened.

"Elizabeth!" Mr. Darcy cried and then he rushed down the steps toward me. He must've seen me from a window, for he ran across the field and met me.

"Miss Elizabeth," he gasped, "You..."

"I'm sorry," I cried, "But I had to see you."

"It is fine."

"I... I must tell you something."

"What?"

"Is it true that you are no longer engaged?"

"No, I am not. I have learned that I cannot marry where I do not love."

"And neither can I. And Mr. Darcy... I love you."

"And I love you!" He rushed toward me, lifted me in his arms and kissed me passionately. When he released me, he lifted me up once more and said, "Elizabeth, I cannot let you go home now."

"I don't want to go home."

"Good. I will marry you, this I promise, but now I will not wait for a reverend, for you are mine already."

⁂

Mr. Darcy carried me around the back of the house and we were met by a portly man.

"Jefferson!" Darcy called him, "Can you make sure that no one sees me bringing her in?"

"Very good sir," Jefferson replied, "I have experience in that field as well." He rushed into the house and then a couple of minutes later, he reappeared. "Everything is well, and the steps and hallways are now empty."

"Jefferson, I have no idea what I would do without you."

"I know, sir."

Mr. Darcy carried me inside and up to his bedroom where he closed the door behind us.

He removed all my wet clothes, laid me down on the bed and I felt very self-conscious, still I stopped myself from concealing my body from him.

"How do I look to you?" I asked him.

"You are perfect, and you are all mine now. For an eternity, you are mine."

He leaned down and kissed me, and then he ran his hands from down my shoulders, along my breasts, pinching the nipples in between his fingers. I wanted to cry out with surprise at the feeling, yet I had to keep my lips sealed.

Then he moved his hands further and further down until he began to stroke me back and forward between my thighs. However, this time, he kissed me to cover my mouth to keep me from making much noise, and then after several minutes of these attentions to my happiness, he whispered in my ear.

"You must tell me to proceed," he whispered. "And you must let me call you my wife."

"I am your wife, now and for an eternity, and you may proceed."

He removed his clothing and then rested on top of me.

"Elizabeth, forgive me, for this will hurt at first, yet it will pass —and I am going very slowly."

He continued, and it was true. It did hurt at first, yet he went with care, only increasing his speed when he knew that I was finally more at ease with it. Then we moved faster and faster until he tensed up and his body released. He lay on top of me and I wrapped my arms around his neck, kissing his hair.

"How did we almost lose each other?" I asked.

"Through my mistakes. Yet no longer shall it keep us apart. No longer will it destroy all that we have. Elizabeth Bennet, you are my fate, you saved me, and I daresay...I owe you a debt."

"And how do you figure that?"

"That's a story for another day."

⚜

My absence at Longbourn did not go unnoticed, yet Darcy and I were so blinded by affection that we no longer cared for our reputations completely. Darcy was able to get me out of Aginfield as stealthily as he had gotten me in when we were done. Then he drove me in his carriage to Longbourn and we simply said that I got caught in the rain and Darcy saw me standing under a tree, so he offered me a ride in his carriage.

Yet he did not leave, but immediately asked for an audience with my parents, which was very brief. He went in tense and came out relaxed and content.

"Then they have given us their consent?" I laughed.

"Of course, they did."

I jumped into his arms and we kissed.

"Elizabeth!" Our mother cried as she stepped from out of father's study, "you must stop that immediately, and Mr. Darcy, you put my daughter down right now and remember yourself."

"Sorry, Mother." I sighed. "We were just so overwhelmed at the prospect of things falling back into place. And being perfect."

PROPER CONCLUSIONS

News spread through Hampshire quickly of my engagement to Mr. Darcy, and I could not comprehend my luck and my guarantee of happiness. For while most women smiled when they got engaged, I laughed!

Mr. Darcy and I did everything together from then on. We were seen walking along the countryside, thoroughly enjoying our brief courtship, and when Charlotte Lucas returned to town with her husband, Mr. Collins, Mr. Collins now could no longer look down on my family, for whatever happiness he thought that he found, I knew I had found a greater one.

⚜

One day, I was visiting the Austen sisters along with Charlotte, Jane, and Kitty, and I finally decided to tell them the whole story of my acquaintance with Mr. Darcy—though I left out the part where Mr. Darcy took liberties he should not have, and that I should not have allowed him to. For there had to be some things that I kept to myself.

When I was done my narration, they all had their own individual reactions. Jane labelled it as miraculous, Charlotte Lucas said it was what I deserved, Kitty called it fate, Maria Lucas called it adorable, Cassandra Austen called it a fairy tale and Jane Austen said that it would make the basis for a wonderful story.

"You think it good enough for one?" I laughed.

"I think it the perfect makings of a good book," Jane Austen said, "with a few details changed, I daresay this is a wonderful idea."

"Well then, if I might make a request," my sister Jane said, "Give me a happy ending in it."

"I believe I can do that."

"And for me," Charlotte said, "keep my ending as it is, so that in the future, every woman will learn from my example and not make the choices that I have. For I now see that I was wrong. It would have been better to have remained unattached all my life than commit to a marriage without affection and mutual respect."

We all felt bad for Charlotte, for her fate was sealed, yet she had walked towards it of her own free will.

"And as for me," Cassandra Austen said, "just make sure that my spirit is in there somewhere, and all I ask for is peace."

"Yet for my part," I said, "make Darcy and I wiser and not so bent on misunderstanding each other."

"Lizzy," Jane Austen said. "It is not possible to make you wiser. Besides, more and more I'm learning that a flaw can be most becoming in a leading character, and while it is best for a hero to have some form of hubris or pride, it is also best for the heroine to have made the mistake of prejudice somewhere. That makes their struggle all the more amazing. The rapture that is rewarded by rebelling against standards placed on you. Yet while I shall change details, towns, estate locations and facts to hide my inspiration, one thing must remain: the names of Bennet and Darcy must be preserved, for I feel significance to them, and a notion that the world shall wish to know them. For those names shall last for an eternity."

THE END

Don't miss out on your next favorite book!

Join the Satin Romance mailing list
www.satinromance.com/mail.html

Good day, Reader, and thank you so much for reading my debut novel. Through your support, if I am fortunate, then perhaps I can go forward with the rest of the series. However, as you have completed this work, I thought it might interest you all to hear the reasons for why I made certain choices that I did. If you are like me, and are quite the curious sort of person, who often ponders why a writer would make a choice that is so unlike what you might have expected, then I wish to elaborate.

First, with this book, I knew that I very much wanted to include Jane Austen in the actual narrative. I had written many 'Pride & Prejudice' inspired works before, ranging from Young Adult to every sort of fiction that one could imagine. The idea to bring Jane Austen into this story sprung from the third novel I had ever written. Originally, it was titled *Girl Races Time*, and then it changed to *Becoming Mary*. It was a story that followed a modern-day version of Mary Bennet, as she discovered that her family was very similar to a family in a book she picked up, called *Pride and Prejudice*. Later, she discovered that Jane Austen had actually gotten inspiration for her book from a real family of Bennets that lived in her village of Steventon. This book was aimed at young women who just graduated college, which is what that version of Mary Bennet was doing in the book.

Well, often my mind wandered back to that idea I had, and then I decided to one day tell the story of the people that the modern-day Mary Bennet had read about. Thus, her book spawned me on another journey, and I began to write *Rapture & Rebellion*. Little by little, I began to fill in the blanks of a story that I had begun years ago, soon after reading Jane Austen's masterpiece.

However, this desire to use previous books of mine as the foundation for this book didn't end with 'Becoming Mary'. No, Reader, it simply began with it. As you recall from this book, when Mr. Darcy Sr. was dying, he told his son about the tradition that was passed down in his family. The message of 'if one were to ever meet a Bennet woman, you owe her a debt', also had its origins in another novel of mine. Originally, it had been titled *Raising the Sunrise, A Pride & Prejudice Origin Story*. It took place in France during the Renaissance Era. It told the story of Jaqueline Bennet, the Englishwoman who a French Prince, named D'Arcy, eventually fell in love with. It was his devotion to her that led to him passing down the saying among his descendants, and Mr. Darcy, in this tale, was descended from him.

This may come across as a strange way of telling a story, but sometimes, what is strange is not wrong—in fact, I believe sometimes it's the most correct thing you can do. I learned a long time ago, that as a writer, I never really fit in, therefore, I learned that nothing was more fun than to stick out. In truth, I loved to connect story elements in my books, but it's not out of a desire to be anachronistic. Yet, rather, it's from a desire to be realistic. When it comes to books, I have found that the most compelling stories have a lot of history in them that could be explored. The writer allows the reader to know that there's a lot of backstory that the book they just read had, and it gives their world a lot of substance. And that substance makes the world feel more real, more tangible, and most importantly, more touchable.

Also, it gives the reader the sense that this is a story that might never end—and that can be quite the encouraging thought. For, let's be honest, when you first read *Pride & Prejudice*, did you really want it to end? Or did you want it to continue, discovering more about these delicious characters, the roads they walked down, or the paths that they almost did, but didn't? When a good book ends, is it a good feeling for you? Yet, if the book gives you moments that have history, and that history can be elaborated on, then is the story ending there? No, it's not. And therefore, that's quite the encouraging thing, and happy thought indeed!

Now, we return back to the primary change in this book: the inclusion of Jane Austen herself. Not only is her presence here, but so is her pen—I spend time in this story showing her devotion to writing the works that make her famous to us. Early in this novel, Jane Austen was working on a book. In the second chapter 'To London We Go!', she asked Elizabeth what her opinion was on the character names of Marianne and Elinor. This is in reference to Jane Austen's first published novel. While she wrote quite a bit of literature before it, she wrote one book called *Marianne and Elinor*, which was written in a series of letters. Yet, when writing the final draft of the book, Jane Austen abandoned her original style, adapted it to standard novel form, and then wrote her first published novel *Sense and Sensibility*.

A couple of pages later, in the same chapter, on pg. 20, Elizabeth and her sister, Jane, are talking and they exchange this bit of dialogue:

"And yet—I am somehow content with my fate, and I can only suppose that I agree with what our dear friend, Jane Austen, said about me once: 'Good-humored, unaffected girls will not do for a man who has been used to sensible women. They are two distinct orders of beings'. And you know perfectly well that I am good-humored and sometimes have no desire to be sensible when it seems sinful to do so. Therefore, I will always be nothing more than Elizabeth Bennet."

"Then," Jane said delicately, "by your logic, I must adhere to Miss Austen's saying about me: But there are certainly not so many men of large fortune in the world as there are pretty women to deserve them."

Reader, this excerpt is two quotes that are from Jane Austen's novel, *Mansfield Park*. This addition of dialogue is a bit of foreshadowing. It's to display to the reader all the potential elements from Miss Austen's other novels that might play a part in the storytelling as the tale of these characters unfold. It also is there to show a known truth about Jane Austen: she often wrote about things that she occasionally saw. Like almost all other writers, she observed the world around her, and used it as inspiration for her stories. Ergo, for her quotes and characters to occasionally pop up in the narrative shows how she would have gathered insight from the world around her and used it to create her legendary works.

Later, in Chapter 16, 'To Be Tossed About', Jane Austen is talking about a man she loved, named Tom Lefroy. This bit is based on her true history. Jane Austen did fall in love with a man named Tom Lefroy, who did not propose to her because she lacked a large dowry. However, Jane Austen's family in this tale is a mixture of truth and pure fiction. Some of the relatives of hers in this book are alive, when historically speaking, at this point in her tale, they would have been deceased. Yet, I allowed this mixture of fact and fantasy to coincide, so that Jane Austen's family life could offer a dynamic to the storytelling.

Next, we come to the inclusion of the Prince Regent. I admit that this was pure fun—and out of that one word that fueled Jane Austen's writing style: irony. The truth is that the Prince Regent was a massive fan of Jane Austen. He adored her writing style. Here comes the irony: she didn't like him. She thought the Prince Regent was, for lack of a better phrase, a complete waste of space. Therefore, in real life, when the Prince Regent asked her to dedicate her novel 'Emma' to him, it became the crowning moment of irony. I know! How deliciously amusing. Therefore, I brought him into the tale for the sake of irony. For here the Prince Regent was, playing a role in her novel, and yet she despised him a great deal. I also did it so that we could, every now and again, hear Jane Austen give her biting criticism about what she felt toward the Prince Regent. What can I say? I just couldn't resist.

That being said, this is a work of fiction. Therefore, since the Prince Regent is a real figure, his true history should be noted here. In chapter 36, 'Can Happiness Be Found So Easily?', when Mr. Darcy took Elizabeth and the others to the ceremony, that was a work of pure fiction. While King George did go mad, this ceremony that takes place didn't happen. Also, historically, King George was not confirmed mad till 1811, and that was when his son was given the title and position of Prince Regent.

Also, onto the subject of Mr. Darcy himself. While it was objectionable to some that I allowed him to be unlikable in a portion of this book...well, to that as well I do not ask pardon for, because of the fact that part of Mr. Darcy's charm is that he was filled with mistakes, and he one day learned how to overcome them. I have always found that it is equally as much about the mistakes that Darcy makes as it is the virtues that he uses to overcome those mistakes. For a virtue, while it is great to always possess, is even more beautiful after one has fought to achieve it after having fought oneself. The battle against one's own nature is where the courage then lies, and as I always felt so with the original Mr. Darcy in *Pride and Prejudice*, that is what I always felt Jane Austen was trying to say. It is very easy to classify her great work as mostly a romance, but often one can miss her subtle messages and meanings. It also is about facing oneself, seeing both the virtues and flaws in one's nature, and overcoming them after you have learned from your mistakes. Also, for those who believe that I should have made Mr. Darcy more likable at first, there was another reason for why I had him as such: it was for the sake of character development. By starting him off in such a questionable place, it would give me a chance to give him more character development in the future—if I was so lucky as to be able to make a series after this book. I can only reply that the constant goodness of a character was not as essential to me as a character learning how to improve over time and having an immense character arc. It's just that sometimes character arcs just take a while to build up to. Therefore, Reader, this was the point of my version of Mr. Darcy, as was my version of Elizabeth who was to be a woman who would fight for what her instincts always told her was something worth fighting for. For her, Mr. Darcy was worth saving, even when he showed her otherwise. I hope you enjoyed this variation series, and found a bit of yourself in these pages, as you were meant to.

Lastly, a political problem that was referenced often was the oncoming war between America and Britain: The War of 1812. This is a war that was doomed from the start for both sides and had a lot of reasons for its happening. During the late 1700s and early 1800s, British ships, due to the poor conditions they were in, were losing sailors who would abandon their posts and secretly join American vessels. This led to British sea captains requesting to always board American vessels that they passed and search their crew to see if they found any British sailors. It was perfectly right for them to do this. Unfortunately, this search became corrupt and British captains would decree that sailors who were never theirs were theirs, and then force the sailors to work on their ship under false pretenses. This was the naval impressment that is said to have led to the War of 1812. However, there is more to it than that. There was also the conflict with America possibly trying to seize land in Canada, land that didn't belong to them. Britain was allied with Canada, and still held land there. On both sides, there was issues of each one's territory being abused by the other. These are a couple of reasons why the War of 1812 is causing a stir in this storytelling. However, in the end, there are even more reasons for why the war definitely ended when it did.

Reader, I hope that you enjoyed yourself when you read this book. With any luck on my side, I hopefully shall see you again, with the next book in the series. Yet, whether I do or not, it's still a truth universally acknowledged that Jane Austen is someone that inspires many of us, and hopefully her inspiration shall push us onward, and sojourning forth with all our hopes, aims and beliefs. I only hope... that I never stop hoping, and that I prove to not be mistaken for doing so.

--*Ney Mitch*

THANK YOU FOR READING

Did you enjoy this book?

We invite you to leave a review at your favorite book site, such as Goodreads, Amazon, Barnes & Noble, etc.

DID YOU KNOW THAT LEAVING A REVIEW...

- Helps other readers find books they may enjoy.
- Gives you a chance to let your voice be heard.
- Gives authors recognition for their hard work.
- Doesn't have to be long. A sentence or two about why you liked the book will do.

ABOUT THE AUTHOR

Ney Mitch has been a long-standing Jane Austen enthusiast, having written forty novels that were inspired by her various works. Since stumbling on Miss Austen's books after graduating from college, she has always dabbled in Austen inspired literature, ranging from writing works for teens to adults. Originally, her desire was to adapt Jane Austen's writing in a way to help young adults connect with her, however over time, she has spread her aims to other genres and styles.

Having received her BA Degree at Desales University, she is a writer, both literary and dramatic, as well as being a Historic Reenactor.

facebook.com/courtney.mitchell.589

twitter.com/CMMitchelPsyche

pinterest.com/shebaanna

www.ingramcontent.com/pod-product-compliance
Lightning Source LLC
Chambersburg PA
CBHW020613260626
47157CB00003B/991